AUTHOR'S NOTE

PREFACE

I began this exercise merely to leave a legacy to my grandchildren. I have wished many times that I had taped conversations with my parents. I didn't and it is an opportunity lost.

My father had a particularly interesting life. He served in the first World War. He was a mortician and a lawyer by profession.

He served as a state representative and state senator in Minnesota over a period of years from 1921 to 1943. He was the first Polish American to serve in the Minnesota Legislature. He and my mother bought Jax – a little bar restaurant in 1943 and helped build it into one of the largest and finest restaurants in Minnesota.

When I mentioned to friends what I was about, i.e. telling my experiences at work and how I viewed them – so that future generations of our family might better know my generation – I was given a great deal of encouragement.

Many people told me that they wished they had more information on their forbears.

I was visiting with a friend . . . a retired golf professional, George Smith, who is ninety-years-old. He said, "I think most people's lives would be of interest to the general public if they only knew how to articulate it."

I have told my story, as I remember it, and from my own perspective.

I realize that others may see certain details differently from their perspective. I fully understand how that could happen.

I have taken excerpts from and updated an article that was printed in the *Minneapolis Argus-Sun* Newspaper in September, 1971. It gives some background on the Kozlak family and tells a great deal about my grandfather, Stanislaw (Stanley) Kozlak, who died in 1916, twelve years before I was born.

John "Jack" Kozlak

1

NINETEEN ENTREES
... without any garnishments

With best wishes.

— Jack Kozlak

The FUN is in the STRUGGLE

by Jack Kozlak

Jax Cafe

1922 - 1928 University Ave. N.E.
Minneapolis, MN 55418 U.S.A.
(612) 789-7292

Kozlak's Royal Oak

4785 Hodgson Rd.
Shoreview (Minneapolis/St. Paul),
MN 55126 U.S.A.
(612) 484-8484

First edition, 1996.

Written by Jack Kozlak.

Edited and prepared by Ed Kaspszak.

ISBN #: 0-9652044-1-3

Printed and Published by Park Press, Inc., P.O. Box 475, Waite Park, MN 56387 (320) 255-8937

DEDICATION

To My Grandchildren

Nick, David, Marlo, Anne, Janelle, Ryan,
Brian, Kate, Peter, Brett, Drew, Nicole

I hope this will give you some insights into what our career in the restaurant business was like. I say "our" because your grandmother and I and all our children shared in no small measure in the demands of the business as well as the frustration, the sorrows, the disappointments, the joys and the rewards.

The history of my family and that of your grandmother's family is really not unusual for many of the people who immigrated to the United States from Europe in the nineteenth century. They came to these shores looking for a better life . . . for an opportunity to work and an opportunity to keep and enjoy some of the fruits of their labor. They had deep religious conviction and faith and they lived according to the rules. They believed that education offered the key to a better life and they were willing to sacrifice so that their children were given the opportunity to further their education.

Naturally, your grandmother and I as well as your parents want you to lead productive lives and to find satisfaction and gratification in your life's work, whatever you choose to do.

I remember the words of my fourth-grade teacher at Holland School, Mrs. Emma Fitch. She told us to, "Try to leave the world a little better place than we found it." Inherent in those words is the hope that we will try to set a good example for others and also offer some service to the community as we journey through life.

My father once gave me a bit of advice that I think bears repeating. He said, "Don't ever do anything that you wouldn't want to see on the front page of the newspaper."

This is a good admonition to recall when you are tempted to do something untoward.

He also said, "Work hard, save your money, and some day you will be a rich man." I think your grandmother and I worked hard for a long time . . . and we managed to save some money so today we are quite comfortable . . . but the rich part comes not from money, but from seeing our children and grandchildren develop as caring and productive citizens.

As I write this I think back to the day I first saw your grandmother. It was 1947. She was seventeen and I was nineteen. We married in 1949 and through the years raised six children and now we have twelve grandchildren.

We have come a long way together and it has not always been easy . . . nor should it be easy.

I had a visit with Stanley Wasie shortly before he died and he was in a reminiscing mood. He told of his early life . . . a virtual orphan. He recounted his meager start in business. He told of some of the trials and tribulations he was forced to endure . . . how hard he worked, and ultimately he became successful. He concluded his story by telling me something that I wish to pass on to you. He said, "When it's all over and you look back, you realize that . . . The Fun Is In The Struggle."

PART

ONE

The Life and Times of the Kozlak Family

Argus-Sun ARTICLE SEPTEMBER 1971

Can a teen-age Polish immigrant land in America with nothing but ambition and a will to work and become the founder of a family dynasty in little more than thirty years?

If his name is Stanislaw (Stanley) Kozlak and he picks Northeast Minneapolis as the place to give his ambition reign he can. And he did.

A little less than ninety years ago a Polish immigrant named Stanislaw (Stanley) Kozlak landed in Minneapolis, taking a menial laborer's job in a sawmill.

Today the Kozlaks are one of the dominant families of Northeast Minneapolis and can count politicians, lawyers, realtors, insurance agents, and restaurateurs among their ranks.

It was a Kozlak who first died in the service of the Minnesota Highway Patrol (William).

It was a Kozlak (Joseph) who had the vision to insist that University Avenue would one day be a major highway in the days when cows grazed where a major regional center is today (Northtown).

It was a Kozlak who brought hundreds of Polish immigrants from the virtual serfdom of Europe to the opportunity of America (Stanislaw).

In talking to the Kozlaks of today (1971), one senses

an air of great respect, bordering on awe, when the topic turns to Stanley Kozlak, founder of the family.

"He was an incredible man, that's all there is to it," said Peter Kozlak, Stanley's fourth son. "It all started with him and today (1971) there are so many Kozlaks in town we'd have to use Bottineau Park for a family reunion."

The saga of Stanley Kozlak and his rise to prominence in the early days of Northeast Minneapolis is a micro-history of the American dream, with all the sentimentality left out.

"He came here when he was seventeen," Peter Kozlak said. His father bade him good-bye by reminding him that the family had always been poor and that there were no prospects for their lot to improve. He told my father, "If it is any better in America, stay there."

The first job Kozlak took upon landing was a labor job in one of the sawmills along the river north of Nicollet Island. He did that for just a short time.

Stanley Kozlak married MaryAnna Jaros, aunt of the famous basketball star of the Minneapolis Lakers, Tony Jaros, perhaps the most famous athlete ever produced in Northeast Minneapolis.

There were six children from this marriage. John, the oldest, was a lawyer. He had passed the bar exam before he was twenty-one years old and by law had to wait until his twenty-first birthday to practice his profession. John served in the U.S. Army in World War I and was gassed while in action in France. He died at age twenty-six in 1920.

Joseph, the next son, father of John (Jack) Kozlak, former state legislator and now a member of the Metropolitan Council, was for eighteen years a state legislator.

"My father was the man who fought to get a four-lane right-of-way for University Avenue from the city limits out to Highway 10 when it was nothing but a dirt road," Jack Kozlak said. Today (1971) Jack and his brother, Bill, run Jax Cafe, which his parents began operating in 1943.

Peter Kozlak told the story of his brother Joe's first attempt at public office.

"This was when Joe was just twenty-two, about the time of the First World War, and he ran against the man who was head of the draft board. And he was drafted!"

For many years Joe Kozlak represented Northeast Minneapolis in the state legislature.

The third son, William, was a member of the Minnesota State Highway Patrol.

"So far as I know," said Peter Kozlak, "My brother was the first Minnesota highway patrolman to be killed on duty. He was run off the road and smashed his motorcycle into a tree. It was during the dust storms of 1934."

The only daughter, Katherine, died in 1947.

In addition to Peter, who is sixty-seven now (1971), there was one brother, Frank Kozlak who died in 1966. Frank Kozlak was an attorney with a combination real estate and insurance agency.

"That's just one line of the family," Jack Kozlak said. "There are many more Kozlaks – I don't know exactly how many, but we are all related.

After his venture into the sawmill trade, Stanley Kozlak decided to go into business, first with a butcher shop and then with a furniture store on Fifth Street and Washington, in 1904.

"We originally lived down by the river, down by Seventh, and Ramsey Streets, near B.F. Nelson," Peter Kozlak said.

"But that's all gone now, it's all changed. We moved up here (to 20th Avenue and University Avenue Northeast) when Dad built his building in 1910."

That building is the home of Jax Cafe today. Ever since it was built by Stanley Kozlak over sixty years ago there has been a Kozlak in business on the corner.

"When my grandfather built on this corner, everyone thought he was crazy," said Jack Kozlak. "This was way out in the country then. The business district was down around Thirteenth Avenue and Fourth Street where my uncle Frank had his insurance office. But he was looking ahead."

Peter Kozlak explained that the building that now houses Jax is a solid building that took a couple years to build. "They just don't build them like this anymore."

Though established on the corner with a variety of

businesses by 1910 – he was the owner and operator of a furniture store, a tavern and a funeral home on the corner – Stanley Kozlak still had time for other interests.

"My father became an agent for the Cunard steamship line around 1900," Peter Kozlak said. "He went back to Poland and got many young men to come to America."

Stanley Kozlak couldn't read or write when he came to this country, Peter Kozlak said. "My mother had worked as a maid in Wisconsin before they were married and her employers had taught her to read and write, and she taught my father."

Stanley Kozlak ran his business in a manner far different from what is customary today, Peter Kozlak said. "He never had a contract, never signed a paper with a customer. But after he died in 1916, we had people come into the store for months, wanting to pay bills.

"A man would come in and say, 'I owed your father one-hundred dollars on some furniture!' We'd look on the books and there was no record. 'I don't care – I owed it to him!' the man would say and that was it."

When he died in 1916, Stanley Kozlak was only forty-six.

"He was a young man when he died," Peter Kozlak said. "But he did more and lived more in his life than I could ever imagine doing in mine. He was an incredible man."

The Kozlaks of Northeast are a testimony to that.

THE ENTRY

by Jack Kozlak

I am told that I came into this world at Swedish Hospital in Minneapolis, Minnesota at 3 a.m. on April 20, 1928. Calvin Coolidge was serving the last year of his term as president of the United States. Theodore Christianson was serving his second of three terms as governor of Minnesota and the start of the Great

Depression was a year and a half in the future.

My parents Joseph Kozlak and Gertrude (Katzmarek) Kozlak had been married seven years and I had an older brother, Joe Jr., age five. My father was engaged in the practice of law; was active in the furniture, hardware and undertaking business with his brothers, and was serving his third term as a member of the Minnesota House of Representatives. My mother was a full-time homemaker. Our house was built in 1925 at 1929-3rd Street in Northeast Minneapolis.

I remember my father telling me that the contract price on the house was six-thousand five-hundred dollars. It was a rather imposing structure for the neighborhood. The exterior was brick and stucco and it had a red tile roof. On the main floor was a kitchen, living room with a fireplace, dining room, breakfast room, sun room and one-half bath. The second floor had three bedrooms, a full bath and an enclosed porch that we called a sleeping porch. The porch was used for sleeping during the hot summer months. The basement consisted of the laundry; an amusement room with a fireplace and a maple wood planked floor; and a room called the vegetable cellar. The "vegetable" cellar contained several shelves that were filled in later summer and early autumn with jars of tomatoes, peaches, pears, jellies, chickens and other food products that my mother "canned" for the months ahead.

The year of my birth was the year that Henry Ford introduced the Model "A". Radio was still in its infancy. (My parents replaced their crystal set with a new Philco). Minnesota native Charles Lindbergh was basking in his celebrity for being the first to fly the Atlantic alone one year earlier. Many urban homeowners were still in the process of converting their gas lights to electric. There were no televisions, VCRs, freeways, supermarkets, talking movies, computers or air conditioners. It was a world without microwave ovens, Waring blenders, water skis, Jetskis, weed eaters, electric toothbrushes and countless other gadgets we take for granted today. And yet before the onslaught of the Great Depression most people in our neighborhood considered themselves very fortunate. Our neighborhood was made up primarily of first- and second-generation Americans who migrated

Wedding portrait of Stanislaw (Stanley) Kozlak and Mary Anna Jaros Kozlak in 1892.

Joseph Kozlak, Sr., and Gertrude Kozlak at the time of their 40th wedding anniversary 1961.

11

The Kozlak Family in 1971. Front Row (L to R): Sue, Ann, Nick, Joel, Carol; Middle Row: Paula, Kathy with Bill, Jr., Katie, Helen, Gertrude, Ruth, Lynn; Back Row: Bill, Sr., Tom, Dan, Mike, Joe, Jr., Paul, Jack, Diane, Mary Lee, Mark.

from central Europe. Most considered that their life and their prospects were infinitely better here than that of their relatives in the "old" country.

Some of my earliest recollections go back to the early 1930s. I remember my sister Gloria who was born in 1932. I can recall her being sick and then her death in September of 1933. Her casket was placed in the living room of our house and friends called there as was the custom of the time.

In the early 1930s the milkman and the iceman pulled up to the curb in their horse drawn carts as did the "Bambi" breadman and other vendors. In the summer Mr. DiMaggio would come down the street with his horse drawn wagon loaded with fruit and vegetables. He would ring a big bell to announce his arrival and the ladies in the neighborhood would come out of their houses and walk to his wagon to make their selections. I can still see Mr. DiMaggio's smiling countenance and hear his cheerful greeting, "How's a da Jack?" as he slipped me a few grapes or a plum.

Most of the neighbors had vegetable gardens in their backyards and many also raised a few chickens and even some rabbits. If you had a telephone you made a call by giving the operator the number of whomever it was you wished to speak with and "she" (it seems it was always a woman in those days) made the connection. Doctors made housecalls as did most music teachers. Public transportation in the city was by street railway and in the 1930s it was both inexpensive and adequate.

I attended John Holland Elementary school. It was located eight blocks from our house. Everyone in our neighborhood walked to school. There was no busing in those days and we thought nothing of it. All my elementary school teachers were women as was our principal, Mrs. Stanley.

I remember all thcsc women as capable, even dedicated, educators. I cannot recall discipline ever being a serious problem in elementary school. I believe most parents taught us to respect our teachers and the importance of doing well in school. Heaven help the misbehaving child whose parent had to be contacted by a teacher.

The Depression years were difficult for nearly all the

adults in some way. There was massive unemployment . . . people with jobs worried about losing them. For
most there was no money for higher education. I can
recall seeing freight trains with dozens of men riding on
the box cars going who knows where looking for work.

Oftentimes men would knock at our door looking for
work or something to eat. My mother would always make
a sandwich for these poor souls and instruct them to step
back while she set it outside the door. The Northeast
Neighborhood House was only a block away and I can
recall unemployed neighbors walking past our house
carrying home loaves of bread that had been distributed
there. I was only five-years-old when President Roosevelt
called the bank holiday. My father was in the nation's
capitol on business at the time. My mother was frightened
until my father called and told her who to go to if she ran
out of household funds.

The Depression was a difficult financial time for my
father and his siblings. The furniture and hardware business was not good. The building they owned needed
updating and repair but there was no money and they were
mortgaged to the hilt. Legislators in those days were paid
five-hundred dollars a year which helped a lot, but even
then five-hundred dollars was not exactly a princely sum.

On Palm Sunday, April 5th, 1936, my brother, Bill,
was born. Our family was now complete. On July 8th my
dad celebrated his fortieth birthday with a party of friends
and relatives held outdoors in our backyard. At my age of
eight, I thought forty was ancient and worried that dad
would not be with us much longer.

I recall the presidential election of 1936. President
Roosevelt was challenged by Governor Alf Landon of
Kansas. My father was a state senator at that time and we
heard a lot of political discussion at the dinner table.
President Roosevelt spoke in Rochester, Minnesota,
during that election season and our whole family made
the trip to see and hear him.

The neighborhood movie theaters did well during the
thirties. Movies were relatively inexpensive, and they
offered adults a few hours of escape from the troubled
times. Saturday children's matinees at our neighborhood
theater cost five cents. We saw a feature movie plus a
cartoon and a weekly serial with stars such as Buck

Ruth and Jack at their wedding reception.

Ruth and Jack at the wedding of Diane Kozlak and Gary Ellis.

Mrs. Fitch's fourth grade class at the historic Godfrey house circe May 1937. Front Row (L to R): Jack Kozlak, Roland Compton, Ray Brytowski, Joe Warhol, Steve Warian, Dick Banick. Second row: Harold Kalina, Joe Grill, Unidentified, Ken Tovsen, Bill Blume, Lynn Lundin, Bob Campbell.

1954: The Kozlak family in the garden at Jax Cafe. Front row: Helen holding Dan, Michael, Diane, Gertrude, Ruth holding Mary, Mark. Second row: Joe, Jr., Joe, Sr., Bill, Jack.

Jones, Tom Mix or Tailspin Tommy.

Even though money was scarce and most adults had to struggle for survival, the children in our area had many activities to keep them occupied. First there were the schools. Aside from the competent instruction we received on a daily basis, there were occasions when we were taken on field trips to historical sites such as the Godfrey House (the first white person's house built in Minneapolis); the Minneapolis Art Institute; or the Sibley House, (the home of Minnesota's first governor). We saw the Minneapolis Symphony Orchestra conducted by Maestro Dimitri Mitropoulos. We even met Harriet Godfrey, who was the first white child born in what is now the city of Minneapolis.

The public park and playground system was also superb. At Bottineau Park we played baseball during the summer, football in the fall and had ice skating in winter. The "warming house" was an old wooden structure heated by a potbellied wood burning stove that glowed red on sub-zero evenings.

The Northeast Neighborhood House was a block from our home and it was a hub of activity. It was here that we learned to play basketball, and in the thirties it was a hotbed of the sport. Edison High School, our local public school, won the state basketball championship in 1937. De LaSalle, the local Catholic high school, had one of the best Catholic basketball teams in the nation, and the University of Minnesota won the Big Ten championship that same year.

Saturdays were "open gym" days and the basketball floor was busy all day with half-court pickup games, one-on-one contests, and boys just practicing to improve their shooting skills. In the evenings and on Sundays during the basketball season we could watch games played by former high school and college stars. There were leagues and tournaments sponsored by the Catholic Youth Organization, local merchants, Amateur Athletic Union, and a season's end all nations tournament. There were organized activities to keep us involved from childhood to young adulthood.

Every year the University of Minnesota invited the Northeast Neighborhood House and other settlement houses to bring as many boys as they wished to attend the first home football game of the year at Memorial Stadium. What a thrill! We walked the three miles to and from the stadium and had seats high up in the bowl end. We saw some of Coach Bernie Bierman's greatest teams in action with players like Ed Widseth, Bill Garnaas, Ray King and later All Americans Bruce Smith and Dick Wildung.

The Minneapolis Park Board sponsored citywide football leagues in various age and weight classifications. When I was twelve-years-old I played for the Bottineau Midgets. We won the city championship but what a scramble it was to get all the players to some of the games. A couple of our teammates had paper routes and on game days we would help them deliver their papers so we could field a team. Transportation too was a problem. If we were lucky Mr. Reiners would take us to our destination in his ice truck. Most of the time we either walked or biked to the game site. We had no equipment such as shoulder pads, football shoes, or helmets. We merely put on an extra sweater or two and an extra pair of pants to help cushion the bumps. When we won the championship we were treated to a father and sons banquet sponsored by the Franklin Creamery Co. We were served wieners and beans plus plenty of milk and ice cream. Each player was presented with a miniature gold football charm as a remembrance.

As the social programs of the Roosevelt administration took hold many changes became apparent in our neighborhood. Many young men went into the Civilian Conservation Corps where they learned a new discipline and performed important work in our national parks and forest lands. The Works Progress Administration and Public Works Administration put people to work building public buildings and improving much of the nation's infrastructure. There were still many constituents calling on my father asking him to help get a job for themselves, or a son or daughter or relative. He had some connections in both the private and public sectors and did what he could to help those in need.

The favorite place for kids in the neighborhood to congregate other than the park or the Northeast Neighborhood House was at the Jaros household. The Jaros family lived a half block from our house. There were twelve children in the family and in the thirties at least eight were living at home. The place was a magnet for every other kid in the neighborhood. Mrs. Jaros was a kindly, easy-going lady who seemed to welcome the activity and sometimes chaos that swirled around her. No one ever knocked on the door at the Jaros house – you just went in. If the family was eating, you were fed something too. If there was a game being played you were soon included. I suppose the family at that time was considered poor monetarily but none of the kids seemed to know or mind. The family shared parental caring and love and it extended to the neighbor kids too.

The Jaros house was next to an empty lot and many a pickup game of baseball or football was played there. In the wintertime the older kids would build a big snow slide and they also built an igloo complete with a small make-shift wood stove. They had a rather large shanty in the backyard near the alley and many a "binder gun" battle was fought there. The binders were cut from worn out inner tubes and the guns were made from wood scraps. The girls in the neighborhood would put on an occasional play in that portion of the shanty that could be used to park a car. No one in the family had a car at that time.

A small backboard and a spring metal hoop taken from an old barrel were attached to the top of the shanty, and spirited basketball games were played there. Some of the kids who played basketball in Jaros' backyard went on to star in high school and college. Marty Rolek was named All American when he played at the University of Minnesota. Tony Jaros starred at the University of Minnesota and later played with the Minneapolis Lakers on several of their N.B.A. championship teams.

A few things that occurred in the thirties and early 1940s are etched deeply in my memory:

In the election of 1934 my father challenged the incumbent state senator for his legislative seat. On the second Sunday before election our family went to Mass at our parish church, the same as any other Sunday. The pastor celebrated the Mass. It was customary for the celebrant to make the weekly announcements before proceeding with the homily. On this day he pointed out that a fresh load of dirt had been spread in the school yard. He then went on to say, "The dirt was donated by our good friend State Senator A. L. Lennon."

My father was on his feet like a shot proclaiming loudly, "That's politics!" He immediately had us on our feet and as we started to walk out of the church he looked directly at the pastor and said, "The Archbishop will hear about this."

As we walked up the aisle, I noticed many other people following the lead of my father. They were walking out in silent protest because of the pastor's indiscretion.

True to his word as soon as we got home my father was on the phone with Archbishop John Gregory Murray telling him respectfully but forcefully what he thought about the conduct of his pastor in this matter.

Nine days later the election was held and my father won handily. Did the flap that occurred at church have a bearing on the outcome? No one really knows for sure but as the news of the incident spread most people thought that dad was treated unfairly and they admired his courage for responding at once.

The early thirties were the days when radio news as delivered by Boake Carter, H.V. Kaltenborn and Lowell Thomas was rife with the exploits of outlaws such as Al Capone, John Dillinger, Alvin Karpis and Homer Van Meter. The stories of the violence committed by these types made every kid fearful but nothing was etched more indelibly on my mind from that era than the kidnapping of the Lindbergh baby. It seems that story was in the news for months – even years. Everyone was relieved when suspect Bruno Richard Hauptman was taken into custody. The trial was sensational and every adult had a theory or an opinion as to Hauptman's guilt or innocence. Hauptman was convicted of the crime and sentenced to die in the electric chair. On the night of his execution virtually every radio in America was tuned in as the announcer described Hauptman's walk from his cell to the room where the electric chair awaited him. Then the graphic description of his being strapped into the chair, the throwing of the switch and the dimming of the lights caused by the power surge. Finally Hauptman was pronounced dead. In retrospect, I sometimes wonder if in incidences such as these, radio is not at least as powerful as T.V.

The rise of Adolf Hitler also made an impression. As war clouds gathered I can recall listening to live

20

shortwave radio broadcasts with my parents at 4 and 5 a.m. when Hitler addressed either the Reichstag or the general populace. My father served in the army during World War I and now less than 20 years later Europe was once again facing the awful prospect of war. My parents and grandparents were deeply concerned for their relatives in Poland and of course they hoped that the United States would not have to become involved in a shooting war.

Nazi Germany was able to grab the Rhineland, the Sudetenland and Czechoslovakia without starting a general war. Then on September 1, 1939, Germany invaded Poland. Great Britain and France declared war on Germany and the process began whereby the world as we knew it was about to be thrown into turmoil.

At first the war had little effect on those of us living in the Upper Midwest. We heard reports on the radio, and newsreels at the movies gave us insights into what was happening in far-off Europe and even farther Asia where the Japanese were embarked on their expansionism. The United States' policy at the time was a commitment to stay out of war. As eleven and twelve-year-olds, my friends and I did not dwell a great deal on world affairs. Our world was filled with thoughts of school and sports.

In the summer of 1940 six of us organized a basket-ball team. The team consisted of George Felegy, John Felegy, Harold Kalina, Pete Leba, Walter "Whoopie" Wronczka and me. We were soon to be seventh-graders. George Hudak, a high school junior, asked to be our coach and we agreed.

The custom of the time was for groups such as ours to ask local merchants to help sponsor your team. If you were lucky you might collect enough money to purchase numbered tee shirts. If you were really fortunate perhaps even a cheap pair of basketball trunks. Our group hit on an idea that no one up to that time had ever tried. We composed a letter explaining that we were from the Northeast Neighborhood House and that we needed help to purchase basketball uniforms for our team. We took our letter and walked to downtown Minneapolis. Our plan was to go into high rise office buildings and present our letter to receptionists at insurance offices, law offices, accountants' offices, etc. In those days most of the prestigious office buildings had manually operated elevators and a dignified uniformed "starter" would be stationed on the ground floor and help load the elevator cars. Another function these gentlemen performed was to see to it that undesirable persons never got above ground level. We quickly discovered that our appearance put us in the "undesirable" category so it was necessary for us to improvise. We decided we would enter the building one at a time and take the stairway to a predesignated floor. Once we had all gathered we would begin our solicitation. Usually we would begin on the second or third floor, and when we completed the canvass of that floor we would take the stairway to the floors above. I can still visualize the women in those offices. They would read our hand-written letter . . . pass it from one to the next and then reach for their purses to give us a dime or a quarter or even an occasional half dollar. We surely looked like ragamuffins and they must have felt sorry for us for these were not the best of economic times. When we finished working the top floor we would all get on an elevator and take it to the ground floor where we would make a humble yet triumphant exit much to the consternation of the starter.

We repeated this process for many days in various buildings, carefully counting each day's collection. Finally, we had all the money we needed. We bought Converse basketball shoes, then we bought basketball shirts with our team name, "Trotters," stenciled on the back. We purchased padded basketball trunks done in kelly green and gray. We each got a kelly green lined corduroy warm-up jacket with our name sewed on the pocket in gray thread. We had enough money to rent the gymnasium at the Northeast Neighborhood House for several weekly practice sessions. Our team was the envy of the "Nut House" as the neighborhood house was affectionately tagged. We played nineteen games that season and won eighteen. The only game we lost was when we stepped out of our class and played a team of high school boys. At season's end we used up our remaining funds by treating ourselves to a "banquet" at the Forum Cafeteria. We had the chow mein luncheon special, fifteen cents, and then took in a "dime dinger" . . . a double feature movie at the Aster Theater, price ten cents. It was a great season.

The war in Europe dragged on. France was overrun in the spring and summer of 1940 and British troops made a miraculous evacuation from the Port of Dunkirk, which would enable their forces to fight on from their home soil.

Radio brought the war to our homes as each night we heard reports from various European capitals by newsmen such as William L. Shirer, H.V. Kaltenborn or Charles Collingwood. And how could anyone who lived during this period forget the unmistakable voice of Edward R. Murrow as he began his report with . . . "This . . . is London!" Murrow's rooftop reports of the Nazi nighttime bombing blitz of London will be studied for generations by prospective newspeople as classic examples of courage and candor.

As England struggled for its life, the Nazi juggernaut consolidated its conquest of most of the rest of Europe. The bombing raids on England raged on but for most of us living in the Upper Midwest the war seemed far distant and hardly an imminent threat to us.

My brother Joe graduated from Edison High School in June of 1940 and in September began his college career at Georgetown University in Washington, D.C. I was now a student at Sheridan Junior High School located at University Avenue and Broadway in Northeast Minneapolis. Brother Bill was still a pre-schooler.

In June of 1941 my parents, brother Bill and I drove to Washington to pick up brother Joe at the end of the school year. We stayed in Pittsburgh one night on our way to Washington and I recall the headlines in the newspaper that day announcing the death of baseball hero Lou Gehrig.

In Washington we visited the Capitol and met Congressman Joseph O'Hara, who was a friend of my father's. We saw the Washington Monument, Lincoln and Jefferson Memorials and many other sights that the district had to offer. A visit to Arlington National Cemetery and the Lee/Custis home was most memorable as was a tour of George Washington's Mount Vernon. I recall vividly that in 1941 a sign over the doorway where the black plantation workers had lived read: "Slaves Quarters". Twenty years later I visited Mount Vernon with my wife and the sign read "Servants Quarters".

One afternoon I went to a movie at the Capitol

23

Theater. I started to walk up to the balcony which was the vantage point I preferred at our downtown theaters in Minneapolis. I was stopped partway up the stairs by an usher who said, "The balcony is for colored people only." In those days there were also segregated rest rooms and drinking fountains. As late as the late 1950s and early 1960s similar evidences of segregation were commonplace in the deep south and even Florida, which was generally considered the least "southern" of the southern states. I was genuinely surprised to witness this blatant segregation on our first trip to Florida in 1958 and felt sympathy for those demeaned by the practice.

On our return trip to Minneapolis from Washington in 1941 we visited civil war battle sites at Frederick, Maryland and Gettysburg, Pennsylvania. During the recently completed school year our history class was required to recite Abraham Lincoln's Gettysburg Address from memory, so being at the site took on a special meaning.

The summer of 1941 was for me much like that of most other thirteen-year-old Midwestern children. I had some duties at home, such as grass cutting, dish washing and trash removal, but there was plenty time for baseball, football, biking and reading. My friend Harold Kalina taught me some of the fine points of caddying and we made countless trips to Armour (later Francis A. Gross) Golf Course where we could earn some money. The caddy rates at that time were eighty cents for eighteen holes. If you did a good job you might get a tip and receive a dollar. Many times we carried doubles and were able to come home with as much as two dollars and fifty cents.

The war in Europe expanded in 1941 when Germany attacked the Soviet Union. The deteriorating relations between Japan and the United States also became more evident as our government tried to bring pressure on the Japanese to halt their expansionism in the Pacific. The Japanese were not taken very seriously by most Americans at that time. It was not uncommon to hear predictions that the U.S. could defeat them in ninety days if war were to come.

When the school year began in September, brother Joe returned to Georgetown and our family settled back into our normal routine. The draft was now in effect and many young men from our neighborhood were inducted into the Army. The pay for buck privates was set at twenty-one dollars per month. The other branches of service were recruiting, and several eligible neighbor boys joined the Navy, Coast Guard and Marines.

The defense industry also came to life. The United States was building arms and selling or "lend leasing" them to our potential allies, and yet the prospect of our entering the war at some time seemed a possibility, it did not appear imminent.

And then on Sunday, December 7th, 1941, the empire of Japan launched a surprise attack on Pearl Harbor, Hawaii. A day later the Congress of the U.S. met in joint session and declared war on Japan. Brother Joe contacted Minnesota U.S. Senator Joseph Ball as soon as he could and requested a pass for the gallery. Joe was there when President Franklin Roosevelt delivered his famed "A day that will live in infamy" speech. He also witnessed Congress voting to declare war first against Japan and later Germany and Italy.

When Joe came home for Christmas in 1941, he told our parents that he wanted to join the Navy. My father tried to persuade him to stay in school. Dad argued that it was likely to be a long war and that Joe Jr. would have ample time to serve after he completed his education. Joe Jr. would have none of it. He wanted to enlist and serve with the young men his own age. At semester's end he joined the Navy and was soon off for basic training at the Naval Training Station at Farragut, Idaho. From there he went to Hawaii, where he served for three and one-half years at the Naval Hospital near Pearl Harbor on the Island of Oahu.

Life at home changed in subtle ways during our country's early involvement in all-out war. More and more young men were taken into the armed forces. Soon many living room windows in our neighborhood had little flags with a blue star denoting each person from the household who was in the armed forces. It wasn't long before there was plenty of work for nearly everyone at home. The munitions plants were flooded with work and unemployment all but evaporated. There was some food rationing and suggested meatless days. Gasoline rationing came next, but it wasn't much of a hardship

25

because the city was still serviced by adequate public transportation, and the suburbs had not yet begun to sprawl. People in essential war work were provided adequate amounts of gas to assure that they could do their job.

As casualties began to mount some of the blue stars in the windows were replaced with gold stars, graphically pointing out that a son or husband had been killed in action. Survivors were referred to as "gold star mothers or a gold star family." Everyone was united in the war effort. Civil defense units were set up – scrap metal drives organized – government war bonds (later called defense bonds) were promoted and sold. The general populace came together in solemn resolve to see the war effort through to a successful conclusion.

As 1942 gave way to 1943, the Allied war effort began to show signs of success. The industrial might of America became ever more apparent as planes, tanks, ships and other war materials began to make a difference. For me, a fifteen-year-old, life was little changed. There was school, sports, and occasional odd jobs such as caddying and grass cutting. Home life seemed secure and predictable. My mother was a homemaker. Dad was home from the office daily at 5 p.m. Supper (as we called it then) was at 5:30. Sunday dinner was at noon. Later we would visit my mother's parents or get together with aunts, uncles, and cousins either at our house or theirs. And then on October 1st, 1943 our cozy predictable lifestyle changed, never to return. October 1st, 1943 was the day my father made a career change. On that date my father and mother began their operation of what was then known as Jax Bar.

Perhaps, I should back up here a bit and set the stage for this event by explaining when the building that houses Jax was built, plus the chronology leading to my parents' purchase of Jax.

PART

TWO

JAX CAFE

CHRONOLOGY: How it started and grew

1910 - Grandfather Stanislaw (Stanley) Kozlak built the building at 1922-28 University Avenue N.E. that now houses Jax Cafe. It was built for furniture, hardware and undertaking on the ground floor. The second floor was a dance hall. There was also living quarters in the building in what is now the south half of the Roundtable Room. Contract price on the building was fifteen thousand six-hundred dollars. My father was fourteen years of age during the construction and he helped out by working as a "water boy".

1933 - My father, Joseph Kozlak, Sr. and his brothers, built a new mortuary building next door at 1918 University Avenue N.E. When the mortuary was moved from the original building that space was rented to Jack Dusenka. The space encompassed about one-eighth of the building as it stands today. Dusenka called his place Jax Bar.

1938 - Dusenka sold the business to Jim Harris and moved to Los Angeles where he opened a place called the Golden Gopher.

1943 - October 1st my father purchased the business (Jax Bar) from Jim Harris. At that time Jax served only sandwiches, hamburgers, pork tenderloin, B.L.T.'s plus fried chicken and beef tenderloin steak. Lunch was *not* served. My parents had no experience in the restaurant or bar business. My father was a mortician and lawyer by profession

and had also served eighteen years as a state
representative and state senator.

Tuesday, October 5, 1943 – My father told me he was
paying a young lad forty cents per hour to wash
dishes on Friday and Saturday nights. He asked if
I would like to make the "big" money. I said yes
and on October 8, 1943 I began a restaurant
career that spanned six decades.

October, 1943 – December, 1945. These were World War II
years and supplies . . . meat particularly, were
hard to come by. Restaurants were allocated only
so many ration points to purchase meat. When
you used your allocation you were done for the
month. By this time the furniture store was
liquidated and the space in the building next to
Jax was vacant.

Dad decided that we should raise our own
chickens, and thus have more points to use for
steak. He bought a brooder and moved it into the
vacant portion of the building. It is the space that
now houses the main dining room at Jax.

He made a deal to buy cockerel chicks from
Ghostley Farms in Anoka for a penny each. He
went to the N.E. feed mill on Marshall St. N.E.,
and purchased mash for feed and we became
urban chicken farmers.

The chickens never left the brooder until they
were ready for the kill. They spent their entire
lives on wire. It took only about ten or eleven
weeks to raise them to the desired weight. You
may have guessed by this time who was in charge
of this operation. I tended the chickens before and
after school and when it was time to butcher them
I did that too.

Spring 1944 – The chicken operation was successful, and
my father decided we should expand it. There was
a huge garage behind the building that once
housed furniture delivery trucks and hearses.
They converted a large part of the garage for the
chickens and raised as many as seven-hundred at
a time to the kill . . . The chicken sexers at
Ghostley's were not always perfect and we ended
up with enough hens to provide eggs for the

restaurant . . . and the business grew. We had meat at Jax when many others didn't and that word spread fast.

The chicken operation was so successful that my father toyed with the idea of using the remaining portion of the garage to raise pigs. After he mentioned this I told my mother that if *that* happened I was going to leave home. She said, "If that happens, I will leave with you."

1944 to 1945 – The business prospered. Both mother and dad worked it. Mother made all the salad dressings in those days, helped greet the customers and took an occasional shift in the kitchen. My duties were now expanded to include stocking the bar and pop coolers on weekends. Plus snow shoveling in winter, and, of course, dish washing and chicken "farming".

December 24, 1945 – Christmas Eve morning. I remember going to the Great Northern Depot to pick up brother Joe who was returning from three and one-half years service in the Navy. Joe came home, (we were living in the little apartment in the Jax building) took a shower, walked next door and began his restaurant career.

At this time Jax was still much the same as when my father purchased it . . . ten wooden booths that could seat four persons each . . . three booths that could seat six, plus ten bar stools.

Brother Joe took an immediate interest in the business. Although he returned to school and earned his degree in history, his real interest became the restaurant. He prodded my father to expand. A new kitchen was designed into the existing building and we opened the next section of the building for dining. We also included a small private dining room. With these additions our seating capacity more than doubled.

We decided to open for lunch. Dad hired John Sawina who lived in the neighborhood and had worked as a cook at Bergseng's Restaurant and the Huddle, among others. Sawina was a Polish immigrant . . . an excellent cook . . . who absolutely murdered the English language to the delight

29

of everyone who knew him. I can still visualize him on the phone: "Hello, Gambling Robbinsdale (Gamble/Robinson) this is Johnny down a da Jax Bar."

Sawina was really our first chef. He prepared the lunches, (cut the meat), requisitioned his supplies and had the basic run of the kitchen. He was an interesting character and at times we liked to have him come into the dining room and greet the guests. His accent cracked everyone up and he added a new dimension to the restaurant.

Our luncheon business grew rapidly. By the fall of 1946 brother Joe and I were both attending the University of Minnesota, but we arranged our schedules so we could be at Jax and help out over lunch. Joe helped tend bar and I bussed dishes, stocked the bars and was a utility man. We were now out of the chicken business because rationing ended with the war.

The word spread that the food at Jax was good. And it was no accident. My father was always basically a day person and he would get up at 4:30-5 a.m. Then he would go to the market and select his produce for the day.

In those days the farmers' market was at its zenith. He got there before his competitors and bought the best quality products available. Next, he would head over to Second Avenue North where the meat purveyors were located and shop for beef, pork, etc. He was back at Jax by 8 a.m., just in time to do the banking and get ready for the luncheon business.

The business began to jell. We had a good combination going for us. My father met people easily. His long career in law and politics served him well in the restaurant business. Soon, political figures from city hall began "finding" Jax. General Mills, Pillsbury, Northrup King, Grain Belt, Glueks, B.F. Nelson, Graco and dozens of other businesses were within minutes of Jax and the businessmen began discovering it.

The Labor Temple was less than two miles from Jax and many of the labor leaders of the day frequented Jax. It was interesting to see people whose work may have made them adversaries set that aside when they met at Jax.

Brother Joe was a great asset. An extrovert and an innovator he soon had people talking about Jax. It was Joe who came up with the idea of providing bus service to the University of Minnesota football games from Jax. Ours was the first restaurant to do this and in a few short years it became a smashing success. We would prepare a short and wholesome luncheon menu so that people could get in and out in good time and make it to the game.

From the mid-fifties until the Gophers switched to night football it was not at all unusual for us to serve seven to eight-hundred lunches in the two hours preceding departure of the last bus.

Another idea Joe developed in the late 1940s was a luncheon menu cover which was a montage of logos and letterheads of our customers' companies. There was no charge to the customer for being included on the cover and it soon grew to six pages. In the center of the outer cover was an outline of the state of Minnesota and within that appeared the phrase, "What Minnesota Sells . . . Sells Minnesota." It was interesting to watch the luncheon customers pointing out their logo to their guests with pride. The menu cover also gave added status to smaller companies who were, in effect, rubbing elbows with the industrial giants in print.

Our employees at that time were outstanding. None of us were schooled or sophisticated in the restaurant business. We were all plowing new ground together . . . and as trite or hackneyed as it sounds, we were a happy struggling family . . . ours and our staff combined.

In the early years, John Scovil was the night bartender. A portly sensitive man, and every inch a gentleman he also possessed an amazing memory both for names and drink preferences. People marveled at how he could have their favorite drink prepared and set on the bar in the

31

time it took them to get in the door and hang their coats. John worked in the county auditor's office during the day at a job my father helped him obtain years earlier. He idolized my dad and worked diligently to make sure the business succeeded.

The waitresses were neighbor ladies who wanted work to supplement their husband's income. Most were young mothers under thirty who came from neighborhood families. The work ethic was firmly entrenched and they responded enthusiastically as we learned together.

Some of the names: Ann Stawski, Mary Holewa, Connie Szczech, Rose Goleski Sundholm, Vickie Arent, Ruth Grupa, Helen Kozlak Martin, Lillian Dulban and Rita Mirocha. The night cook was Anna "Mama" Lipa. She was Mrs. Five-by-Five and waddled when she walked. She wore Granny glasses and the harder she worked the farther they slid down her nose. She cut her own french fries, made her own hashbrowns . . . boiled the potatoes and chopped them with a tin can before frying. She also was a genius at cooking steaks to the guest's specifications.

Pilferage? Theft? This is a bugaboo of many restaurants. We never experienced it in those days. We were small. We were growing. We all struggled together. At times it seemed more like a crusade than just a business. We were young and we wanted to succeed and be recognized.

One night waitress, Lillian Dulban, found a one-hundred dollar bill on the floor under a booth. She turned it in to my father. The next day a man called and asked if it had been found. He got his hundred dollars. Lillian received a twenty-dollar reward, and Jax got hundreds of dollars in positive word-of-mouth advertising.

1949 – I became engaged to Ruth Wichmann on December 27, 1948. The wedding date was set for September 12, 1949. It was decided that the reception would be upstairs at Jax, but that space had laid dormant for years. My father contacted Pat Seydel who was with Cook Paint Company and a good customer. Dad placed him in charge of freshening up the room.

The room was really barn-like to begin with, but Pat made it look good. He had the walls painted a rich burgundy. All window trim, as well as the benches that lined the walls, done in gray. There was a stage at one end of the room with spindled railings and those too were done in gray. The entire floor in the room was of maple boards and those were sanded and polished. A florist provided ferns for a backdrop on the stage and flowers for the tables. Brother Joe hired Wes Barlow and his orchestra for the music and saw to it that a myriad of other wedding details were tended to from proper attire to transportation.

Ruth and I were married on Monday morning, September 12, 1949 at Holy Cross church. A breakfast followed the wedding and a reception and dinner for some two-hundred fifty guests took place that evening. We spent our wedding night at the St. Paul Hotel. The room cost four dollars, and because it was our wedding night the hotel opened up an adjoining parlor room at no charge.

We drove to Chicago and spent five nights at the beautiful Edgewater Beach Hotel. Room cost seven dollars per night plus fifty cents for a radio. It was delightful. We had very little money, but we could open the window of our room. We could see and hear the Wayne King orchestra and the Dorothy Hild dancers perform on the Beachwalk at the hotel.

We drove back to Minneapolis on Monday, September 19th. I had to be at work by 5 p.m. because we had booked a big party for the newly painted second floor.

It was a party to honor the mayor of Minneapolis, Eric Hoyer. About three-hundred people were in attendance. It was the biggest function we had handled up to that time. Mayor Hoyer attended our wedding the week before and I had a lot of admiration for him.

He was a painter years earlier when he was

an alderman. He was still working with his painting partner Albin Carlson while performing his aldermanic duties. My father hired the pair to wash and paint the walls of the main floor kitchen. It was summertime so I was out of school and had the opportunity to work along with them.

The first day on the job I arrived after Mr. Hoyer and Mr. Carlson. They invited me up on the scaffold and showed me what to do. Both men were dressed in coveralls, the traditional painter's garb. At about 10 a.m. Mr. Hoyer said in his best Norwegian accent, "Well Albin, I gotta go to the council meeting." He bounded down from the scaffold and removed his coveralls.

I was amazed to see that he was dressed in business suit trousers, white shirt and tie. Everything except his suit coat which he had in his car. While he was gone, Mr. Carlson and I carried on. At about 1 p.m. Hoyer returned, donned his coveralls and resumed the job of washing the walls.

This made a big impression on me because even at that time most aldermen did no other work. To me it underscored his inherent honesty. He worked hard at public service and he continued to work at his trade. He also lived very modestly in his Northeast Minneapolis home.

When he became mayor many narrow-minded people criticized him because he spoke with a foreign (Norwegian) accent, but no one could challenge his ability to think or his integrity. Eric Hoyer retired to Seattle many years ago to be near his daughter. He usually made it a point to stop at whichever restaurant I was at when he visited Minnesota.

University of Minnesota football was the big autumn sports attraction through the forties and fifties. This was before the Twins, Vikings, or North Stars came to town and the limelight was always focused squarely on the football Gophers. I noticed that each year the Rainbow Cafe hosted a dinner at season's end for the Gopher "A" squad. It always got good press. This is fine but I wondered why no one ever honored the "B" squad. I mentioned this thought to brother Joe and my father and they said, "Go ahead and do it."

The 1949 football Gophers were an outstanding team, with soon to be N.F.L. stars Clayton Tonnemaker, Leo Nomellini, Gordon Soltau among the stars. They looked like potential national champions until they faltered twice late in the season. Little did I realize as I planned the "B" squad dinner that the "A" squad would slip and ultimately the Gopher "B" squad would end the 1949 season as the only unbeaten football team in the Big Ten.

I first contacted coach Sheldon Beise and told him what we had in mind. He said "Great." We set the date. Next I contacted Pat Seydel and asked him to be master of ceremonies at the event. Pat was a singer and front man for some bands before he got into the paint business. He weighed well over three-hundred pounds, sported a classy mustache and was a natural wit. Next, I decided that we should have a Most Valuable Player award and enlisted the help of a few business people to defray the cost of an appropriate trophy.

The night of the dinner we closed the entire main dining room for the "B" squad. We served huge tenderloin steaks, oversized baked potatoes, big salads plus pie à la mode for dessert. The squad devoured everything. Pat started the program with a few jokes and everyone was at ease and having fun. Coach Beise talked for a bit and announced that the winner of the most valuable player award by a vote of his teammates was Kenny Simmons.

The trophy was brought into the room. It was magnificent, remindful of the Chicago Tribune's trophy for the winner of the College All-Star game. Beise said it was a good thing none of the squad saw it before the balloting or they all would have voted for themselves.

Pat closed off the program with a couple of rather risque jokes. He told of the fellow who advised his friend to "put a rubber on the organ"

35

if he got intimate with his girlfriend. About a year later the advisor saw his friend wheeling a stroller down the sidewalk. He inquired, "Didn't you put a rubber on the organ?" His friend replied, "I couldn't find a rubber and I didn't have an organ, so I put an overshoe on the piano."

Most of the "B" squad in 1949 were World War II veterans and many of them became instant fans of Jax. The younger men too became customers as they reached maturity and became active in their businesses and professions. In the short run we received excellent press for honoring the "B" squad, and in the long run we made many friends for life.

In January of 1950, Ruth, Joe and I were invited to a wedding reception held at the old Andrews Hotel. When we walked into the room, Joe noticed Walter "Lefty" Tomczyk tending bar. Joe said, "Lefty! What are you doing here?" Lefty had only had one other job in his life and that was working for John Rapacz's Bar. He had been laid off at John's and this was his first night as a temporary at the hotel.

Joe asked him to stop in at Jax to discuss permanent employment. Lefty was hired the next day and worked at Jax until he retired in 1985. As a bartender Lefty had no peers. He was quick, squeaky clean, polite, entertaining and honest beyond question.

Later, as the business expanded Lefty became a maitre d'. Here too he was always the "house" man. He worked most nights and we never worried when we left the place in his care. Many of the guests thought he was one of our family and we always considered that a compliment.

One warm spring afternoon, a few months after Lefty came on board, I watched a lady walk in the door and sashay down the aisle to where I was standing. She flashed a pretty smile and said she was looking for waitress work. Her entire manner reminded me of Ann Southern's Maisey character. We were well staffed and I told her we had nothing available.

She smiled again and said, "Can I talk to your father?" I located my father and brought him toward the lady. "Rosie" he exclaimed, "what can I do for you?" She told him she was looking for work and he turned to me and said, "Hire her." I didn't realize it at the time but Rosie Goleski Sundholm was practically a legend as a waitress. She had worked at the East Hennepin Cafe when it was one of the most popular places in town.

It seemed that almost everyone knew Rosie. She loved people and this showed. Beyond that she had the most "upbeat" disposition of any human being I have ever known. Even when she had serious problems she never allowed them to interfere with her work. Her generosity was unparalleled. She was always willing to help those who needed it. One person who liked to tell of the help and kindness he received from her when he was a poor and struggling student at the University was Hubert Humphrey. He never forgot that Rosie would cover his bill at the East Hennepin to tide him over back in the late 1930s.

Hubert Humphrey and Rosie remained friends for life. He stopped in to visit her as often as his schedule would permit. He invited her to his inauguration as Vice President and the day she retired he called the restaurant as we were honoring her to congratulate her and spend a few minutes reminiscing.

(The following article on Rosie appeared in the *Minneapolis Tribune* on November 26, 1972.)

By Robert T. Smith

It was 30 years ago. The young University of Minnesota student was poor. Often he ate at the old East Hennepin Cafe.

One day his hunger was bigger than his pocketbook and he was short for the bill.

"That's OK, Sweetie," said Rosie, the waitress. "This one's on me, including tip."

The other day Rosie celebrated her sixty-fifth birthday and noted her forty-fifth year as a waitress. A phone call from Washington came to Jax

Cafe, where she's been for twenty years. It was for Rosie.

"Hey, Rosie, happy birthday," said the voice of the former university student, former vice-president and now Minnesota senator.

"Oh, Hubert, you gorgeous creature," said Rosie. "How are you, Sweetie?"

Later, Sen. Hubert H. Humphrey talked about Rosie Sundholm: "She was the queen of all of East Hennepin. She made the profession of being a waitress a skill and an art."

Humphrey and his wife, Muriel, often went to the old cafe, which no longer exists. When he was elected mayor of Minneapolis, he held his first party at East Hennepin with Rosie in attendance.

Jack and Bill Kozlak of Jax Cafe threw a birthday party for Rosie on the day Humphrey called. All the employees of the cafe attended. They talked over old times, including the fact that Rosie used to put Jack and Bill into high chairs when their parents brought them to the East Hennepin.

Rosie, well known in Northeast Minneapolis, was born in Poland. At six, her parents brought her to Minnesota and she grew up in Columbia Heights. Even as a small girl, she loved to wait on tables. She started at the East Hennepin in 1928 and stayed there twenty years.

Rosie knew many of the Gopher football players. She had a deal with Babe LeVoir: For each touchdown he made, she would buy him a beer.

"There were all sorts of politicians around," said Rosie. "And Hubert was the poorest little kid you ever saw. I campaigned for him for mayor so he would have some money for food."

Rosie also knew some characters on the other side of the law: Kid Cann and Tommy Banks, to name a couple, "My son, Richard, used to caddy for the Kid's brother, Yiddy Bloom, who ran a liquor store across from the East Hennepin," she recalled.

Rosie, who's had some heavy personal problems, never brought them to work. "To be a good waitress, you must love people and forgive them all their faults," she said.

Early in her career, she devised a method to handle cranky customers. She would really hustle to serve them so she could get rid of them in a hurry. But she abandoned the plan. The bitchy customers would be so impressed with the fast service that they would return to the cafe and demand Rosie.

The old bit about eating and sleeping one's job directly applies to Rosie. "I often have nightmares about being a waitress," she said. "I sit bolt upright, and say things like 'Did I bring him the mustard?'"

(End of *Tribune* Article)

Brother Joe and I felt that Jax had just scratched the surface of its potential. We prevailed on dad to expand farther into the building and buy more parking which we sorely needed. He was slow to respond. He had struggled through the Great Depression, suffered many reverses and now for the first time he felt somewhat financially secure. He was in his mid-fifties and reluctant to take new risks. We continued to push, and finally he agreed to buy our first bit of off-street parking – plus an additional dining room expansion into the building.

1950 – We went to the H.J. Nelson Fixture Company and had them design what was to become the Roundtable Room. The room was done in blond oak panels and had a bar at one end. We were able to incorporate a fireplace into the room. Then we had W.S. Nott Company build a spit with a geared down motor so we could do suckling pigs, hams, and rounds in the fireplace for special occasions. The Roundtable Room turned out beautifully. It had indirect lighting which was just becoming the rage plus solid oak round tables and captain's chairs with red leather trim. The carpeting was a beautiful thick pile red wool scroll.

It was Joe's idea to make it "For men only" at lunch. The idea caught on immediately. Remember, this was 1950 and "For men only" was an acceptable idea. It wasn't long before many companies asked if they could have the same table every day. There was a B.F. Nelson, Coast to Coast, Bemis Bag, Graco, and other "company" tables. The only time these people called us was when they could not make it for lunch and we would then release the table.

About this time our parents began taking two or three week Florida winter vacations. This gave Joe an opportunity to test his promotional skills without clearing his ideas with anyone but me . . . and I usually thought his ideas were great.

As I mentioned earlier, Joe spent three years in Hawaii during the war and he thought it would be fun to have a luau. To the best of my knowledge no one had done one in the Twin Cities up to that time. But that didn't stop Joe. He decided to have it on the second floor. He contacted Northwest Airlines and borrowed a grass shack that they used for promotional purposes. We used it at the top of the stairs on the night of the luau. He promoted the party through our mailing list and sold out a January night long in advance.

He had ti leaves, flower leis, vanda orchids, lomi lomi salmon, and poi flown in from Hawaii. He had our waitresses outfitted in mu mus and made up with deep sun makeup. The luau was quite authentic with roast pig, french fried bananas and many other delicacies. Through the University he found two Hawaiian girl students whom he hired to give hula lessons. He hired the Hawaiian musicians from the Waikiki Room at the Nicollet Hotel. Everyone had a great time. This event was so successful that we ran many of them through the years.

Joe loved a party and Valentine's Day was a natural for him. He promoted a fixed price dinner complete with flower corsage for the lady and cherries jubilee for dessert. Ever the romantic, he hired strolling musicians for the evening. He realized that weather in Minnesota was unpredictable at best, so your check became your reservation.

On that Valentine's night we were hit with six

inches of snow. About 7:30 p.m. my father called from Florida. He said, "I understand you are having a heavy snow so I suppose it is slow there." Joe said, "I'm sorry I don't have time to talk. We have a full house and a waiting list. Call us back tomorrow."

The new Roundtable Room did extremely well at noon but it needed some promotion on week nights. I thought of a pig roast, and together with our chef we developed a nice menu with soup, cole slaw, oyster dressing, vegetable, potato and peach flambé for dessert. These dinners were by reservation only and sold out consistently. We usually did two in the fall and two in the spring.

One day I picked up a suburban newspaper and saw a heading: *Church Sells Out Pheasant Dinner*. We decided to try a pheasant dinner on a Tuesday night in the Roundtable Room. Once again we struck pay dirt. Two in the fall and two in the spring. They helped make our Tuesday nights. Next we did mallard duck dinners and these finally evolved to Hunters Dinners where we sold out the entire second floor, serving combination dinners including pheasant, duck, goose with wild rice and all the trimmings plus a flaming dessert. Strolling musicians also added to these affairs. We were turning lemon nights into lemonade.

At about this time we got our first break from the Minneapolis daily newspaper. Will Jones wrote a column reviewing restaurants and he came out and reviewed one of our pig roasts. He enjoyed things that were a bit off-beat and he wrote a sparkling review. It enhanced our image and also helped our bottom line. In the years that followed, Will Jones treated us kindly whenever he chose to critique us.

1951 – We were getting more calls for parties on the second floor, but we lost a lot of potential business because the decor was not up to par. We finally convinced dad that something should be done. He agreed to new lighting, another paint job and improvement of the restrooms and kitchen. We got the job done just in time for my five-year high school class reunion.

1952 – In 1952, Joe married Helen Dunne. The business continued on a growth curve. Joe and I shared the majority of the work load and now youngest brother, Bill, at age fifteen, became available for occasional dish, bus, and stock duties.

1952-53 – We continued to plod along for the next couple of years. Ruth and I and Joe and Helen began raising our families. Joe and I continued to push for improvements at Jax. I dropped out of school after Ruth and I got married and Joe kept prodding me to go back and get a degree. One day I was in the vicinity of St. Thomas College and I stopped in and visited with the registrar, Father Wittman. He too urged me to come back and earn my degree. I remember saying, "I'm married, a father with another child on the way . . . even if I do come back it will take two years and I'll be twenty-five by the time I finish." He looked me squarely in the eye and said, "How old will you be in two years if you don't come back?" I enrolled, carried a full academic load . . . worked full time, paid my own tuition and got the best grades I ever had. I had no time for the social aspect of college life, but I have never been sorry that I expended the effort to get my degree.

Joe and I both enjoyed special promotions and the next thing we tried was a German Night. Chef Norbert Helget was of German extraction and when we ran the idea of a German Night past him he was delighted and enthused. We developed an authentic menu for the evening complete with such offerings as sauerbraten, wienerschnitzel, and hassenpfeffer. Of course sauerkraut and sweet sour red cabbage were choices as were soups with spaetzles. For dessert we had a specialist bake some of the most exotic tortes imaginable.

A German Night needs German music, and we were able to engage Fezz Fritsche and his band. Fritsche was from New Ulm, Minnesota, a German community of some ten-thousand people located about seventy miles from the Twin Cities. His group was well known throughout the state. When we announced the date of our German Night the reservations poured in.

The combination of authentic German food with specially selected beers, wines and spirits plus foot stomping oomp-pah-pah German music was magic. Everyone had a great time and over the years we promoted many more extremely successful German Nights.

I worked many night shifts at Jax during my student days and many times I would get an opportunity to study between the hours of midnight and 1 a.m. As the business wound down and we prepared to close for the night, I would usually spread my work out on one of the back booths and sit so I could see the front door and the bar.

On one of these occasions waitress Ann Stawski stopped by to chat. I don't remember how we got on the subject but I learned that she was not a U.S. citizen. Her parents immigrated to the United States from Poland when Ann was just a baby in arms. Her father secured his "first papers" on the road to citizenship but died before attaining full citizenship. Ann did not know where her parents had entered the United States nor the ship that had brought them here.

Because of this and some other quirks in the law she was denied citizenship even though she was married to a U.S. citizen and had borne three children who were also U.S. citizens. She told me that she had spent a great deal of money with attorneys in hope of getting the problem corrected but it was all to no avail.

I offered to write a letter to Senator Humphrey outlining her problem and requesting his help. She said that would be fine but I thought I detected a sense of defeatism in her attitude. I wrote the letter.

One week later we received a reply signed by the senator acknowledging receipt of our letter together with his assurance that he would work

43

on the problem. Annie's spirits brightened. And then nothing. Days turned into weeks . . . weeks into months and just when we were about to abandon hope another letter arrived.

Ironically, it was almost a year to the day from our first correspondence. The senator advised Annie that his staff had identified the ship that brought her parents to North America. It had docked at a Canadian port. They had located and documented the place at which her parents had entered the United States. Further, all the red tape was now satisfied and she could proceed with the application for citizenship. Annie was ecstatic. Soon everyone in the restaurant, her church, and the entire neighborhood knew what Senator Hubert Horatio Humphrey had done.

Annie went to night school to learn about the Constitution . . . Bill of Rights . . . court system . . . separation of powers and all the other things a new citizen should know. I am convinced that no one in Minnesota was ever a more serious or dedicated candidate for citizenship.

The day she went before the judge and was granted citizenship was indeed special for Annie and all who knew and loved her. Her husband was granted the day off from work so he could accompany her to the proceedings. Her children were excused from school so they too could observe this important occasion. The entire restaurant staff and all of the customers were delighted to share her happiness.

That evening Ruth, my mother, dad and I were guests of Annie and her husband for dinner at Jax. I can still visualize Annie on that evening. She wore a red, white and blue corsage compliments of H.H.H. and a countenance that told the whole story.

1954 – Then suddenly something happened. One of our neighbors who had not been a serious competitor took the plunge, building a big new dining room plus a new bar, private party facilities and parking.

Our competitive juices began running and it

was much easier to convince our father who still controlled the purse strings, that if we wanted to stay on top in our area we had better spend some money.

I suggested we build a complete new kitchen and convert the existing kitchen to dining area. We had all visited the Ivanhoe restaurant in Chicago and been impressed by their dining room and adjoining garden. We discussed the possibility of razing the huge garage in the back of the building . . . putting in big windows on the west end of the dining room and building a garden for the diners to look out on.

The idea gained strength as we discussed it. We also knew the dining room itself needed a going over but we couldn't quite decide what to do. One day I was discussing our dilemma with Dale Stanchfield, a customer and county commissioner. He told me of a man named Sam Wentworth who did nice work designing areas that were remodeled at the courthouse.

I contacted Mr. Wentworth and he was delighted at the opportunity to design a dining room. He did all the work laying out the room. He located the windows, specified the beautiful walnut paneling, selected the moldings and trim and did just a superb job.

Aaron Carlson Company did the millwork and it looks as good today as it did the day it was installed. Mr. Wentworth sent a bill for two-hundred twenty-five dollars, which had to be the best buy since the Louisiana Purchase. We had a new modern kitchen designed to service both the first and second floors. The new building addition also had a full basement and a large elevator that services all three floors.

When it came time to build the garden we were fortunate to hear about a man named Paul Bass. Mr. Bass, a landscape architect, designed the Minnesota Pavilion at the Century of Progress Exposition in Chicago in 1933-34. And he was available. When laying out the garden he discovered a drain in the center of the old garage. He came forth with the idea of building a waterfall and trout stream as long as we had a drain in such an appropriate place. In order to have a waterfall we needed a well and Mr. Bass drove a sand point and hit good water at twenty feet. He built the falls, laid out the stream, selected the trees and shrubs and positioned the flowers.

When the project was completed it was the talk of the town. Diners could net their trout and we would whisk them to the kitchen for preparation. Colored lights illuminated the garden at night and when winter came the more it snowed, the prettier the garden became. My mother selected the carpeting and coverings for the new dining room chairs and her eye for color proved exquisite.

At this point I convinced my father that we should change the name from Jax Bar to Jax Cafe and buy a new sign for the building. I also hired a local artist, Ed Zajac, to design a crest for us. He was working for Brown & Bigelow and was delighted at the opportunity. He did the job for one-hundred twenty-five dollars.

I remember the day dad and mother went to the bank to pay for all we had done. They put their name on a one-hundred thousand dollar loan, but it must have seemed ten times as big to them because they experienced the bitterness of the Great Depression and dad was now pushing sixty. I'm sure he remembered the original price for the entire building at fifteen-thousand six-hundred dollars, and here we were now spending six times that figure. We all worked hard and now that we had a large, well-equipped facility the money came back.

During the winter of 1955 we got a big break when Cedric Adams did a little story on the garden in his column in the Minneapolis daily newspaper.

(Following is what Cedric wrote:)

I don't gasp at a sight very often, particularly at one I see in or from a restaurant, but I let out a big one and stared with my mouth open at Jax Cafe at University and Twentieth Avenue NE the other night. The Kozlaks, hosts at Jax, have built what they call their Old World Garden. You see it through the window walls of the main dining room. In it are Colorado blue spruce, Austrian pine, junipers, and dozens of other trees and shrubs. During the summer months, a trout stream flows through the garden. Guests net their rainbows for dinner. The holiday season, however, tops everything. The trees are filled with colored lights, Santa and his reindeer are in the garden, right now there's fresh snow on the trees, snow covers the water wheel and the whole scene looks like a Currier and Ives. If you plan to dine at Jax while all this is in evidence, may I suggest you arrange at least an added fifteen minutes to your eating schedule for nothing but reflection as you look out on this breath-taking scene.

Cedric Adams was an extremely popular writer for the Minneapolis Star. His column, *"In This Corner"* was a potpourri of information of local interest. He also did the noontime news and 10 p.m. news on WCCO radio.

WCCO was one of the most powerful and popular radio stations in America and Adams was their top draw. Airline pilots flying in the Minnesota, western Wisconsin, and northern Iowa areas said they could tell when Cedric Adams signed off on the 10 p.m. news because they could see the lights go out in the farm houses on their route.

Adams had a legendary following and when he gave a plug it translated immediately into extra business. He didn't tell us in advance that the story was going to run. So the first night we were caught a little shorthanded. But we adjusted quickly in the days that followed and were able to gain many new friends.

I took the liberty of going to our storerooms and picked out many canned delicacies, some of our monogrammed glassware, and a few bottles of choice spirits and cordials. I took this to our local florist and had it arranged in a very large wicker basket with some poinsettia plants. We covered the basket with cellophane and tied it with a big red bow. The florist's husband and I (it took two to lift it) delivered it to the Adams' residence. Mrs. Adams answered the door and was amazed at the gift. She said she had never seen anything like it. Neither had we.

A few days later I received a call from Cedric. He thanked "all the Kozlaks" for the gift and then asked if we had space for a party of about two-hundred fifty people. I assured him that we did and he explained that he and Mrs. Adams together with Dr. and Mrs. Paul Larson were interested in hosting a party for their friends. Both couples were much in demand socially and with their busy schedules a yearly party was a nice way to satisfy their obligations. They had done the country club and private club bit and were looking for something different.

I met with both couples and showed them the second floor. The room was still a bit barn-like. I didn't know how they would react but Cedric thought it was just great. He wanted to do a costume party with a chuck wagon dinner. We designed a menu and they left all the other details up to me.

Brother Joe and I, Chef Norbert Helget and Pat Seydel worked together. Pat designed a covered wagon . . . Norbert had some old wagon wheels. And by laying out the buffet tables with the covered wagon as the center of attention we created an impressive effect. Keith Powell, one of our cooks at the time, did two beautiful ice carvings. The buffet table contained many accompaniments, but the center of attention was big beef rounds.

It was somewhat difficult for the staff to

48

concentrate on their duties as the guests arrived because many guests were local celebrities and they were in costumes as well. The crowd enjoyed a social hour, and when it was time for dinner we had our chef and four assistants march out of the kitchen together. They wore their "whites" with red neckerchiefs. They each carried big carving knives and sharpening steels. They positioned themselves behind the table and in unison raised their knives and steels and speedily sharpened their knives. The click-click-click got everyone's attention and the guests began their dining experience.

About this time Charlie Saunders, the owner of Charlie's Cafe Exceptionale and the premier restaurateur of his day, came to me and said, "Hey kid, how about showing me the rest of the place." I was ecstatic. We went into the second floor kitchen and took the elevator to the main floor kitchen.

It was very busy but everything was operating smoothly. He observed our cooking line in operation and complimented our new kitchen. We walked out to the Roundtable Room and every table was filled. We proceeded to the main dining room and he saw the garden and a sea of people occupying the tables. We walked to the bar area where Joe was working the podium. The bar area was wall to wall with people waiting to be seated. Mr. Saunders and Joe exchanged greetings, and we started back upstairs. On the way he said, "Geez, you got quite a place here . . . how come nobody knows about it?"

There was dancing after dinner and Cedric Adams capped off the evening by presenting a door prize. We had the prize in the kitchen and it was a gorgeous package. It was about six feet, six inches high and thirty inches wide. It was wrapped in shiny pink paper and had a wide lavender ribbon that went from bottom to top and around the sides. A huge bow adorned the center of the package. Cedric took the microphone and did a big buildup to the actual award. He described at great length how the Adams and Larsons scoured the countryside to find an appropriate prize for such an important occasion.

Finally, he announced the winners and as the winning couple came forward we carried the package into the room. The crowd oh'd and ah'd as they saw the package. It looked like something from Nieman Marcus. Cedric presented the prize and the winners couldn't wait to open it. The crowd was rife with expectation. When the wrapping came off, the room erupted in laughter because behind the beautiful packaging was the sorriest looking outhouse door complete with crescent that anyone had ever seen!

We felt that there was plenty of business available but our customers told us that the second floor was not in keeping with the main floor. Joe and I continued to pressure our father to decorate the second floor. Finally in late 1957 he agreed to look at a proposal. I went to the Aaron Carlson millwork company and met with Aaron Sr. and his son, Paul.

I went to them for three reasons: Their company was renowned for its workmanship; they were located in our part of the city, and they were customers. They were familiar with the space we proposed to remodel, and they questioned me as to what we would like the room to look like. I told them that we all appreciated beautiful wood.

I suggested that since the ceilings were thirteen feet high we might like some massive beam treatment on the ceiling. They asked if we had a preference for the paneling. I replied that whereas the Indiana walnut in the main dining room and the Philippine mahogany in the bar were outstanding, we might like to try something entirely different on the second floor.

Their designers went to work. Meanwhile, I contacted a bar supply company and had them redesign, spec and price an entire new underbar and back bar setup. New sinks, mixers, coolers, back bar steps plus whatever else was needed.

It didn't take Paul Carlson long to get back to

me. For the sake of getting a price on what he proposed to furnish, we agreed on cherrywood paneling in the main room, hallway, and stairwell. For the bar we chose oak planks and for the small dining room butternut paneling. The designers showed the rooms done with an eleven-foot wainscot. The large dining room showed the massive beams with ample space between them for acoustical treatment. Pilasters below the beam settings broke the monotony of the long walls. The plan looked beautiful. The price for all the paneling prefinished and delivered was quoted at sixteen-thousand dollars. This doesn't seem like a lot today but in 1957 you could still buy a very nice home in the Twin Cities for that amount of money.

Next, I contacted Ernest Ganley Construction Company and obtained a bid for the installation of the paneling. I also had a custom lighting company design chandeliers for the rooms. The chandeliers were expensive, eight-thousand dollars. But you would not see them anywhere else. And because of the size of the rooms, we needed something bigger than could be found at conventional lighting companies.

Selecting chairs was no problem. We purchased new chairs for the main floor in 1955 and we wanted the same frame with a different cover for the second floor. In 1955 they cost twenty-eight dollars . . . they were now thirty-two dollars. Three-hundred chairs, tables, carpeting, a luminous ceiling in the hallway and it was soon decision time.

My father was always a tough sell. He could think of a dozen ways to say *no!* Joe and I would not take no for an answer on this one, however. In the early spring of 1958 father finally gave the project his blessing. The project was primarily mine to coordinate and complete and I loved the challenge. We accepted no bookings for the second floor between June 30th and September 13th. All contracts were let. All subcontractors and workmen were apprised of our deadline. They absolutely had to be ready on the 13th of September because we had a wedding reception booked for noon that day.

The millwork company promised timely delivery beginning the first week in July and they were true to their word. The carpenters began their work on July 1st with their preparation, removing the old wall benches and ripping out the old door frames and window casings. We knew we were on a tight schedule, but we were dealing with responsible people and felt confident that the job could be completed on time. We asked all of our employees to stay off the second floor. We understood they would be curious to check the progress of the project, but we wanted no distractions whatever to the task at hand.

The weeks sped by and the job took shape. I was the expeditor and scheduled the times at which one trade followed another. As September approached it became clear that we were cutting it very thin on completion time.

I rechecked with our suppliers. The carpeting was scheduled to be laid on September 12th. The chairs were to be delivered in the late afternoon of the twelfth, as were the tables. Our electrician had possession of the chandeliers and he agreed to hang them late Friday night on the twelfth if necessary. We pushed ahead. Finish carpentry work is very precise and the men on our job were artisans of the highest order. The only problem is that to do the job correctly takes time.

On the morning of September 12th the carpenters still had a few odds and ends to finish, and as they worked little patches of sawdust accumulated. The room looked far from finished. The wood floor was not yet carpeted. The tables were in town on a truck waiting for my call to be delivered. The chairs were on a truck somewhere between Ohio and Minneapolis. The light fixtures were at our electrician's shop. It was about 9:30 a.m. and I was on the main floor writing up the reservations for the lunch hour.

Enter: Tomorrow's bridegroom to be. He had

walked upstairs to see the room. When he confronted me his face was as white as his shirt. What he had seen was what I have just described and he said, "You forgot about my wedding." I tried to reassure him, but I don't think he thought it at all possible for us to be ready.

The carpenters finished at 10:30 a.m. and the carpet layers arrived on the scene. I called for the tables and asked for the latest delivery possible on that Friday afternoon. I checked on the chairs and was assured they would be at our dock by 4 p.m. The carpet layers projected that they would be done by 5:30 p.m. I scheduled the chandeliers for 6 p.m. delivery.

Everything fell into place. By 10 p.m. Joe and I had the new tables and chairs arranged for the party the next day. The rooms looked exquisite and they still do.

We called to the main floor and invited the employees to come and take a quick look as time permitted. What they saw was the newly named Cosmopolitan Room done in beautiful cherrywood with massive beamed ceilings. A heavy pile red wool carpet with an interesting beige and gold scroll design covered the floor. The tabletops matched the walls and the chairs were black anodized frames with gold seats and backs. The new barroom with walls of solid oak boards was not only beautiful but built to be functional.

The luminous ceiling in the hallway near the coatroom was a rather new innovation at the time and everyone was fascinated by the effect it gave. Some of the employees remembered the second floor from the old dance hall days. Some had their wedding dinners and wedding dances in this space. They could not believe the transformation. I remember Rosie and Annie as they looked over the rooms. They said they couldn't imagine that it could turn out so beautifully and tears of joy streamed down their faces.

The next morning Donna Kopp and Owen Kane were pronounced husband and wife and they made their way to Jax for what they hoped would be their reception. I remember Owen as he walked up the stairs. The joy of his wedding did not fully mask the apprehensive look as he walked toward the dining room. When he saw the room he broke into a broad grin turned and said, "I didn't think it could be done. Congratulations and thank you."

The reception and dinner went off beautifully and the word-of-mouth advertising about the exquisite new facility began to spread. We now had a restaurant facility that we felt was second to none, with the possible exception of Charlie's Cafe Exceptionale. However, even Charlies best private dining room was not as posh or as large as our Cosmopolitan Room.

We had another advantage as well. Our second-floor facility was serviced by its own kitchen. Most restaurants at that time, and many today as well, service banquet rooms from the same kitchen as their main dining room. This arrangement can sometimes be made to work, but the way we were set up, our large private parties could be served on time without disturbing the flow and tempo of service on the main floor.

This enabled us to develop and expand our banquet and dining room business simultaneously. When we totaled up the cost of the second-floor project, it came in at eighty-thousand dollars. At the time it seemed expensive, but today you can easily spend three-hundred dollars for a good restaurant chair, so to outfit that facility in chairs alone could cost ninety-thousand dollars in today's dollars.

1958 – Brother Bill graduated from Holy Cross College in 1958 and was now working with us in the business. He was a business major and he came on board with suggestions that reflected his training. For years our father told us that he was going to sell us the business. We thought that now that Bill had completed his schooling the time was at hand. It made a lot of sense to Joe and me. We were both married and had growing families. Our fifth child, son Paul, was born in June. Joe and

54

Helen were expecting their fourth child. We were both at the stage of life where we yearned for ownership. I was thirty . . . Joe thirty-five.

Bill was only twenty-two, but we were willing to make the business a three-way partnership if only we could buy it. We didn't care about owning the building. We knew mother and dad could extract a nice income from the rent plus the sale price. I often wondered how many family businesses face this situation . . . this dilemma. Our parents could not bring themselves to sell.

It got so it could not even be discussed. It was too emotional . . . too painful. We continued to work together but Joe had reached the point where he was looking for the right opportunity to make the break.

The "new" second floor was a big bite. We began booking some monthly dinner meetings for groups in the one-hundred to two-hundred person range and it was great business. The menus were almost always of the pre-set single item variety. These groups had a cocktail hour before dinner and a business meeting after dinner. We booked the American Foundry Men's Society, National Association of Accountants, Petroleum Credit Association, Investors Diversified Services Men's Club and many other similar societies and associations.

They helped fill the space from Monday through Thursday. We were able to book the room on weekends with wedding dinners, class reunions, dinner dances and assorted other quality functions. When we did not have a booking for a weekend night, we would promote a special evening on our own.

The summer after the second floor was remodeled, a group of Polish American business and professional people had a convention in the Twin Cities. They scheduled a dinner at Jax for two-hundred seventy-five people and the featured speaker was to be Senator Hubert Humphrey.

I worked the party and as the guests arrived the cocktail hour conversation in various groups turned to Humphrey. I couldn't help but pick up bits and pieces of chitchat and it seemed to me that Senator Humphrey had few friends in the crowd. Phrases like "too glib," "ultra liberal," "brash" and even "motor mouth" were used by some in attendance to characterize Humphrey. If he had any supporters in the group, they were silent.

Dinner time arrived and the guests were seated . . . Humphrey had not yet arrived, but he had sent word that he was detained and asked that the dinner proceed on schedule. The dinner service was well underway when Humphrey bounded up the stairs, stepped into the cocktail lounge, and asked for me. None of the guests could see him and so they were not aware of his presence.

One of the bartenders came into the dining room and whispered that the senator wanted to see me. I proceeded to the cocktail lounge and the senator asked, "Is there anyone on your staff who can teach me to greet these people in Polish?" There were several because we had assigned all our Polish speaking waitresses to the party. I went and found Rosie and brought her to the cocktail lounge. Humphrey was delighted. Not only was he going to be tutored in Polish, but his teacher was his dear friend Rosie.

We sat at a little table and he explained that he wanted to open his speech with a Polish greeting. Rosie thought for a moment and proceeded to teach him to say, "Dobrie Vietur, Polazie, Posdraviam Voss." It took several minutes of repeated efforts for him to get it down perfectly. He must have repeated it twenty times: "Dobrie Vietur, Polazie, Posdraviam Voss."

When Rosie and the senator were both satisfied with his proficiency at speaking the phrase, Humphrey proceeded to the head table just in time to enjoy some dessert and coffee. When he walked through the dining room to take his place at the table there was no applause . . . no stir of excitement . . . no emotion from the crowd whatsoever. The master of ceremonies rose from his chair, shook hands with the senator and they both sat down.

When the time came to start the program the master of ceremonies rose and gave the usual flowery introduction concluding with, "It gives me great pleasure to introduce Minnesota's senior Senator, Hubert Horatio Humphrey." The applause was polite and restrained as Humphrey made his way to the microphone. No one rose to their feet . . . it was a chilly reception at best.

Humphrey adjusted the microphone, scanned the crowd for a moment or two, leaned forward and began: "Dobrie Vietur, Polazie, Posdraviam Voss." The room erupted. Everyone was on their feet cheering. I have never heard or seen such a spontaneous outpouring of emotion. The crowd loved it . . . Humphrey had hit a sensitive responsive chord and instantly made over two-hundred new friends. Translated to English all he said was: "Good evening my fellow Poles and a heartfelt welcome."

His speech was marvelous. He told of his admiration for the Poles and the tenacity of the Polish people. He showed his knowledge of their plight of being squeezed between the Germans and the Russians throughout modern history. He told them what they wanted to hear and he concluded by contrasting the Soviet and United States attitude toward Poland. In Krakow the Soviets had built a monument to the Soviet war machine. In Krakow the people of the United States had contributed the money to build a new hospital. It was vintage Humphrey. He had stepped into a potentially hostile group and won them over.

PART
THREE

Continued Growth
of
JAX CAFE

The "new" Cosmopolitan Room with a seating capacity for over three-hundred guests presented us with opportunities and challenges. We had the opportunity to book business meetings, weddings, private luncheons and many other special events. The challenge was to do a good job and be competitive so that we could get repeat business.

It is comforting to know that some groups have been holding monthly meetings at Jax for over thirty years without interruption. An additional challenge was to fill the nights that were difficult to book with private parties. I mentioned some of the things we did before the Cosmopolitan Room was completed . . . but now with the big investment and a correspondingly bigger financial nut to crack it became increasingly important to fill the space with customers.

Among the special nights we promoted was a Viennese Night. I contacted the Minneapolis Symphony Orchestra (forerunner to the Minnesota Symphony) and asked if it were possible to put together a group that could provide appropriate music for the function we were planning.

I was referred to Misha Breggman. Misha had been with the orchestra for many years and he welcomed the opportunity to put a group together. He selected ten of the symphony's finest musicians including his brother Joe.

The group represented a total of almost two-hundred years experience with the Minneapolis Symphony and they were outstanding. They provided beautiful, sophisticated listening music during cocktails and dinner plus dance music par excellence for the remainder of the evening.

The menus for these affairs were standard Viennese fare that we varied nominally from one Viennese Night to the next. Some of the items that received the most praise were the wienerschnitzel, the green spinach noodles, and the fabulous tortes that we served for dessert.

Soon, we were receiving requests to do a Polish Night. We didn't need much coaxing because of our heritage, and we joyfully complied. We served golumbki (cabbage rolls stuffed with ground beef and rice), pierogi (made with a dough similar to ravioli then stuffed with cottage cheese, sauerkraut or prunes). And then, of course, we served Polish sausage, roast pork, and plenty of sauerkraut. We included authentic Polish poppyseed bread, nut bread, and cheesecake made with cottage cheese and graham cracker crust.*

The dessert finale was colorful marzepans (ground almonds with vanilla sweetened with powdered sugar) in the shape and color of strawberries, bananas, pears, carrots, miniature oranges and apples.

Poles, and those who wish they were, love to dance. And dance they did. Polkas, mazurkas, schottisches and the butterfly were played. The floors at Jax are steel reinforced. However, on these nights the chandeliers in the main dining room below jiggled more than a little as the people danced on the floor above.

These special nights gave the Cosmopolitan Room great exposure and they also showed the public that we had the expertise and the facilities to be more than a steakhouse.

Brother Joe really hit on a winner when he instituted bus service from Jax to the University of Minnesota football games.

It was only logical that our next step would be to provide lunch and dinner and bus service to the state high school basketball tournament. We followed the district

* See recipe section for Polish cheesecake recipe.

and regional high school tournaments with great interest. When the state tournament field was set we fired off
ads to the local newspapers of the participating towns
that would be represented.

In those days the tournament was held at Williams
Arena at the University of Minnesota, so we were in a
prime spot to provide meals and bus service.

State tournament week, in late March, quickly
became one of the busiest weeks of the year. The adult
population of small towns follows its high school teams
with a passion. We made it easy for them to attend all the
sessions of the tournament and still enjoy good food and
drink.

The tournament ran on Thursday, Friday and
Saturday. Thursday presented the greatest challenge for
us because all eight teams in the tournament, as it was
then structured, were in the championship round on
Thursday. This meant that Williams Arena would have
from thirteen to sixteen-thousand people for two games in
the afternoon and eighteen-thousand plus for the two
games played in the evening.

For Jax it meant two floors packed with customers at
lunch and a logistical headache for the limited time
between the afternoon and evening sessions. The majority
of our guests who attended the afternoon session on
Thursday also attended the evening session.

The second game of the afternoon session was
scheduled to begin at 3:30 p.m. This meant that if it
started on time—and all went well—we would have
roughly two and one-half hours to get the people back
from Williams Arena to Jax . . . serve them and get them
back for the evening session.

This may not seem like a particular problem in the
fast food era, but Jax was then, as now, a white tablecloth
restaurant. Remember also that the tournament is held in
March, and March is Minnesota's snowiest month. It was
almost an article of faith that heavy snow accompany the
state high school basketball tournament. I can visualize
more than once the scene—where it snowed—customers
would push a bus to get it around the corner on
Twentieth Avenue, so it could proceed on University
Avenue to the Arena.

Bill, Jr., Kathy, and Bill, Sr., greet guests at Jax.

(Above, left) Thea Stay. Over four decades a dedicated manager, teacher, and friend of the Kozlak family and their employees at Jax. (Right) Walter "Lefty" Tomczyk. From 1950 until his retirement in the late 1980s, Lefty personified everything about Jax that made it a great restaurant. A trustworthy loyal friend to our family.

Jack, Governor Wendell Anderson and Bill in the Roundtable Room at Jax. Joe Sr.'s picture is in the background.

Bottom row (L to R): Joe Strauss, Rudy Soroka, Harold Kalina, Pat Doughterty. Top row: Stan Fudro, Dick Miller, Bob Hanna, Sam Sivanich, Governor Wendell Anderson, John Skowronski, John Kozlak, Al Hofstede.

We were always concerned with the time constraints. We fretted over the snow. But what we really dreaded was overtime games during the Thursday afternoon session, because they further reduced our time tolerances.

How do you get six hundred to six hundred-fifty people all arriving within fifteen minutes of each other into a two-story restaurant? How do you offer a varied menu, serve cocktails as well, and get them from Williams Arena to Jax (three miles each way) and back in such a short time?

First, we took reservations. This gave us a good indication of the size of each group, and let us know when we reached our capacity. The size of the groups dictated how the dining rooms would be set, and we were able to determine this early in the day.

Next, we would draw a table diagram of each floor and assign waitress/waiter stations. As soon as lunch was finished we began setup for the between sessions meal. Once we knew which groups would be on the first and second floors, we mimeographed sheets with the alphabetized names of the reservations. The sheets indicated on which floor each group would be seated. We took these mimeographed sheets to our buses that were parked at Williams Arena, so our customers would each get one as they boarded the bus for the return trip to Jax.

We further instructed that there were coat check facilities on each floor. This alleviated a jam up at the front door. It relieved guests of the bother to make their way to the podium, to find out to which floor their group was assigned.

The menu was planned days in advance. We offered a short, quick wholesome menu. The entrées served were braised beef tenderloin tips in wine sauce; roast chicken with wild rice; baked stuffed pork chops; prime ribs of beef; walleye pike.

The dinner price included a round-trip ticket for the bus. The bus ticket was located at each place setting. Only people who were not having dinner found it necessary to purchase a bus ticket. We had them available at the podium and at the coat checkrooms.

To properly staff the restaurant we had on duty thirty-five waitresses, nine bartenders, six line cooks, four salad persons, five bus persons, four host/hostesses,

63

three checkroom attendants and six dishwashers. Other employees who worked in the afternoon in anticipation of the between-game rush were the cleaning crew, laundry personnel and stock person.

These were exciting days because we had an opportunity to see just how much we could do. Many times we would have large groups scheduled for service after the basketball crowd headed back to Williams Arena in the evening. Our crew always responded to the challenge. Most of them looked forward to the tournament with relish. They were proud of the fact that they were part of a smooth working team.

* * *

In 1959 it was announced that John Kundla, former University of Minnesota basketball star and former coach of the world champion Minneapolis Lakers basketball team, would assume the coaching duties at the University. Kundla was a popular figure, and his appointment caused a great stir of excitement among basketball fans.

For years there had been a downtown quarterback club for U of M football fans but there was no similar club for basketball. I discussed this with brothers Joe and Bill and we decided to see if we could get something going for basketball.

First, I paid a call on Dick Cullum, who was the master of ceremonies for the Downtown Quarterbacks and one of the nation's most knowledgeable sports writers. He liked the idea of a basketball club and said he would help us in every way he could.

He acquainted us with the workings of the Quarterback Club and provided us with valuable advice on how to set up the basketball luncheon club. He even volunteered to be its master of ceremonies.

Next, we set up a meeting with Otis Dypwick, who was in charge of University sports promotions, and Coach Kundla. We approached them with the idea of having five luncheon meetings at Jax during the basketball season.

We proposed a season ticket arrangement for the club. We would add enough over the normal cost of the luncheons, so that the club could present a scholarship to a worthy high school basketball player at season's end.

Brother Joe came up with the name Back Court Club.

Kundla and Dypwick liked the idea. Coach Kundla felt confident that visiting coaches would attend the meetings when possible.

We also came up with the idea of honoring the high school basketball player of the week at our meetings. The selected player and his coach would be invited to sit at the head table with Kundla, Cullum and other visiting dignitaries.

When we obtained final university approval we set a schedule with Coach Kundla. Next, we designed a mailer explaining the proposed club and included an application to join. The completed applications and the money poured in.

Former college and professional stars were among the first to join: George Mikan (Mr. Basketball for the first-half of this century) along with other former Lakers, Don Carlson, Tony Jaros and Vern Mikkelsen. Business and professional people responded with enthusiasm too. And before we knew it we filled out our membership at two-hundred sixty people.

Dick Cullum did a beautiful piece in his column following the first meeting. He not only reported the items that made the meeting an entertaining and fun experience, he also gave a sterling endorsement to the fine food Jax served to the members.

The Back Court Club flourished for many years and the members got to see and hear many entertaining guests. People like Coach Al McGuire (Marquette), Joe Hutton (Hamline), George Mikan (De Paul and Minne-apolis Lakers), Bobby Knight of Indiana and scores of other well-known coaches and players.

Dave McMillan, the gentleman who coached the 1937 Gophers, was on hand too. Dave was one of the original New York Knickerbockers and, although retired, still had a keen interest in the game.

He told a story about taking his Gophers to Madison Square Garden in the mid-1930s. He told how many of his players had never been to New York and that they were from poor homes.

He promised that if they won the game they could order anything they wanted for dinner. They won and proceeded to a fine hotel dining room. The last person to order dinner was Marty Rolek (Marty later was named All-American). He ordered shrimp cocktail. Dave explained that Marty had a silly grin on his face when he ordered.

When the waiter set the shrimp cocktail before Rolek, he looked amazed and said, "When I read shrimp cocktail on the menu I thought they were kidding."

Each meeting featured a question and answer period. Sometimes these generated a lot of laughs. I recall one of the fans asking Kundla if he thought Vern Mikkelsen had good speed when he played with the Lakers. Kundla answered, "He wasn't slow and he wasn't fast . . . he was half fast."

Al McGuire was always entertaining too. He explained his recruiting policy, saying he liked to look for strong, tough kids from big city ghetto areas. He told how he would receive letters from small town priests telling him about boys five-foot-ten-inches or five-foot-eleven-inches who averaged twenty points per game for their schools. McGuire chuckled as he said, "I'm not looking for altar boys, I want animals."

At the final meeting of our second year we honored the 1937 University of Minnesota Big Ten championship basketball team. Coach Kundla had been a member of that team and it was the only Big Ten basketball championship that Minnesota had won up to that time.

It was a fun reunion for the team members and it added stature to the burgeoning Back Court Club.

A spin-off of the Back Court Club soon followed. George Lyon, a leading Minneapolis businessman and hockey buff, called and inquired about starting a University of Minnesota hockey club.

Brother Bill worked with Lyon and Coach John Marriucci and the Blue Line club was born. Marriucci was a great draw for the club. He was Mr. Hockey in Minnesota. In addition to his knowledge of and dedication to hockey, he was an entertaining speaker.

Marriucci also had a sparkling sense of humor. He and Kundla were close friends. They made guest appearances at each other's meetings, where good natured debates and kidding over the merits of their favorite sport delighted the crowds.

Who else but the noble Roman, John Marriucci, could stand up before two-hundred and fifty Back Court

66

members and greet them by saying, "I have noticed by observing the people here that our Blue Line members are much younger and much more intelligent than this group." The crowds loved it.

Some of the hockey players who came to the Blue Line meetings as student athletes went on to successful careers in professional hockey. Louie Nanne became general manager of the Minnesota North Stars, as an example.

Herb Brooks coached the Minnesota Gophers, New York Rangers and Minnesota North Stars. Brooks will probably be remembered as long as hockey is played for his part in coaching the U.S. Olympic team to a win over the Russians and ultimately a gold medal at the 1980 Winter Olympic games.

Both the Blue Line and Back Court clubs are still going strong. The interest in them rises and falls, at least in part, depending on the fortunes of the teams and the personality of the coaches.

When Bill Fitch came in as coach of the Gopher basketball team, he told me he wanted ten season meetings of the Back Court Club. I didn't think we could fill ten meetings. He not only filled them but ended up turning people away because of space constraints.

Fitch had enthusiasm and style that caught the imagination of the public. He was a good recruiter and coach. He soon had people swarming to Williams Arena. Fitch later coached the Cleveland Cavaliers, Boston Celtics and the Houston Rockets.

The Back Court Club helped many young athletes through its scholarship program. The club made it possible for many youngsters, who might never have otherwise seen a live session of the state basketball tournament, to get there.

At one of the meetings, member Charlie Pyle stood up and pointed out that hundreds of tickets for the Friday afternoon consolation session at the tournament went unused. He explained that tournament tickets were sold in sets.

And if your team advanced to the championship round, you would not be inclined to have a great deal of interest in the consolation round. Charlie suggested that the Back Court Club make a project of collecting and distributing the Friday afternoon tickets that would otherwise be unused. Dick Cullum and Sid Hartman wrote it up in their Minneapolis sports columns. Don Riley did the same in the St. Paul paper.

Jax became the clearinghouse for the tickets. We collected them. Then coaches and physical education instructors from throughout the metro area picked them up and saw that they were used.

The sports luncheons were not only good for business on the day they were held, but Jax benefited in other ways too. We now provided dinner and bus service for all Gopher home basketball and hockey games.

It was not unusual for us to serve dinner to one-hundred-fifty to two-hundred people before a sports event and then transport them to the game. It was added business.

The Minneapolis and St. Paul daily papers and many of the suburban papers announced the time and place of each meeting. The meetings were also mentioned on powerful WCCO radio during morning and evening drive time.

Even if you were not a sports fan, the name Jax was in print and on the air. The best part of it was there was no cost for us to bear.

One good thing leads to another, and we provided dinner and bus service to other events that presented an opportunity. The Metropolitan Opera came to Northrup Auditorium each year and parking there is never easy. So we decided to run buses.

I called the Transit Authority and asked how much a bus cost new. At that time it was about sixty-seven thousand dollars. So we ran an advertisement in the paper:

"Sixty-seven thousand dollar motorcoach with uniformed chauffeur will transport you from Jax to the Metropolitan Opera. Reservations 789-7297."

It worked. We ran buses to the Opera for many years. I couldn't help but chuckle as the opera crowd boarded the "motorcoach" dressed to the nines.

Years earlier, when Jax was still emerging from the corner bar category, we would occasionally have a very slow night. When someone would come in and see a dearth of activity it was only natural to ask, "Where is everybody?" Lefty's stock answer was, "The opera hasn't let out yet."

Vintage Jax Restaurant Menu

PART
FOUR

A Dramatic Change

During the winter of 1960-61, Joe Jr. was approached by a group of developers who were building a new motel at the corner of Prior and University Avenues in St. Paul.

They wanted a restaurant in the facility and they offered Joe an opportunity to own and operate it. Joe was now nearly thirty-seven years-old and he had five children.

He longed for ownership . . . a business he could put his exclusive stamp on and call his own. This was a turning point in our family business relationship. It would have been nice if our parents could have understood that this was a favorable time to expand for the benefit of our entire family . . . an opportunity to spread our risk . . . to grow. This was not to be.

They were not at all supportive of Joe's venture. They actually felt threatened by it. I do not think they understood that the Twin Cities was growing at a fantastic pace. Instead, their thoughts harkened back to their days of financial insecurity . . . of struggle without reward.

Joe plowed ahead with plans for his restaurant. He arranged his own financing. He designed the motif and selected the furnishings down to the last detail. He organized a professional staff. He did a superb job and to his enduring credit he did it completely on his own.

In the summer of 1961 the new Midway Motor Lodge was opened. Mr. Joe's Restaurant became a new and important addition to the Twin Cities dining scene.

By the time Mr. Joe's was ready to open, our father had become accustomed to the idea of Joe Jr. being on his own. By then I think his disappointment in Joe leaving Jax gave way to admiration of his determination and courage.

On the afternoon that Mr. Joe's opened I stood with my father and brothers at the bar. We watched as our dad bought the first round of drinks for the sizeable group that had gathered for the unofficial opening.

Joe Jr. continued to be an outstanding innovator. It wasn't long before he brought fresh seafood to town on a grand scale that had never been done before. His fresh seafood buffets were constantly jammed with contented diners.

He also worked diligently as a "minuteman" giving much time and effort to the task of bringing major league sports to Minnesota. His work schedule was always frantic, but he still found time for his wife and sons.

Joe was a familiar and most enthusiastic rooter at sports events where his boys were participants. They were good students and good athletes, and his all-consuming pride and joy.

Joe operated Mr. Joe's until 1968 when he suffered a heart attack and decided to sell the restaurant. He then engaged in less demanding and less stressful pursuits. A second heart attack proved fatal. Joe Kozlak, Jr. died February 1, 1972. He was forty-nine years-old.

FIVE

JAX and its employees

From its first beginning Jax Cafe has been fortunate with many trustworthy, hardworking and loyal employees. Several have volunteered their thoughts and impressions of Jax. Their statements are printed as follows:

Thea Sletkolen Stay:

"I taught school at Montevideo, Minnesota, from 1937 to 1940. I had grades one through eight. I married Bernie Stay in 1941 and we moved to Clearbrook, Minnesota, where he had a good job.

"We had a nice place to live and I thought I would never have to work again. My son, Doug, was born in 1943 and Bud came along in 1944. Not long after this Bernie began having a problem with alcohol. He had no tolerance for liquor and gradually his work and our marriage began to suffer.

"I finally left Clearbrook and came to Minneapolis with my sons in 1951. I moved in with my sister Olga. I needed a job so I could maintain my family. I couldn't take the necessary time to wait for a teaching job.

"Ollie (Olga) was a waitress at Little Jack's. Little Jack's is a bar restaurant located six blocks from Jax. There is no connection between the two places other than that they are friendly competitors. Ollie thought I could learn to do waitress work, but thought it might be better if we didn't work at the same restaurant. She took me to Jax and I applied.

"Joe Jr. interviewed me and he knew Ollie. He called me about a week later and I went to work. I found waitress work interesting and challenging and the money was good. I have always enjoyed being with people and at Jax every day was different.

"I liked my job. I stayed at Jax until I retired in 1985. Even now at my age – I go in and help out on a part-time basis.

"I went out to Royal Oak and worked for Diane when she was on maternity leave and that was fun too.

"Some people do waitress/waiter work and they complain about the hours and they complain about the customers. I tell these people that the hours go with the job . . . when you do restaurant work you are on duty while the customers are enjoying themselves. And if you don't enjoy being with people you shouldn't do restaurant work, because you just complicate matters for the folks that you work with and those you serve."

Ann Stawski:

"I took a job as waitress at Jax in 1941. This was before Mr. and Mrs. Kozlak bought Jax. My sister-in-law, Bernice, was working there and she trained me.

"I worked to supplement my husband Chester's income. He had a good job in the accounting department at Jenney Semple Hill. (It was a large wholesale hardware company.) Business took a turn for the worse at Jenney Semple Hill and Chester lost his job.

"He was over 40 when this happened and he was never able to land really good steady work again. He did odd jobs and picked up whatever work he could get. I took all the time I could get at Jax.

"It got me out of the house . . . I could be with people. Even though Chester wasn't fully employed, and though we had three children, we still managed to build a new house. Everybody in the family helped as best they could . . . and the house . . . some people might think it's a dump, but to me, it's my castle. (The house is a comfortable modest structure on a quiet street in an older section of the city six and one-half blocks from Jax.)

"I remember when Mr. and Mrs. Kozlak (Joe Sr. and Gertrude) bought Jax. Mr. Kozlak didn't know much about fancy drinks. When he was behind the bar he asked us *(the waitresses) what went into the drinks. He and John Scovil would read the bartender's book. When they had time they would practice making the fancy drinks.*

"Mrs. Kozlak made all the salad dressings from her own recipes, and she helped in the kitchen too. We worked hard . . . real hard, but I can honestly say I loved it . . . every minute of it."

Ann retired in 1973. We had a little farewell ceremony. Bill and I presented her with a diamond watch. Ann and Chester celebrated their fiftieth wedding anniversary on June 12, 1978. They renewed their marriage vows at Holy Cross church where they were married. They then had two-hundred guests for dinner and drinks and an old fashioned wedding dance at Jax.

Chester had been fighting cancer for many months, but that night it was as though he had never been sick. He and Ann must have planned and saved for years in anticipation of this special night. Ruth and I were at the party and were amazed at how well Chester looked.

The party was a huge neighborhood reunion. For Ann and Chester it was the crowning glory of fifty years together. They were as happy that night as two new-lyweds. Chester died three months later. He had set a goal to enjoy his fiftieth anniversary and he made it.

Connie Szczech (pronounced "check"):

Connie came to work at Jax in 1948. She was an extremely energetic and enthusiastic person who looks at least fifteen years younger than her age. She was seldom at a loss for words.

"I worked in receiving at Dayton's department store before I became a waitress but I found it dull. In 1943 I took my first waitress job at John's Chinese Restaurant in downtown Minneapolis.

"Waitresses were looked down on in those days. Dining out wasn't something people in our neighborhood had an opportunity to do. And if you worked in a place that served alcoholic beverages they thought of you as a barmaid.

"Joe Jr. hired me at Jax. We used to sit around on Tuesday nights late and try to think of ways to drum up

business. Joe Jr. was very creative. It was at one of these Tuesday night meetings that he developed the idea of lunch and bus service to the football games.

"We were the first restaurant to provide that service and it caught on very quickly.

"I remember one night in the early years when we got swamped. This happened before the dining room was really decorated and we just had some old tables and chairs that Mr. and Mrs. Kozlak had purchased at the Goodwill store. The waitresses were taking turns in the dining room and I had my hands full.

"Just when I was busiest Mr. and Mrs. Kozlak (Joe Sr. and Gertrude) sat at one of my tables. I couldn't get to them and after a few minutes Joe Sr. became irritated and stopped me saying, 'Why can't we get any service here?' I told him to look at the dining room and said: 'There are your customers . . . do you want me to take care of them or stop and serve you?' He said, 'Of course, you are right. Take care of them first.'

"I loved working at Jax. We had a good group of people to work with and the customers were very nice. I still enjoy waitress work. I stayed home for a while and got bored so I took a job waiting tables at the Court Bar restaurant in downtown Minneapolis. It reminds me a lot of Jax back when I started there . . . stained glass and dark seasoned wood. And it's not too big. I can still run the legs off the younger people who work there too.

"My daughter does waitress work. She graduated from high school and went two years to college. She makes more money as a waitress than she could in her field. The image of service people has improved a lot since I started. Almost everyone dines out nowadays, and the public is generally more sophisticated and appreciative of professional servers.

"What would I think if a grandchild decided to make food service a career and goes to Cornell or Stout? I'd be proud as punch."

Mary Holewa:

Mary did waitress work at Jax from 1947 until 1974. She became the consummate professional server elevating her job to a near art form.

She never wasted a step or motion. Mary maintained

a calm demeanor and always provided unobtrusive service in even the most tense and demanding situations.

Mary: *"I had never even been in a restaurant until I met my husband-to-be. I was nearly 18. The public image of waitresses was not good at that time. I used to think I would be willing to do nearly anything but waitress work. I got a job at Woolworth's and I was there for five years.*

"One day I ran into Connie and she talked me into applying at John's Chinese Restaurant. She convinced me the money would be better than I was making, and she said the owners were nice to work for . . . she was correct on both counts.

"One day a friend asked me why I went downtown to do waitress work when there was a nice restaurant called Jax much closer to where we lived. I had never even heard of Jax at that time but I decided to apply. Mr. Kozlak (Joe Sr.) hired me. Jax was a busy place. The money was good and the hours were compatible.

"My father was living with us at the time. He worked nights so he could be with the children during the day. The luncheon shift at Jax started at 11:30 a.m. Before going to work I would serve an early lunch to my baby son and put him down for a nap. Usually when I got home from the lunch shift he was just getting up.

"I could also be home to greet my children when they came from school. And I could have dinner prepared for them before I went on the dinner shift.

"My husband, Andy, was with the children on the evenings I was at work. It was a good arrangement. What did my father think of me doing waitress work? He was from the old country and to him a job was a job. Andy didn't like the idea at first but, once he saw the surroundings I worked in and observed the fine clientele, his objections fell by the wayside.

"We had a fine group to work with at Jax. In the early years bartender John Scovil moonlighted from his job in the county auditor's office. We also had Phil Harris. They were two fine gentlemen.

"Phil worked as a bartender while studying for his chiropractor's license. A Navy veteran, husband, and father he had his office open less than a month when he was struck down by bulbar polio. He died in a matter of hours.

"Ilow Mrs. Lipa could cook those steaks. She formed the tenderloins beautifully and got them done just the way the customers wanted them. When I was on the job I really didn't feel like I was working. I liked the challenge of being busy.

"On the days we ran buses it was fun to serve all those people in such short time and make sure they got on the bus and saw the kickoff. Then we would be extremely busy throughout the evening too. I would be tired when the night was over but I felt good, knowing we did a good job and provided a pleasant experience for so many people.

"The time at work went fast. Those super busy days took a lot of organization and concentration. I missed the action for years after I retired. I guess I still do."

Violetta Rootkie (Vi):

Vi joined the staff at Jax in 1951 and worked until 1961. She had performed secretarial work.

She was also an accomplished seamstress. Vi became a server in the Mary Holewa mold . . . well organized, intelligent and extremely proficient.

Vi: *"Marty, my husband, never really wanted me to be a waitress. Waitresses were not held in very high esteem in the early '50s. Jax was somewhat unique in that they only hired married people in those days. I did waitress work because of the flexible hours. I could see my children off to school in the morning and be home when they came from school.*

"I think we benefited as a family by this arrangement. I think it was much better than the latchkey system that many families must live with today. When someone asked me why I did waitress work, I told them I'm here because I like it here. For the most part we had very good people to work with. At the end of a busy day I felt fulfilled.

"The image of servers has improved since I started. And it's about time. Part of the improvement is probably due to a more mobile society and more disposable income. Even back when I did waitress work we had waitresses who had taught school or done nursing, or worked successfully as stenographers and bookkeepers.

"Cecelia (Cecelia Leimgruber) was valedictorian of her graduating class of over four-hundred students, and we had others who were honor students too. We even had a bus girl (Eugenia Strunke) who could speak six languages fluently. If anyone thinks that people doing server work are incapable of anything else, they are mistaken."

PART SIX

The Darker Side

or

Cops and Robbers

It wouldn't be fair to allow you to think the restaurant business is all fun and games . . . a party every night type of existence. I wouldn't want you to go out and sink the family jewels into a restaurant in the present day climate. Without sound preparation you might become one of the thousands of restaurant entrepreneurs who fail each year in the United States.

There are even worse things that can happen than financial failure. One winter morning in the early 1950s Joe drove from Jax to the Fidelity State Bank on Central Avenue Northeast.

It was snowing and there was no room in the parking lot. So he parked about one block away. He went into the bank, made a deposit and picked up some change to conduct the day's business.

It was snowing heavily when he returned to his car. He got behind the wheel. But before he could start the engine he felt cold steel at the base of his neck.

Robbery! The robber had been hiding on the floor of the back seat. The side and back windows were obscured by the snow so Joe did not notice anything unusual as he entered his auto.

The robber instructed Joe to start the car and drive to a quiet side street and park. Once there, he had Joe lay facc down on the seat with his arms behind his back.

He tied Joe and took the bag of money. The bag contained mostly change and a few hundred dollars in bills, which were necessary to do business before the advent of plastic. The robber looked into the bag and, seeing his booty, explained, "Boy, I really got a bum steer." He locked Joe in the car and departed.

It was freezing cold outside and the interior of the car quickly cooled down too. Joe struggled to free himself. It didn't do any good to call out for help . . . there was no one within earshot.

He was now cold and fearful of freezing. He continued to struggle. Several minutes later he began to slip one of his hands free. He persisted in his efforts and finally succeeded in getting free. He made his way back to Jax.

The robbery was reported in the newspapers and the police investigated. But they came up with nothing. Now, it's bad enough to be held up at gunpoint. It is a severe emotional shock at best. However, when the perpetrator of such a deed is at large, another unpleasant dimension is added.

And then, of course, when you are working with the public there is the inevitable unthinking joker who comes up from behind, pushes a forefinger in your back and says, "Stick 'em up!" It was not the most pleasant of times for Joe.

Winter gradually gave way to spring and spring to summer and Joe's nerves returned to normal. He was newly married, and he and Helen had a nice little house on 36½ Avenue Northeast.

* * *

On a warm summer evening Joe worked until closing, locked the restaurant and drove home. When he reached the driveway he stopped his car, opened the door so that he could proceed to the garage, to open the overhead door. (Joe did not have an automatic garage door opener at this time.)

He was barely out of the car when a man darted from behind the bushes brandishing a gun. He held the gun on Joe and told him they were going back to Jax to open the safe.

The distance from his house to Jax was little more than two miles. But with a gun pointed at him, it must have seemed like a cross country trip. It was about 1:45 a.m. when they pulled up on 20th Avenue alongside Jax.

The robber told Joe en route that they would enter the restaurant through the side entrance on 20th Avenue. When the car came to a stop, the robber glanced to the right to open the car door on his side.

At this precise moment Joe bolted out the door on the driver's side and ran through the bushes and into the yard of the house behind the restaurant. As he ran through the yard he yelled, "Ray! Ray! Call the police . . . call the police."

Ray and Eleanor Julkowski lived in the home behind Jax. It was a warm summer night and they were sleeping with their windows open. They responded immediately. Lights began to come on throughout their house. The robber fled. The Julkowskis had Joe come in, and the police were soon on the scene.

It was many months later that Joe's assailant was apprehended. It was through interrogation, after being apprehended for yet another crime, that the culprit was identified.

* * *

In 1952 we refurbished the bar room at Jax. We replaced the old wooden booths with the more comfortable upholstered variety, carpeted the floor and had a new bar top made to replace the old worn mahogany original.

We also purchased a new safe. The safe was very heavy and was just the right size to fit under the bar at the front end of the room. Most people were never aware of it being there.

It had a combination dial on top that, when engaged, provided access to the inner portion. Once the top was lifted open there was an inner cylinder that could be opened by using two keys.

During normal business hours the top was not locked. One key remained in the cylinder and only my father, brother Joe, and I had a copy of the second key. It was possible to slide money, guest checks and papers into the cylinder but you could not get anything out without the second key.

The best feature, as presented by the salesperson,

was that even if some unauthorized individual succeeded in opening the top, it would do them little good. Without both keys the inner cylinder was virtually impenetrable. The only way to get it open, we were all told, would be to torch the cylinder top off. And if someone did this they would burn the money . . . so why would anyone bother?

Delivery of the new safe was timed to coincide with the removal of the old bar top. It was only while the bar top was off that the new safe would fit through the narrow opening at the west end of the bar. Once encased, and with the new bar top set, glued and screwed in place, we figured we would be protected for years . . . even decades.

A few months later, my father entered the restaurant at about 6 a.m. on a Monday. He walked through the opening at the west end of the bar and walked toward the front of the room. Here, he kept an adding machine, check-out forms, money wrappers and other items needed to check out the previous day's receipts. He used the bar top to the right of the area where the safe sat as a mini-office. There was a telephone on the back bar in the same area. It was handy for him to talk to suppliers when they called as he "checked up".

He removed the adding machine from a shelf, where it was stored, and plugged it into the electrical outlet. Next, he removed his check-out forms from a drawer across from where the safe was placed. He had his money wrappers, pencil, forms, and desk light all positioned.

He was now ready to open the safe and remove the money and guest checks from the previous business day. He turned around and leaned over to open the safe. It was gone! Gone!

At first, he couldn't believe it. Where was it? How could anyone get it out without dismantling the bar? He walked back to the narrow opening to the area behind the bar. Nothing had been moved. Not a scratch anywhere. The front, side, and garden doors showed no signs of being tampered with. Ditto the kitchen door.

There was only one other possibility. In those days there was a tiny bottle shop occupying a part of the building where our living quarters had once been. The burglars had taken the safe from behind the bar, through the dining room, and into the kitchen.

They broke the door between the kitchen and bottle shop. They got the safe up two steps that separated the areas and through a side door of the bottle shop to the outside. It appeared that they had made a successful heist.

The mystifying part of the whole episode is how the burglars managed to get the safe over the bar without causing any damage. They also maneuvered it through the dining room and into the kitchen where they had to squeeze through very narrow passages flanked by stationary equipment. The police, friends we have in the moving business, everyone, was impressed and a bit in awe to think the safe could be removed so cleanly.

A few days later, the phone rang and a man asked for Joe Sr. My father took the call and the voice on the other end said, "Joe, we have your safe. If we can arrange to get the key to us we will see to it that you get the checks that must be inside!"

My father told the caller that in no way would he do such a thing, and thus become an accomplice to the crime. The voice thanked my father politely and to this day we do not know if the safe's inner cylinder was opened. We do know that none of the checks were ever cashed.

* * *

It was a busy Friday summer evening. I was on duty at the podium at about 6 p.m. when I was approached by two men in their twenties. They asked if they could cash their paychecks. I looked at one of the checks and it was from a china and restaurant supply company located on Washington Avenue North.

The checks were nicely printed and looked authentic. However, I declined to cash them for two reasons. One was that our house rule was not to cash payroll checks for people we did not know. The second reason was that, although the check was for a restaurant supply company, I had never heard of it.

I apologetically explained that I was not permitted to cash payroll checks. They thanked me and departed. I didn't give the episode another thought.

In those days many of the neighborhood bars made it a practice to cash payroll checks. The bar owners would borrow large sums of money from their bankers on Friday so that they could cash checks for their customers.

They would deposit the cashed checks to their accounts and repay the loaned money to the bank on the next business day. So the interest they paid was minimal.

Many laborers felt much more comfortable going to a bar in their work clothes than they did going into a bank lobby. (Drive-in tellers had not yet become popular.)

Some bars actually had little teller's cages where the check cashing was done. The customers would cash their checks and then have some beverages. Friday afternoon and evening were busy for the straight bars.

Jax was not into check cashing. We were more restaurant than bar. We did not care for the exposure of having a lot of cash on the premises.

About 11 p.m. two men and a woman came in the front door. They glanced about and walked past me to our coatroom. At that time we had a black light sign over the cloakroom that said checkroom. They must have thought it was a room to cash checks because they walked into it. I walked over to them and asked if I could help them.

They wanted to cash their paychecks, and offered them in unison. I took them and noticed that they were for the same china/restaurant supply company that I had seen earlier. Once again, I explained why I could not cash them.

One of the men said something to the effect that they never had any trouble cashing their checks at the bars in the area. Once again, I declined apologetically and they departed. I walked out the door very soon after they left and saw them drive away from the curb, proceeding south on University Avenue. I noted their license number. My suspicions were aroused.

I went inside and called telephone information and asked for the number of the company on the checks that I had seen. Information had no listing for a company by that name. I called the police. I gave my name to the desk sergeant and told him I thought there may be a group passing forged payroll checks.

He said, "Call the forgery or bad check division on Monday morning." I said, "No! This is right now." He showed more interest. I gave him a description and license number of the car and its occupants that had just left Jax. He closed with "O.K. . . . thank you."

At closing time, 1 a.m., the trio that I described was arrested as they left Andy's Bar just seven blocks from Jax.

A few minutes more and the bad check artists would have been gone for good. They were part of a group that had cashed thousands of dollars in worthless checks at bars, grocery stores and other businesses on that Friday afternoon and evening.

The police recovered most of the money, and the merchants in turn received most of their money back.

Buzz Winslow was chief of police in Minneapolis at the time. When he received a report on the incident he stopped in and personally congratulated me for "being alert."

I also received warm thanks from many of the merchants who would have been stung had the ring not been apprehended. One such merchant was Ed Widseth, a University of Minnesota football All-American in the 1930s. At that time, he was owner/operator of a popular Northeast Minneapolis supermarket. Ed, too, stopped in to express his thanks. That had a special significance for me because Ed Widseth was one of my role model heroes when I was a young lad.

* * *

It was a busy Friday evening. The dining room was filled and people were at the bar waiting for tables to become available. Thea and I were at the podium.

Waitress Cozette Cosette or "Cozy", as we liked to call her, approached us and asked if three men had gone past us. She had their guest check in her hand. We did not recall seeing them but I checked the men's room to see if they had stopped there. They were not in the building.

Cozy showed us their check. They had enjoyed two cocktails each, appetizers, porterhouse steaks with all the trimmings, and a bottle of expensive wine. When Cozy asked if they would like dessert they ordered three different selections.

When Cozy went to the kitchen to pick up their dessert they departed the restaurant. Three men wearing business suits about thirty years of age. At first, we thought they may have stepped outside for air. However, as time went on we became convinced that they had skipped out on their check.

Cozy felt terrible about it but it was an obvious fraud, and she was not to be blamed. She told us, "I will never, never forget that one guy's laugh. If I ever hear it again I will know it." Many months later on another busy night Thea and I were again at the podium. Cozy's station was in the main dining room. On one occasion Cozy cut through the back portion of the Roundtable Room on her way to the kitchen. She heard a strange laugh and stopped dead in her tracks.

She looked across the room and saw the men who had defrauded us months before. She hurried to the podium and told me where they were seated. We located their waitress and examined their check.

Sure enough, the same pattern was emerging. Two cocktails, appetizers, lobsters, expensive wine. We told the waitress to come to the podium if they ordered dessert.

I also called Lefty on our intercom (he was upstairs) and told him what was happening. This time the trio did not order dessert. When they finished their dinner and saw their waitress go to the kitchen, they left the table.

I didn't see them until they were but a step or two from the podium. They were walking fast. Once they passed the podium and entered the bar area they bolted out the side door.

There were a couple people in front of me so I lost a little time in pursuing them, but I made it out the door. Two of them were half-way down the block when they let out a whoop and a holler. They thought they had got away.

The third man, a big bruiser, was a bit slower. He ran to his car which was parked across the street facing west for an easy getaway. As I ran toward him he entered his car, trying to get the key in the ignition. When I reached the car I slammed my hand down on the hood of the car, making a loud noise and shouted, "Stop!"

In the next instant I realized I was on a dark street performing a citizen's arrest on a big dude who may be armed. I glanced over my shoulder towards the restaurant and there like an angel of mercy running toward me was Lefty.

We marched the man back to the restaurant. Thea had called the police and they arrived quickly. The police were questioning our quarry when his two buddies returned to the restaurant. They put on an indignant act. They claimed they merely took a little stroll. How dare we accuse them of running out.

The police asked if I wanted to file charges. I said if they paid their bill and promised never to come back I would not press charges. They paid and I never saw them again. An interesting sidelight: When they paid the bill they did not include a tip. The senior police officer reminded them of their "oversight." They then decided they had better not push their luck any further. The waitress received a "gratuity."

In retrospect, I think I should have charged them because the next day I contacted managers Don Ryan at the Lexington Cafe and Jerry Murphy at McCarthy's. When I described the men both Ryan and Murphy said they answered the description of a trio that had done the same to them.

* * *

Early on a Saturday morning during my election campaign in 1968 a masked robber entered Jax Cafe. My brother Bill and Chef Wayne Fyle were the only others in the whole building.

The robber demanded money at gunpoint. Bill opened the cash drawer and put all the bills in a bag. He asked the robber if he wanted the rolls of change too. The man said he did. We always had a large supply of change for the weekend and Bill filled three bags with rolls of quarters, dimes, nickels and pennies.

The robber now had a heavy load. Next, he ordered Bill to walk through the dining room and out to the kitchen. When they entered the kitchen, the robber brandished his gun at Wayne and ordered both Wayne and Bill to the basement.

Once the robber got Bill and Wayne to the basement he ordered them to stay put. He then tried to nail a basement fire door shut, perhaps thinking there would be no other way for Bill and Wayne to get out. His tools (a hammer and nails) were no match for the steel fire door, so he gave that up and left the premises.

On one side of the basement there is a delivery chute that opens up to the sidewalk. Bill opened the door of the chute a crack and saw the robber running down the sidewalk. He wasn't going very fast because the bags of heavy change were awkward to handle. Bill opened the chute and climbed up to the sidewalk. The robber was unaware that Bill was free. Bill then ran alongside the sidewalk on the grassy boulevard so that his footsteps would not be heard.

When he got within proper range of the robber Bill executed a perfect flying tackle. The robber was stunned. Bill disarmed him and held him at gunpoint until the police arrived. All this was duly reported in the daily press and television. And while I had nothing to do with it, the news report placed the Kozlak name in a most favorable light during the election campaign.

PART
SEVEN

Jax
of
Golden Valley

I received a call in the fall of 1975 from Frank Wolinski. He was a former Minneapolis alderman and was a business broker, specializing in restaurants and bars.

He had Michael's restaurant in Golden Valley for sale and wanted Bill and me to take a look at it. I had heard rumors that Michael's was for sale in months gone by, but the figures accompanying the rumors were clearly out of our reach.

I mentioned this to Wolinski and he told me the situation had changed completely.

The owner of Michael's restaurant was Michael Crakes. He built and opened the restaurant in 1952 and was very successful. In the latter years of his ownership he had tired of the business.

He fell in love with Florida and spent much of his time there raising race horses. His employees described him as a kindly man with a penchant for being a bit impulsive.

One day he posted a notice to his employees saying that as of August 31, 1975 all food service personnel would be terminated. He quit the food business. He kept the bar open for a couple weeks and finally closed that too. It was only then that he placed the property in the hands of a broker.

Bill and I had kicked the expansion idea around for many years. We looked at a couple properties but nothing had materialized up to that time. We discussed Wolinski's approach and decided to take a look.

I was not at all familiar with Michael's. I only knew that place by reputation, and its reputation was good. The first time I walked through the building I was surprised at how small and compact it appeared.

Jax took up three floors of a large building with thousands of square feet, several dining rooms, two kitchens, seven restrooms and over one-hundred employees. By comparison, Michael's was small and it seemed to me that it would be easy to manage.

Bill and I discussed the pros and cons of the location and the property. The fact that the restaurant had been closed did not bother us at all. We would be buying land and building and would have an opportunity to assemble our own staff. Further, the normal "good will" charges for a going business should not apply because the business had ceased operation.

After considerable soul searching we decided to begin the negotiating process. The decor needed refurbishing, and much of the kitchen and bar equipment needed replacement. We made certain that our knowledge of these facts accompanied our offer.

There was considerable interest by others in the Michael's property. We learned that at least one person had made an offer considerably in the excess of ours. Bill and I discussed this and decided that we would stick with our offer.

We were now in the midst of the holiday season and Jax was extremely busy. We took the attitude that if we acquired Michael's, that would be fine. However, if we didn't, it wouldn't matter.

During the entire process we had never met, seen or heard from Michael Crakes. His attorney, Mr. Gustafson, contacted us once on his behalf, but that was it.

On a cold day in December, while sitting at the kitchen table at home, I received a call from Florida. It was Michael Crakes. He informed me that if we would increase our offer by ten thousand dollars he was prepared to deal.

I explained that Bill and I had put a lot of thought

into our offer and that it was a firm offer. I also told him I knew that he had an offer for more money than our offer. It was for him to decide who had the best chance of succeeding, and thus being able to pay him.

He said, "How about increasing your offer by five-thousand?" I replied that we would not be able to do that. He said, "All right, you have a deal. I will have my attorney, Mr. Gustafson, contact you."

I called Bill at Jax and gave him the news. I don't think either of us was particularly elated. We were in the midst of our busiest season, working long hours and now we had obligated ourselves to a substantial new venture.

Prior to the official closing on the property, which was to take place on December 30, 1975, we hired Bill Bowen, an excellent interior designer, to help us with restyling the restaurant. We set a budget and Bowen went to work. I also contacted my dear friends, carpenter/contractors Bob Sappa and Harold Kujawa and lined them up to do the carpenter work that would be necessary.

We agreed to start on January 2nd. We didn't have title and we didn't have a plan, but we did have the wheels in motion. We closed the deal on December 30th in lawyer Gustafson's office. Michael Crakes was not there . . . he was in Florida. After the closing Bill and I stopped at the Ambassador to toast the deal. We ran into Pat Moore, Jerry Wahl, Charlie Ashford and a few other friends. They congratulated us on our acquisition. At that moment the word that we were expanding to Golden Valley began to spread.

Bill and I excused ourselves and went back to Jax. The next day was New Year's Eve, our busiest day of the year, and we had much work to do.

The morning of January 2, 1976, Bill Kozlak, Bill Bowen, Bob Sappa, Harold Kujawa and I met at the "new" restaurant. Bowen had his plan ready and we approved it. There was considerable carpentry work involved. We were to move two walls and build a new wall at one end of the bar. Some areas took a wood wainscot and others had to be framed for proposed stained glass windows.

We also refaced both sides of the fireplace, remodeled the front entry, covered the ceilings with acoustical tile, had banquettes built for one dining room and recarpeted the whole place.

89

The wiring and lighting needed attention too. We brought the wiring up to date and introduced new light fixtures to the dining areas. We had the kitchen equipment checked and replaced items that were worn out. The restaurant had an old Champion conveyer dishwasher that our inspector pronounced fit. We thought we were spared a big expense.

Bill and I agreed that I should stay with the Golden Valley operation. I would supervise and coordinate the remodeling. Bill ran the Jax Northeast operation and I concentrated on getting the Golden Valley operation going.

Selecting a name for our new enterprise was not easy. We just couldn't decide what to call it. Then one day while telling our meat supplier, Jack Kirschbaum, about our dilemma he said, "There is nothing wrong with telling people who you are and where you are."

That did it! It was *Jax of Golden Valley*. We ordered a new sign for the front of the building. Not only was there the remodeling to coordinate, but I also had to interview and hire a staff, select and order uniforms, menus, cocktail napkins, office supplies and innumerable other items.

Michael kept an office person, Doris Schoen, on his payroll until we took over. She stayed with us. Having someone who knew the building was very helpful during our remodeling and start up. Bill would stop by every day to see how the project was progressing and help with decisions that had to be made.

We decided to give the chef's job to Ken Wolf, who had worked at Jax with Chef Wayne Fyle for many years. My son, Mark Kozlak, came on board as maitre d'. He helped with the organization of the restaurant. Once we opened he put his flair for public relations and promotions to work. He came up with many ideas for special parties and special nights. He even published a Jax newspaper. Daughter Lynn joined us a few months later as a hostess. My son-in-law to be, Mark Satt, was hired to be the luncheon cook early on. He trained under Chef Fyle at Jax Northeast until Jax of Golden Valley was ready to open.

The remodeling came together quickly. In mid-January we set a target date for opening as the first Monday in February. I have found that it pays to set a target date, to inform all suppliers of it, and to stick to it.

The carpenters and electricians increased their

efforts when they understood our goal. Sappa and Kujawa brought in extra help and we kept on schedule.

We decided to advertise our opening to only those people who had house charges at Jax. We prepared a nice letter telling about the new Jax of Golden Valley and inviting them to try it.

We also made them aware that the facility would be new to us and most of the employees. We did not want to raise their expectation level too high. We mailed the letter the week before we opened.

The hiring process went well. The winter of 1976 found a lot of excellent people looking for work and we were able to select many truly professional people. One such person was Lenny Daniels.

He had been Michael's bar manager since 1957. We hired him on the spot. It seems that nearly everyone in the area knew and admired Lenny. Always the perfect gentleman, he gave service with an extra touch of class. He made every customer feel important.

We were able to hire a good experienced group of waitresses and waiters, including Betty Kane and Ella Ahlstrom, who had worked at Michael's until it closed. Later Vi Nash and Val O'Brien, who had also worked for Michael's, joined our staff.

Our family had an excellent relationship with the folks at Fidelity State Bank. When we bought Michael's and needed money to remodel we just signed notes to obtain the money to pay current bills.

We did not want to set up permanent financing until we were off and running. Bill had become acquainted with "Chug" Pohlad of the famous banking family and he wanted to visit with him about the possibility of permanent financing. I said okay and we met with Chug and his brother Carl at their downtown Minneapolis office.

I had never met Carl Pohlad before. They asked some questions about our project and about our financial health. Carl Pohlad was cordial to a fault but he did not seem the least bit interested in our business. No harm done . . . it was at least an experience.

A few days later I was working the podium at Jax Cafe when Walter Rasmussen, president of the Northeast State Bank and Guaranty State Bank, came in for lunch. As I seated him he asked, "Have you arranged your permanent financing yet for Golden Valley?" I responded, "Not yet." And then I heard the strangest sound. He said, "Can I bid on it?" We arranged a meeting and before long we struck a deal for the Golden Valley loan. Walter Rasmussen continued to be our banker, a valued customer and friend until he died.

A week before our projected opening we rented a private dining room at the Holiday Motel Restaurant which was located next door. We had the staff in for training sessions. The remodeling was nearly done. Bricklayers had completed the fireplace refacing, carpenters were followed by painters. Electricians were hanging the new light fixtures. Glaziers were setting the new stained glass.

On the first Friday in February we had the new carpeting laid, set the tables and chairs in place and thanked everyone involved for doing such a big job in so short a time.

We decided to open the bar on Saturday evening. We brought in Lenny and two waitresses and turned on the new sign. We did a brisk business and had an opportunity to hear what the customers thought of the decor.

The comments were very positive. On Sunday we had many of Jax Northeast employees and their spouses for dinner at Jax of Golden Valley. We gave them gift certificates that could be used toward any item on the menu. This was our dress rehearsal. It went surprisingly well.

Bill and I agreed that when Jax of Golden Valley opened he would go there and I would return to Jax Cafe for an unspecified period of time. Jax of Golden Valley opened for lunch and dinner on the first Monday in February 1976.

The business took off like a rocket. The place was packed for both luncheons and dinners all week long. The lounge was busy until late at night. Popular entertainer Jeannie Arlan Peterson opened with us. Her piano and vocal stylings were a big hit.

After we had been open for a couple weeks the advertising campaign I designed kicked in. We ran small ads in the Minneapolis daily papers with the message that Jax of Golden Valley was hard to find.

We challenged the people to find it. We told them our guests had to be very intelligent because we were hard to find. We invited them to call our "control tower" if they needed to be zeroed in. Later, we switched to the tag line, "'Tis Hard To Find But Once."

Bill and I were amazed at the amount of business Jax of Golden Valley was doing. People were virtually fighting to get in. I received a call at Jax Cafe from Minneapolis Alderman Dick Miller. He said a Minnesota Supreme Court Justice wanted to know if he could get him a reservation for dinner at Jax of Golden Valley. Of course, we obliged.

The restaurant was not without its problems. The old conveyer dishwasher needed constant repair. By March we knew we would have to replace it, but we were also cramped for space in the kitchen.

We decided to build an addition to the kitchen area to provide for a new dishwashing machine and dish storage. We got at it as soon as the frost was out of the ground. When the job was completed we felt that a big problem was solved.

No sooner was this done, however, than hot weather arrived and we began having trouble with the air conditioning unit that services the lower dining room. It was an old water cooled unit. The water was supplied from a well. Aside from the fact that the machine was old the water temperature from the well kept creeping up over the years.

The repair people did their best to get the dining room cool. However, once we got a big customer load the temperature just went up and up. I called Jim Eldorado, whom I considered an expert in solving the type of problem we were having.

He surveyed the situation and gave me his recommendation. He said, "It won't do any good to pour more money in that old unit. Sometimes you just have to bite the bullet and put in a whole new system."

He had his recommendation ready including the price. It was expensive but we had no choice. We ordered the new system.

The late spring and summer of 1976 were very warm. While we waited for the new air conditioning system to be installed, I'm afraid there were times when our guests became uncomfortable in that warm dining room.

It was very hard on the servers too. We pleaded with

Eldorado to hurry the job to completion. He did his best. On a hot Friday afternoon in early July, sheet metal workers were installing the ducts on the roof and electricians were wiring the new unit. Jim Eldorado came to me and said it didn't look like they would be able to finish until Monday. I asked if his men would work overtime.

I promised some treats if they got the job done that evening. The tradesmen stayed on the job. At about 6:15 they were ready to throw the switch. The dining room was already very warm even though we had not yet seated anyone.

The waitresses and bus people who were to service the room that evening were standing about with apprehensive and even worried looks on their faces. They didn't want to go through another hot, uncomfortable night.

Jim Eldorado engaged the switch. The air came through the diffusers. The first rush of air was hot because the ducts were filled with hot air. In a few moments we felt the hot air turn cold. What did the employees do? The same thing I did. We cheered!

Michael's/Jax of Golden Valley has been operating since 1952, with but one brief interruption, when Michael Crakes closed the restaurant and sold the property to us. The percentage of restaurants that have had longer runs are really quite rare throughout the United States. Similar operations in the Twin Cities with greater longevity would be Jax, Murray's, The Lexington, Little Jack's and a handful of others.

Tom Kozlak, one of my brother Joe's sons, now owns the restaurant – thus continuing the "family" ownership at that location. However, it has been renamed "T.K. Nicks".

When you examine the establishments that have withstood the test of time you find that they have managed to maintain a solid core of dedicated employees in an industry that is rife with turnover.

Jax of Golden Valley had many such superb people on its staff. Let's meet some of them.

Val O'Neil: *"I have been doing waitress work for forty-five years. Prior to that I worked as a private secretary. I did typing, shorthand, filing. Back then, that job paid about fifty cents an hour. I had to buy clothes in keeping with the* job, and that was a substantial expense. There was more money to be made in waitress work.

"Also, I wasn't happy in the office environment. I felt stifled. I worked downtown at Osterberg's restaurant for a few years before coming here in 1957. I have enjoyed the public. I know ninety percent of my customers every day. They call for reservations and ask for me. I consider it a great accomplishment. They appreciate the service. It makes me feel good – important.

"Have I waited on celebrities? Sure. Mitzie Gaynor, Tennessee Ernie Ford, Mickey Mantle, Rod Carew, Harmon Killebrew. I can't remember them all. They were all nice. But as far as I am concerned, all our customers are celebrities."

Lenny Daniels: "When I got out of the service I went to work at the Covered Wagon restaurant in downtown Minneapolis as a busboy. Next, I became a barboy and then a service bartender. I was going to school to become a sheet metal worker. But I really enjoyed the restaurant business. At the time I got married, I decided to make bartending my career.

"My wife and I bought a house and settled down. We both worked. The Covered Wagon closed in 1957 when the block was taken over for a redevelopment project. I started work in this building (Michael's/Jax of Golden Valley) as a bartender on August 5, 1957. I became bar manager some weeks later. I have only worked at two locations. We were all pleased when we heard Jack and Bill Kozlak purchased Michael's. It meant new life to this facility.

"I have been happy and proud to work at the Covered Wagon and here at Michael's and Jax of Golden Valley. I am officially retired but still enjoy coming in on a part-time basis."

Vi Nash: "Before I moved to Minnesota my twin sister and I worked in Reston, Washington, helping build Boeing B-29's. I helped put the wings on and she was an electrician. We were the first twin sisters to work in aircraft assembly. My first waitress job was at the Sky Room at Dayton's department store. I served many of the Dayton family. I came to this restaurant on July 6, 1954. I wanted to work here because it was closer to home. I wouldn't have to *travel all the way downtown. I didn't know a thing about liquor service when I started but the other servers trained me. I've put a lot of years in this building.*

"So many interesting things have happened over the years. I wish I had kept a diary. If you don't write things down you forget. What advice do I have for young people considering a restaurant career?

"You must like people or stay out of the business. You must love a daily challenge. Every day is different than the next and you must have the ability to adjust to various situations.

"If a customer seems crabby . . . be twice as nice. Be happy even when it hurts. Be a loyal employee. If you can do these things you will feel as fulfilled and rewarded in your work as I have been in mine."

The three people you just met have an aggregate total of well over one-hundred years of serving the public. I wish those of you who may never know them personally could see how good they look and how active they are.

They have spent their lives in difficult, demanding jobs that can be very stressful. Yet, they are physically, mentally, and emotionally strong and sharp.

I have great admiration for these people and others like them. Today, we hear a good deal about "burn out" from youngsters half their age in many different fields of endeavor. I think the success of Vi, Val, and Lenny underscores the importance of doing work that you find satisfying and enjoyable.

PART
EIGHT

Kozlak's
Royal Oak

It was a Sunday in mid-July, 1977. Ruth and I were at our cabin at Balsam Lake, Wisconsin. Ruth was in the kitchen preparing lunch and I was in the living room looking through the St. Paul and Minneapolis Sunday papers. I glanced at the classified section and noticed a heading: Auctions.

There was an ad for an auction to be held nine days hence for the property known as the Sandpiper Restaurant. The Small Business Administration was disposing of the property "as is". The ad listed the ground rules for the auction and the times in the week ahead when the building would be open for inspection.

I had never been to an auction. I was only vaguely familiar with the property being advertised. I had never dined at the place. I *did* know that it was located in a developing suburb called Shoreview, and it was rather close to the posh residential community of North Oaks.

I showed the ad to Ruth. She said, "Why don't you take a look at it?"

The next Tuesday afternoon I drove from Jax to Shoreview to take a look at the property. As I entered the Shoreview community, I noticed a sign listing the population at just over ten-thousand. The homes I saw on my way were modest and well-maintained. There did not seem to be much business or industry in the area, which would not bode well for luncheon business.

97

The grounds accompanying the building to be auctioned looked sad and neglected. There were many mature oak and elm trees on the property, but the fallen leaves from the previous season lay everywhere. The lawn had gone to weeds. Old discarded pieces of restaurant equipment (broken tables, chairs, light fixtures, etc.) were outside along the back portion of the building. Outside the restaurant a dilapidated stockade fence surrounded a huge replica of a sailing schooner that was in a state of vandalized disrepair.

As I entered the building I was virtually assaulted by a wretched odor. It was my understanding that the building had been padlocked by the government for certain defaults in payments. The place had been closed for weeks, but there were partially filled glasses of highballs, beer and cocktails that had been left sitting on the bar. The deep fryers in the kitchen were filled with grease that had become rancid. The hood, steam table, stoves, ovens, and everything else needed either a thorough cleaning or replacement.

The main dining room was a large rectangular room that was terraced at one end. There was not one window in the room. There was no natural light whatever. The chairs were oak painted black with black fabric seats. The backs of many were torn.

The roof showed signs of leaking in several locations. All the carpeting on the main floor was worn out.

I walked downstairs to the banquet and office area. It was a sorry sight. The banquet room had poor lighting and worse ventilation. The public access to the area was through the main dining room. The banquet room chairs were cheap, worn-out folding chairs. The decor was not only non-descript . . . it was non-existent.

The office too was a mess. Someone had strewn papers in every direction and even managed to tip over the safe. The only restrooms in the building were located in the downstairs area. The walk-in coolers and small food preparation area were located downstairs too.

A dumb waiter was in place; it went from the main floor kitchen to the banquet room. But it was inoperable.

I walked outside and took another look at the ship. There was a stairway in the ship that went down to a basement area. It was a smallish room with a bar at one end. There was only one stairway in or out of the room, which I assumed was not in accordance with current safety standards. There were no restrooms on board.

I dismissed the ship as a gimmick that should go. As I prepared to leave I noticed horses grazing on the lots to the south. A pheasant flew up on the back portion of the Sandpiper property, which remained in its natural state, except for those places that were strewn with old building materials and discarded bedsprings.

The site and the building were a neglected mess. Yet, I was intrigued by the possibilities. There were, after all, four and one-half acres of land. There was an eight-thousand-square-foot building. If it could be bought "right" maybe it could be put together properly and become a winner.

I contacted the Shoreview city manager, Gary Dixon, to see what information he could give me regarding population trends and commercial and industrial developments. He was very helpful and said that Shoreview would welcome a Jax-type operation. He rolled out the welcome mat and offered much encouragement.

I learned that three family groups had been unable to make the Sandpiper succeed. The present building was about thirteen-years-old. It was built before the metro freeway system was in place. It seemed to me that a restaurant that large in a community that was just beginning to develop had to be a long odds gamble. I also learned that the previous owners did not have a great deal of restaurant experience . . . at least not for the size and scope of the Sandpiper operation.

All the previous owners were fine, hard working people, but it seems a combination of bad breaks denied them the success they worked so hard to achieve. Aside from the fact that the restaurant may have been premature for the area, the previous owners I visited with indicated that they were also plagued with the problem of under capitalization . . . a sad fact that leads to the demise of many aspiring restaurateurs.

On Thursday morning (Bill's day off was Wednesday) I told brother Bill that I had looked over the property to be auctioned, and reported on what I had seen and learned. I asked him if he might be interested in it as a place for us to expand.

His first reaction was a categorical *no*. As the week wore on I suggested that he at least take a look at the property and try to gather more information.

The auction was to be held the next Tuesday morning. I came on duty at Jax on Saturday afternoon to relieve Bill. Before he left for the day I told him I would be in very early on Tuesday morning in case I decided to attend the auction. Once again I suggested he take a look at the property. He seemed disinterested.

Ruth and I went to the lake on Sunday morning. We discussed the impending auction. At that time four of our children and one son-in-law were working at Jax or Jax of Golden Valley in either full-time or part-time capacities.

We tried to evaluate our family situation. Many of our children were at or near the age where they were making career choices. Some were gravitating toward the restaurant business. Bill and Kathy's children were much younger. We had no way of knowing if the restaurant business would interest them in the future.

At the time their oldest child was barely fourteen. I also had the impression that Bill and Kathy felt somewhat overpowered by the imbalance of my family in the business.

As Ruth and I discussed our situation the idea evolved to buy the Shoreview property ourselves. We talked about the possibility of a partnership arrangement with some of our children, if we bought the property.

I felt that if we had time to get the new project going, I would be able to sell the Jax Cafe business to Bill after a year or so. It seemed that we were approaching the time when it might make sense for Bill and I to split.

I arrived at Jax Cafe about 7:30 a.m. on Tuesday morning...the day of the auction. I was surprised to see Bill there with Dick Doran and Dick's son, Steve. The Dorans were customers and friends who operated warehouses in the Twin Cities. Evidently, Bill had taken the Dorans with him to look at the Shoreview property.

The Dorans and Bill were discussing the property with great enthusiasm. I got the feeling from the conversation that we may have been headed for some type of partnership in the project with the Dorans. At this point I explained to Bill and the Dorans that when I last saw Bill it was quite evident to me that he had no interest in the projcct.

I told of the subsequent discussion Ruth and I had at the lake. I then said to Bill that if I bought the property and remodeled the building, and had about a year to get it going with my family, I would then be willing to sell him my half of the Jax Cafe business. Bill didn't hesitate for a moment. He said that would be fine.

The Dorans were very understanding and the conversation quickly shifted to developing a strategy to use at the auction. Dick Doran had considerable experience with auctions and I was grateful for his help. First, he told me to select a figure beyond which I would not bid and stick to it. He warned of the dangers of getting swept up in the competitive atmosphere of an auction.

Next, he concocted a plan of action. He suggested that I get involved in the early bidding and then withdraw. He reasoned that there would be many people there who knew Bill and me. As long as we were bidding they might think the real value had not been reached. He suggested that Steve pick up the bidding when I stopped. Steve was only in his early twenties. Dick thought it would be unlikely that any other bidders would know him. The time for the auction to begin was approaching, so Bill, Steve, Dick and I got into Dick's car and headed for Shoreview.

We decided to drop Steve off about three blocks from the property so that no one would know we were collaborators. Bill, Dick, and I drove to the property and Steve arrived some minutes later. He did not come anywhere near us.

The auctioneer conducted the sale from what was then the kitchen loading dock. I began the bidding. It was very slow at first but gradually all the serious bidders became involved. I was in the forefront of the bidders and I ran the price up several thousand dollars.

Then I quit with a bit of a flourish. I threw my hands down and stepped back into the crowd. Steve now began bidding. The auctioneer looked at me and motioned to me every time there was a break in the action. However, I merely shook him off and stepped back farther.

Steve was fantastic. As the bidding progressed he took off his suit coat and hung it on a picket of the stockade fence. The gesture had dramatic effect. It was like a statement that he was there to stay.

The auctioneer called a recess. Steve challenged him immediately. He loudly proclaimed that there was nothing stated in the rules that permitted a recess. The auctioneer prevailed and a five minute recess was held. The recess was called after Steve's last bid.

When the bidding resumed someone topped Steve's bid by five-hundred dollars. Steve quickly countered with another five-hundred dollars. Then silence except for the chant of the auctioneer trying to encourage additional bidding. Finally, he said, "Going once, going twice. Sold!!"

Bill was standing next to me at the back of the crowd. City manager Gary Dixon was close to us. When the auctioneer said, "Sold," Bill extended his hand to me and said, "Congratulations." A puzzled Gary Dixon said to Bill, "But that young fellow over there won the bid." Bill smiled at Gary and said, "He's ours."

I went into the kitchen of the restaurant and wrote a check for ten percent of the purchase price and gave it to the auctioneer as was required. Over and above the purchase price was a sixty-thousand dollar real estate tax liability with Ramsey County that would be necessary for us to satisfy. A closing date was set with the Small Business Administration for one week later.

The S.B.A. agreed to provide round-the-clock security on the property until the closing process was finalized.

We returned to Jax. I called Ruth and gave her the news. I recall thinking that once again our lives would be changed. What was Ruth's reaction?

Ruth Kozlak: *"I was excited at the prospect of working with our children and our son-in-law, Mark Satt. I liked the idea of doing something on our own. I always helped out at Jax when asked. I did hostess work at lunch . . . worked many football Saturdays, New Year's Eves . . . I felt I could be helpful with this new venture.*

"I was confident in the abilities of our children and particularly confident of Jack's business sense. On the other hand, I was frightened at the thought of the huge debt we would surely incur. I knew that three groups had failed to make a go of the place and that troubled me.

"Was there something wrong with the location? Everything happened so fast. I had not seen the property or the

building before we bought it.

"Once I did see the property I was excited by the potential beauty. There were several huge oaks and elms on the property. Most of the land was rough and neglected, but we could visualize lawns and flowers and a patio garden dining area.

"There was plenty of space for parking too. I knew what a struggle it had been for Jack and his brothers to obtain parking at Jax. That would not be a problem here.

"The building needed a lot of work but I liked the basic layout. Here too the possibilities seemed limitless. The restaurant itself was big enough to keep us all busy if we could attract customers, and yet it was laid out so that portions of the dining room could be closed off on slow nights to keep it intimate."

* * *

I began working on the project immediately. The very evening of the auction I called my friend, carpenter Bob Sappa, and asked if he and his partner Harold Kujawa would be available to work on the remodeling. Luckily, they were just finishing a job and they were available to start on Monday.

Next, I called John Neal. John designed the Roundtable Room for us at Jax. He also designed the Wig and Bottle restaurant, King's Inn, and several others. He agreed to meet me at the new property the next Tuesday.

Ruth and I called a meeting of our children to be held at our lake cabin on Sunday. At the Sunday meeting we discussed ideas for operation of the restaurant. Those who were interested could buy shares in the business. We discussed who would be eligible to own stock.

It was agreed that only one person from each family could own stock in the business. This posed an immediate problem for our daughter, Lynn. Both she and her husband, Mark Satt, would be working at the "new" restaurant but only one of them could hold stock. Lynn said she wanted Mark to have their family's stock in his name.

Each one of our children or their spouse who was coming into the business would be required to purchase twenty-five hundred dollars in stock. The money was much less important than the lesson it would give them in the workings of our system. Everyone involved would be required to go to a bank and borrow the money to purchase their stock, and that added to their sense of commitment to the project. It was also decided that when a stockholder wanted out of the business the remaining stockholders would buy their stock.

We agreed that I would be in charge of the remodeling project. I would contract it myself. The rest of the group would stay at their existing jobs until we got close to our opening date.

We also decided that the name and the image of the Sandpiper must be changed. Mark Kozlak suggested we run a contest at Jax of Golden Valley offering a prize of a one-hundred dollar gift certificate to the person who came up with a name we would choose for the new restaurant.

It was an excellent idea. The contest would allow hundreds of people to know that there was another restaurant in the offing, and we were rewarded with a good name for the property.

* * *

I met carpenters Bob Sappa and Harold Kujawa at the restaurant on Monday morning. We toured the building and began noting things that needed immediate attention. Ruth stopped by and joined us.

I mentioned earlier that the only customer access to the banquet area was through the main dining room. Ruth asked if it would be possible to relocate the stairway so that there could be a direct access to the lower level from the lobby. What a great idea, if it were possible. Harold and Bob got out their tape measures and began checking bearing walls, head room, stairway depth and everything else that was necessary.

They showed us where the stairway would begin in a new lobby, took us downstairs and pinpointed where it would end. We knew at once that this was an important change to the building that must be made.

The next morning we closed on the property. There was no turning back now. I met designer John Neal after lunch. We toured the building and looked over the grounds. I told John that we wanted to put windows in the dining room and build a patio garden.

I explained Ruth's idea to relocate the stairway to the banquet area. Bob and Harold showed him how it could fit in. John approved. I explained our desire to build restrooms on the main floor and asked him to locate and design them.

Then he said, "Do you realize this is the first job I have ever been involved in where the carpenters were working before the designer?" John was not familiar with the neighborhood; I drove him through North Oaks, Shoreview, and nearby Arden Hills, so he could get a feel for the area.

As we headed back to the restaurant, John said, "I think I know what I want to do with the place." I explained that time for me was of the essence . . . the interest was running on the money we had borrowed, plus we would have to borrow much more.

Whatever we did I wanted to be open before Thanksgiving so we could capture the holiday season business. John said, "You can start by tearing out all the carpeting. Find out what kitchen equipment you can salvage and get rid of the rest. Get ahold of a roofer and see what will be needed to correct the leaks. I will be back to you in about a week."

The cleanup and cleanout began. Son Mark Kozlak assembled a crew of young men who worked part-time at Jax Golden Valley as dishwashers and bus boys. Ruth worked with them as they cleaned the grease out of the kitchen fryers and washed the dishes, cookware and glasses.

There was only one burner on the stove that worked. They had to heat water over that burner and wash everything by hand. The dish machine and hot water heater were inoperable and not worth repairing.

I called a used restaurant equipment company and asked if they were interested in buying any of our cooking equipment. They took a look and pronounced most of it junk.

I had to pay to have it hauled away. We would need a new broiler, new stoves, grill top, hot top, steamer, and dishwashing machine. There were only a couple reach-in refrigerators that we could salvage. The kitchen floor was covered with asphalt tile squares in poor repair, and the walls were painted sheetrock.

I decided to have the walls covered with pale yellow ceramic tile and the floors with red quarry tile. I contacted a friend from a leading restaurant supply house and we discussed the cooking equipment needed to prepare our proposed menu.

Their kitchen engineers set about the task of designing the necessary equipment into our limited space. I quickly learned that the existing kitchen exhaust system would be inadequate. So we had to adjust to that problem.

Adjust became synonymous with spend . . . a new exhaust system was the only solution. As long as we were going to install an entire new cooking line I decided to cover the entire wall behind the cooking line with stainless steel. We installed gas and electrical connections on the equipment that could be easily disengaged and moved for thorough cleaning behind.

The roofing company was quick to respond to my call. Their recommendation was to replace the entire flat roof. They also recommended insulating the roof with beveled insulation. This would save on energy costs and bring us right up to code. Price: Twenty-thousand dollars. Ouch! I let the contract.

Mark's crew helped tear out the old carpet and deposit it into the huge commercial dumpster that we had rented. Next, they began raking the grounds and cutting the weeds on the property.

It was past mid-August when John Neal showed us his preliminary plan. It called for windows on the entire north wall of the main dining room . . . seventy-two feet of windows. Guests would be able to look through the windows to the garden that was yet to be designed or built.

The upper portion of the windows would be rounded and etched. He called for brass railings where appropriate, and brass pots for live plants. A light metallic finished Formica was to be used on both salad bar and huge cubes on which to set plants.

He also introduced large terra cotta vases and lavabos. He selected new acoustical material for the ceilings. He showed the colors to be used for wall coverings, carpeting, and the refinished dining room chairs.

A beautiful functional canopy was designed for over the bar. He had relocated the check room and maitre d' stand. Two new restrooms were shown. There would also be more closet and storage space. It was an excellent plan and we quickly adopted it.

John instructed Bob and Harold to start ripping out old railings and identified those walls to be peeled down to the studs. He told me to have the heating, ventilating and air conditioning systems checked. He also recommended that I look into the possibility of having an automatic fire prevention sprinkling system installed in the building. As long as we were going to be torn up, now would be the time to do it.

Now that we had a plan we were off and running. John Neal brought in more detailed drawings almost daily and with these I could open up bids.

I don't know if I have ever been busier. I was still trying to cover my shift at Jax while putting this new project together. I took bids for tile work, millwork, kitchen equipment, chair refinishing, liquor dispensing systems, carpeting, acoustical tile, cabinets, vanities, and on and on.

I had to let the contracts and then coordinate the trades so they could follow each other without losing time. I would wake up in the middle of the night and think of things to do. I kept a pad and pencil at my bedside so I could make notes when this happened.

Ruth was a big help. The weeks that I was on the day shift at Jax, she would drive to the new project and open up the building for the tradesmen. She knew who was to be there each day and what was to be done.

She set up a preliminary set of books and paid bills as they came due. If something came up that she wasn't sure of, she would call me at Jax for clarification.

I called Jim Eldorado to check the heating, ventilating and air conditioning systems. He reported that most of the duct work located on the roof was in bad shape. It was deteriorating and it wasn't even insulated.

The air conditioning/heating unit that serviced the bar and cocktail lounge was not worth repairing. I agreed to all new insulated duct work, a new improved air distribution system and an entirely new heating/cooling unit for the cocktail lounge and bar.

Jim Eldorado also did something else for me that turned out to be a big favor. He noticed on our plan that we did not show a full basement under the new restrooms. He asked me why not. I explained that I was trying to save some money.

Jim said, "Jack, I know you and I have watched you operate. I predict you will need that space for something in a very short time. As long as you are going down to the frost line anyway, please let them dig deeper and put in a full basement under those restrooms." I went along with his suggestion and I don't know how we could have gotten along without that space.

The wiring too was out of date and it would be necessary to practically rewire the entire building. I took bids on a sprinkler system for the building and learned that the reduced cost of insurance would pay for the system in four years.

I let the contract. I often thought of the movie, "Mr. Blandings Builds His Dream House". This was the same situation revisited. It seemed that one problem led to another and another, ad infinitum.

We installed a new hot water heater and discovered we also needed a water softening system. We added new gas cooking and heating equipment and discovered the gas pressure to the building was inadequate.

In the midst of everything two huge elms on our property were tagged for Dutch elm disease. I had to pay to have them cut down and removed. Price: Seven-hundred-fifty dollars.

Gradually the job began to take some shape. I contacted Park Nurseries and was able to hire Ed Reed to lay out our patio garden. He had been trained by Paul Bass and had worked with him when the garden at Jax was built a quarter century earlier.

My friend Don Lucker stopped by to look at the building. He asked me what I was going to do with the ship that was outside. I explained that I wasn't going to use it but I hadn't decided how to dispose of it.

He offered to take it away. He had it hauled to the state fair grounds, where he hoped to use it for some type of commercial venture during the fair. He paid two-thousand dollars to have it moved, but nothing ever came of it.

It cost me seven-hundred dollars to fill the excavation under the ship and level the area.

In early September I saw that Marie Kalina had died. Marie was the wife of Peter Kalina. Peter was well-known as an accomplished chef. He had held chef jobs at the

Minneapolis Athletic Club, Golden Valley Country Club, and Majestic Oaks Country Club.

He retired early to care for his ailing wife. He is an older brother of my good friend, Harold Kalina. Although Harold and I were lifelong friends I only knew his brother Peter casually. I was well aware of his reputation as one of the leading chefs in town.

The day after Marie's funeral I called Harold Kalina and asked if he knew whether Pete might be interested in going back to work. I explained that I was involved in the new project and thought Pete might want to get involved in some capacity.

Harold said that it was just what Pete needed. I asked if I should wait a few days before approaching him. Harold said, "Go to him right now, today."

I drove to Pete's house. He came to the door and I explained that I was in the midst of a new project and needed help. I told him that if he was interested he could determine his own level of involvement.

He could tutor my son-in-law Mark Satt . . . be a consultant . . . do whatever he chose. Peter stood at the door and said, "I will help you. I'll come out to see you in a few days." That was all there was to it. I was delighted. We would have an outstanding experienced person to assist us. It was a tremendous stroke of good fortune.

The next day my uncle Peter Kozlak took Peter Kalina to lunch at Midland Hills Country Club. Bill Bell was in the dining room. Bill had the management contract for food and beverage at Midland Hills. A knowledgeable executive, he also was associated with the Rosewood Room at the Northstar Hotel and the Mendakota Club, among others.

When Bell spotted Pete Kalina he stopped at his table to visit. In the course of their conversation he asked Pete Kalina to come to work for him as a consultant. Pete answered, "No, I am not available. I promised Jack Kozlak that I would help him."

* * *

Peter Kalina stopped the next week for his first look at the restaurant. We were still in the tearing-out phase. The heating and air conditioning units had been swung off the roof by cranes and roofers had begun their work. We had disposed of the worn out kitchen equipment.

The carpenters were removing interior walls that had to be relocated. The place was a dusty, dirty mess. Dumpster after dumpster was filled and hauled away. Before the job was completed we had filled nine huge commercial dumpsters to overflowing.

Pete looked over the various rooms in the building and returned to a long table in the dining room where the remodeling plans were laid out. He examined them for a very long time. When he was finished he came to me and pronounced the plan "superb."

He predicted that the dining room with the new windows would be particularly beautiful. He offered suggestions for positioning our cooking equipment to facilitate a steady production flow. He would visit once or twice a week to monitor the progress of the project.

The contest to name the restaurant attracted scores of good suggestions, but the name Royal Oak was in a class by itself. Paul and Pat Brink, customers at Jax of Golden Valley, submitted the name and everyone in our family was delighted with it. On September 20, 1977, the old Sandpiper restaurant became the new *Kozlak's Royal Oak*.

By October 1st I had let all contracts. Roofers, block layers, electricians, carpenters, tile setters, plumbers, and sheet metal workers were now busy putting the restaurant back together. The dining room chairs were sent out to be refinished. This helped eliminate clutter in the dining room work area.

Construction of the garden also began. A concrete block wall was built around the area to be planted. Huge boulders were hauled in along with truckloads of soil. By mid-October trees and shrubs began arriving at the job site.

In mid-October we called all the subcontractors together and told them we had to be ready for a November 15th opening. We explained that the date was critical for us if we were to be able to capture the holiday season business.

They all pledged to do their best to get us open. I now had my daughter, Diane, cover my job at Jax and I stayed with the new project full-time.

We placed ads and began interviewing prospective

Diane Kozlak and Gloria Minke at Kozlak's Royal Oak.

Keith Hargadine, and Randy Schade, culinary experts at Kozlak's Royal Oak.

(Above) Romelda Kascht ("Melda,") along with Carol Braun handle the office duties at Kozlak's Royal Oak.

(Right) Mark Satt, pictured at Royal Oak, on one of his visits from the kitchen to the dining rooms.

111

(Above) Cherie Pederson and Bette Bowes – "servers extraordinaire" – have been at Kozlak's Royal Oak since opening day in 1977.

(Right) Carol Kozlak Braun can best be described as versatile. Find a job at Kozlak's Royal Oak and she can probably accomplish the task.

employees. The applicants found it difficult to believe that we would be open by November 15th. They walked through sawdust, over extension cords, and sidestepped building materials to get to our office.

Happily, we were attracting many quality people who wanted to join our staff. One lady, Ruth Larson, applied for waitress work. I offered her a position and said we expected to be open by November 15th. She said that would be fine, but asked if I had any work she could do before then. I asked, "How are you at cleaning?" She said, "I am very good at it and I will be glad to help."

She started the very next day. She scraped the steam table clean with razor blades. She cleaned the refrigerators in and out so they sparkled like new. She polished the brass bar rail on her hands and knees. She picked up and swept each day so that the tradesmen could come into a clean, orderly environment.

Ruth stayed with that job until we opened for business. She has been doing waitress work for us since the first day.

Between the 15th and 20th of October we ordered our outdoor sign; selected and ordered uniforms for waiters, waitresses, bus people, and bartenders.

Pete Kalina, Mark Satt and I put the final touches on the luncheon, dinner and banquet menus. Mark Kozlak helped name the banquet and party areas and we made up our reservation book. I wrote and inserted ads that pointed to our opening.

The "Ma Bell" ad was an attention getter, and it led to many inquiries about our facilities.

Our son, Paul, though only 19-years-old, had considerable experience working at Jax at various jobs in the kitchen. He was also an accomplished bartender. He became the bar manager at Royal Oak and did a fine job of getting the bars organized.

The positioning ad where we paid tribute to our potential competitors also generated many calls. We were building some suspense. Several people called to comment favorably on this ad and to say that they could hardly wait for our opening.

We began booking holiday season business. The first party I booked was the Northway Construction Company holiday party. Clyde Rehbein, the president of Northway, came in to see if our facilities could accommodate his group. We were still terribly torn up, but he looked at our plans and booked space for one-hundred twenty-five guests. Other bookings quickly followed.

Pete Kalina saw what was happening and he said, "Jack, we have to provide a banquet kitchen downstairs. More expense was about the last thing I needed but I knew he was one-hundred percent correct. In typical Pete Kalina style he had his recommendation and the numbers ready. I approved it and the banquet kitchen was ready by the time we opened.

* * *

As October wound down the pace of the remodeling picked up. Sappa and Kujawa brought in more carpenters. The new windows were installed. Decorative mouldings arrived and were being fitted around all the exposed beams. Lattice work was being built right on the job. All carpenters began working Saturdays in order to get the job done.

Sappa and Kujawa worked on Sundays too. They passed up pheasant and duck hunting. Their wives were shocked. Bob and Harold always looked forward to hunting season. However, they knew how important our target date was, and they wouldn't let us down.

It was fun to watch everything come together. When the tile-setters finished in the kitchen, we called for our new cooking and dishwashing equipment to be installed. Once the tile was set in the new restrooms, the cabinetmaker delivered the new vanities and the plumber was there to install the fixtures.

Gradually, sheet metal, electrical workers, and plumbers gave way to acoustical tile installers, painters, paper hangers and carpet layers. The kitchen was completed during the first week in November. Pete Kalina and Mark Satt made sure they acquired all the pots, pans and utensils they needed.

They checked their new cooking equipment, refrigeration and dish washing machine. They began ordering in the staples they would need. Our official opening would commence with lunch on November 15th.

The way the project came together in time for our target date was truly amazing. We cut it close . . . extremely close . . . but every tradesman, every supplier and every employee gave us their very best effort.

114

Jack (a.k.a. Jax) Kozlak has reincarnated the former Sandpiper restaurant as a swan; it's called the Royal Oak and it's one of the most gracious dining spots in the Twin Cities.

Comfort with a touch of real class is evident throughout, and the result is a rare combination of subtlety and opulence, grandeur and good taste. In the bar earth-toned geometric carpeting blends with lush brown suede walls. Gleaming brass and sparkling glassware form a glowing halo above the blond wood bar. And elegantly etched glass separates the main bar from a cozy lounge where a singer-pianist dispenses mellow middle-of-the-road music nightly.

Colors in the two-level dining room are soft, neutral and understated. The tables are beautifully set. Large, sweeping palms rustle as guests and staff move past. There is ample space between tables, and the lighting (which includes candles) is perfect—low enough for intimacy, bright enough to see and be seen. One wall is tall, with arched windows that overlook a garden decorated with holiday lights.

The menu is standard and well-prepared, with prices ranging from $6.50 for walleye pike to $10.50 for a large filet mignon. There is also pheasant ($8.95), Long Island duckling ($8.75) and sole with almonds ($6.50). Six oysters were large, fresh and $3.50. And it wouldn't be Kozlak's without live Maine lobster, priced surprisingly low—$13.95 the night we were there. The salad bar offers iced plates. The carafe wine is Ridgecrest burgundy, zinfadel, rose and chenin blanc (which is perhaps too sweet for the house white).

The service is remarkable for a restaurant that is newly-opened—friendly, efficient and knowledgeable.

Everyone seems to have a good time at the Royal Oak. It's the kind of place that's worth getting dressed up for without diminishing your fun.

KOZLAK'S ROYAL OAK—4785 Hodgson Road. Shoreview—484-8484. Open Tues.-Sat. noon-midnight; Sunday from noon to 7:30 p.m. Closed Monday. All major and Jax credit cards accepted. Reservation advised.

circa 1978

Mpls. StPaul

The Magazine of the Twin Cities

115

On the Friday afternoon before our opening, men were laying fresh sod in the new garden as a fluffy wet snow fell to the ground. Bob Sappa's wife, Patty, stopped by in the morning to take a look at the restaurant.

My wife was busy with last-minute dusting and cleaning. Patty began helping Ruth and stayed with it for the remainder of the day. That typified the spirit of the entire project.

* * *

We held some staff training sessions in advance of our opening. These were vital and productive sessions where everyone had an opportunity to get acquainted. Our management staff outlined our objectives and expectations. We answered questions regarding the day-to-day operation as well as employee benefits.

As I surveyed the nearly four-score people we had hired I was struck by their diversity in age and experience. I was also impressed by their attentiveness and earnestness. As we completed our agenda I pondered the responsibility we assumed as employers. I thought of how people like Bette Bowes, Cherie Pederson, Sandy O'Connor, and many others, left secure positions at restaurants where they had seniority and steady customers.

I wondered how some of the young people (dishwashers and bus persons), many of whom were in their first job, would perform. I felt that we had a bright and attractive group of people but I wondered if we could quickly shape them into a smooth-working team. Many thoughts raced through my mind as we completed our training. How would we do?

Would the public like the new Royal Oak? Would we be busy? Would we be able to fulfill the obligations we had assumed when we hired all these good people? The moment of truth was at hand. Tomorrow we open.

* * *

Lunch hour approached. It was Tuesday, November 15, 1977. We had a few luncheon reservations on the book . . . very few. The dining room was set and ready. The cooks, bartenders, wait staff, coat checker and every other staff member was at their station.

We really didn't know how much business to expect,

but we were staffed up just in case. I tried not to display my nervousness. The emotion I was feeling as I waited for the first customer was a cross between my wedding day, the birth of our first child and election day in 1968, when I was a state legislative candidate.

From the dining room I could see the garden. Through the pickets of the fence outlining the garden, I could see people walking from the parking lot toward the front entrance. It was 11 a.m., our announced opening hour.

By 11:30 the dining room was half filled and at noon we had a nearly full house. The comments of the people, as they saw the restaurant for the first time were warm expressions of approval. Repeatedly, we heard, "It's beautiful," and "You have done a great job."

The salad bar and luncheon menu received their share of raves too. The service suffered a glitch or two because of the newness of the operation, but the affected customers were understanding. On balance, our first meal was a great success. We were as busy as we dared be for openers and the guests approved of the cuisine and the surroundings.

Our first dinner hour was busy also. Lighting is extremely important in a fine dining restaurant, and John Neal did an outstanding job of lighting Royal Oak. Guests commented on the warmth and beauty of the restaurant and the soft romantic lighting in the dining room.

Customer reaction to the new Kozlak's Royal Oak was very favorable. And the word spread fast. Minneapolis-St. Paul Magazine did a column on the restaurant soon after we opened.

The business took off like a rocket. It was wonderful to be so busy and to see a new staff perform so well. I remember one of our first weekends. I was working at Jax and hustled out to Royal Oak when we cleared our waiting lists.

Royal Oak was extremely busy. I walked into the bar and observed the smooth orderly flow of service. I stepped into the kitchen and watched the activity. Everyone was a study in concentration. Cooks, servers, busers, dishwashers . . . everyone was doing a professional job.

There was very little noise or clutter. The newness of the operation required that everyone concentrate on their

117

jobs totally. For a new group they did more than succeed . . . they excelled.

We also had a problem or two. During one of our early lunch hours I was helping tend bar. The dining room and bar were both busy when the quiet conversation in the restaurant was interrupted by the loudest, longest crash of dishes that I had ever heard.

I rushed to the kitchen to see two dishwashers standing ankle deep in expensive broken china. A shelf that had been erected to store dinner plates and platters came loose from the wall and the result was over a thousand dollars in breakage. Luckily, no one was injured.

From the time we opened in November until the first of the year I seldom had an opportunity to visit with Pete Kalina or Mark Satt. We were so busy in the front of the house that our communication was confined to sending messages with party orders and projections for the amount of business to expect from day-to-day.

I didn't worry about the kitchen. Pete was there with Mark Satt at his side. The operation seemed to get smoother with each day. Pete's experience was priceless. He kept the kitchen properly staffed but did not waste labor. We seldom ran out of a menu item, yet we did not have wasted product. He set the tenor of the kitchen . . . calm, relaxed efficiency.

Peter Kalina: *"I never saw a place that got off the ground so fast and stayed there. Actually, the business went up-up-up. Mark Satt and I worked twelve-hour shifts for months. The first year we did this seven days a week. The restaurant was closed Monday but we came in to do prep work.*

"I had been away from the business for a year and one-half before Marie died. I wanted to see if I could still do the work . . . if I hadn't lost the touch.

"Royal Oak has done well because it had a good base. It started well . . . everyone knew their job and stuck to it. They knew the importance of taking care of the customers and didn't worry about the hours. We defined our market and stuck to it.

"Mark Satt was a good student. He sucked up knowledge like a sponge. I taught him to do the buying. How to make everything from scratch; to watch food and labor

costs. I impressed the old adage on him that there is only one-hundred percent in a dollar.

"If you spend more, you lose. Mark has a nice personality. He knows how to treat people. He is a willing worker. I stop in to visit with him often.

"I receive great satisfaction in seeing people like Mark and Randy. (Randy Schade started at Kozlak's Royal Oak as a teen-age dishwasher. He was thought to have a learning disability. Pete Kalina worked with Randy and developed him into a top-notch cook, and he took off on a successful culinary career.)

"I feel proud when I hear the good reports about Kozlak's Royal Oak. My friend Terry McGovern summed up what many feel about Kozlak's Royal Oak. He said, 'When you dine at Royal Oak you feel like you really went out.' I enjoyed being a part of it."

* * *

Mark Kozlak always had an eye for a worthy promotion or a quality idea. He had visited New Orleans and attended the Jazz Brunch at the famous Commander's Palace Restaurant.

He thought that the decor at Royal Oak would lend itself beautifully to a similar brunch and he wanted to try it.

We decided that Ruth, Pete Kalina and I should go to New Orleans and take a look at the Brennan's Commander's Palace Jazz Brunch. We flew to New Orleans in late January of 1978 and reserved a table for their Sunday Jazz Brunch.

It was delightful. The menu featured two appetizers, choice of one of a dozen New Orleans brunch entrées plus hot French bread and dessert. Three strolling musicians made their way through the dining rooms, adding musical spice to the event.

That afternoon and evening we discussed what we had experienced at Commander's Palace and decided it was the kind of brunch we should do. I came up with an idea for an ad to promote the Royal Oak New Orleans Jazz Brunch. However, I would have to clear it with the owners of Commander's Palace, Dick and Ella Brennan.

On Monday I made an appointment to meet the Brennans and we proceeded to their office. It was our first-ever meeting and I explained that we wanted to institute a brunch similar to theirs at Kozlak's Royal Oak restaurant in Shoreview, Minnesota.

I had sketched out an ad I hoped to run that read: *Two Ways to enjoy a New Orleans Jazz Brunch.* On one side of the ad it would direct people to fly to New Orleans and visit Commander's Palace. On the other side it directed people to Royal Oak.

Both Dick and Ella Brennan were very gracious but he asked if we would come back the next day so he could have time to mull it over. Dick then led us on a complete tour of their fabulous facility.

The next day we returned to the restaurant and met Dick Brennan again. I didn't know what Dick's response would be to my request, but I was prepared for a mild turn down. He said, "George Connor and Bob Wetoska were in for dinner last night. (Both Wetoska and Connor were legendary football stars at Notre Dame and the National Football League.) I knew Wetoska was from Minnesota so I asked if he knew you. You have my permission to run any ad you wish linking our restaurants and the brunch," said Brennan.

Bob Wetoska's father, Steve, was a chef for decades at the Donaldson's North Shore restaurant in Minneapolis. He and my father were close friends. When my parents entered the restaurant business Mr. Wetoska helped them organize their kitchen and later helped them expand it.

Bob Wetoska was an occasional customer at Jax before he moved to Chicago. I recall we had the pleasure of hosting his wedding rehearsal dinner.

The go-ahead from Dick Brennan was a good break. It provided us with an opportunity to be associated with one of America's great restaurants. In later years I served on the National Restaurant Association board of directors with Ella Brennan and more recently with her nephew, Ralph Brennan.

Before we boarded the plane back to the Twin Cities, Pete Kalina had our brunch menu roughed out. I called my son Mark from New Orleans and asked him to begin the search for some good jazz musicians.

We set a target date for our first Royal Oak New Orleans Jazz Brunch for the first Sunday in April, 1978. As soon as we got home Pete and Mark Satt began testing

The Royal Oak Stomp

The eggs came over easy on a lazy afternoon.

And the sunnyside was decidedly up at the foot-stomping, toe-tapping, table-hopping New Orleans Jazz Brunch Sunday at Kozlak's Royal Oak Restaurant in Shoreview.

Moving table-to-table with extraordinary enthusiasm was "The Wandering Three," a strolling Dixieland band which is curiously — and understandably — devoid of a drummer and a piano player.

But Dixieland groups don't stroll, a sophisticated young man protested mildly.

"But they march," was the smug response of Welton Barnett, a graying and elderly gentleman who is one of the finest guitar players in the Twin Cities areas.

Not entirely saintly, a horde hungry for food, booze and the sounds of the South started marching into Kozlak's promptly at noon, the time to legally begin service of liquor on Sundays in Minnesota.

Some came from church. Many came from their beds.

Welcomed warmly by two Kozlak women, their appetites were tickled by mellow hors d'oeuvres presented by Barnett, Dick Pendleton, clarinet, and Dick Norling, upright bass.

And the name of the tune was "Way Down Yonder in New Orleans."

Frothy drinks and fancy dishes poured from the bar and kitchen. The band offered an exciting menu: "St. James Infirmary Blues," "St. Louis Blues," "Basin Street," "Someday You'll Be Sorry" and the inevitable "When the Saints Go Marching In."

"We play mostly Dixie," Pendleton, leader of the trio, noted proudly.

But the band did not resist requests — for "Hello, Dolly" and "And Times Goes By." Nobody shouted "Play Melancholy Baby."

The guests devoured the songs and some elegant entrées — eggs sardou, eggs benedict, omelette pontalba, gulf shrimp au gratin and chicken rochambeau, which basically is boned butter fried chicken breasts hiding slices of ham and topped with mushroom and tarragon-flavored bernaise sauces.

La Caille Au Chambertin was an early-afternoon challenge. It is southern quail braised in a red wine sauce with pearl onions, bacon and fresh mushrooms.

The menu at the Royal Oak, 4785 Hodgson Road, boasts fizzy cocktails and rich desserts.

Among the "eye openers" are a ramos fizz, a New Orleans gin fizz and mimosa, which is comprised of equal parts of champagne and orange juice.

The dessert list includes hot-buttered pecan pie and bananas foster — bananas sautéed in butter, brown sugar, cinnamon and banana liqueur and served over vanilla ice cream. The delight is flamed in rum at tableside.

Sunday brunch begins at 11:30 a.m. The final seating is at 2:30 p.m.

All three members of the band, which works until 4 p.m., are veteran musicians who studied and worked with Doc Evans and Harry Blons.

Formerly The Sandpiper, the Royal Oak is run by Jack Kozlak, who also is an owner of the Jax cafes in Northeast Minneapolis and Golden Valley.

The Royal Oak, a bright and airy supperclub rich in live plants and etched glass, opened in mid-November. The Sunday brunch started April 2. A huge patio should open in a couple of weeks.

The bosses at the Royal Oak are young. Three of Kozlak's children — Diane, Lynn and Paul — make up the managerial team. Lynn's husband, Mark Satt, is chef.

Diane said that the Sunday brunch at the Royal Oak is much like those served daily at Brennan's and the Commander's Palace in New Orleans. The Royal Oak is less expensive, however.

Only the Sunday music is old. The dining concludes with a soulful rendition of "Do You Know What It Means to Miss New Orleans?"

"It makes you wanna dance," said waitress Cherie Pederson.

Don Delfiacco reviewed our brunch in the St. Paul Dispatch *(May 4, 1978) and we were off and running.*

their brunch recipes. We soon settled on our brunch menu. Mark Kozlak was able to book the Dick Pendleton trio to supply the mellow jazz music we were looking for. I ran this ad before our first brunch:

The brunch was an instant success. It is now in its eighteenth year and going strong. Dick Pendleton continues to lead the group. I don't think he has missed a single Sunday in all those years.

The menu is varied a bit from time to time but the basic format is the same. Our guests tell us they concur with our original ad. "There are two ways to enjoy a New Orleans Jazz Brunch. Fly to New Orleans and Commander's Palace . . . or . . . in the Twin Cities visit Kozlak's Royal Oak."

* * *

THROUGH THE YEARS AT ROYAL OAK

The spring and summer of 1978 were exciting at Royal Oak. Our huge canvas canopy was installed over the dining area in the patio and the garden was planted with a myriad of colorful flowers. Attractive patio dining furniture arrived just in time for the outdoor season, increasing our seating capacity by some seventy seats.

The guests loved it. In good weather the patio garden became a favorite place for many folks at both lunch and dinner. The business was doing very well. We were paying our bills on time and meeting our commitments at the bank.

One part of the building that we felt needed upgrading was our banquet area on the lower level. We had installed a new acoustical ceiling in the banquet area and replaced the old folding chairs with more attractive banquet chairs before we opened the previous November.

We also had the room freshly painted, but the area was not at all in keeping with the main floor.

At one of our management meetings we decided that we would try to make a meaningful improvement to the property each year. The banquet area was the obvious first choice for our attention.

Once again John Neal did an outstanding job of design. He specified a wide oak chair rail to ring the dining room. Below the railing would be a soft brown suede wall fabric. From the top of the railing to the ceiling smoke mirrors covered the walls. He selected attractive chandeliers for the ceiling and a complementary patterned carpet for the floor. We also decided that it was time to upgrade our air distribution system and air conditioning in the area. We installed a new twenty-ton air conditioning and air handling unit.

When the job was completed, we had a beautiful room that we could sell with pride and an area where we could easily control the climate.

As our first year drew to a close we decided to hold an appreciation dinner for our staff and their spouses. The single people were allowed to bring a guest. We had a social hour where we met many of the spouses and guests for the first time. Mark and Pete prepared an excellent dinner that was enjoyed by all.

The program was short. Just a few remarks on the "State of the Restaurant" and a sincere "thank you" to the staff.

Music and dancing followed. We all enjoyed the evening so thoroughly that the Appreciation Dinner became an annual affair. Everyone looks forward to it. We invite many of our alumni and retirees too.

I think it helps to draw us together as a team . . . to build esprit de corps.

As it happens, we head into our busy holiday season soon after our appreciation dinner. I think the timing proved to be ideal.

* * *

The business continued to prosper and we quickly became cramped for space. The coat check room was often overloaded. We had no place to store our summer furniture. The records we must keep for the government began piling up.

We decided to build a storage building that would be detached from the restaurant. The building is little more than a garage but we made it look like a carriage house.

We included windows with muton bars and planter boxes below them. The roof and exterior of the building matches that of the restaurant. We placed a cupola with a weather vane on the roof and Ruth made curtains for the windows.

The building sits to the side of our property in a grove of mature oak trees.

At the same time we had the carpenters build an addition on the front of the restaurant that more than doubled the size of our checkroom. We also built a concrete ramp to provide easy access to the restaurant for the handicapped.

In September of that year I sold my half of the Jax and Jax Golden Valley businesses to my brother, Bill. I did not retire, as many people suspected, but what had been a frantic work load was reduced to a much more manageable level.

I devoted more energy to Royal Oak and the Minnesota Restaurant Association. Also, Ruth and I had more time together.

* * *

At the beginning of our third year Larry Hokanson from Land O' Lakes called to inquire about a party they hoped to hold for some of their very important distributors. Land O' Lakes had recently opened their spacious new corporate offices in nearby Arden Hills.

Larry thought a New Orleans theme might be exciting. He wanted us to come up with some ideas for the projected summer party. I asked for a few days to work on it and we set a date for our next meeting.

Pete, Mark Satt and I went to work immediately. We saw this as an opportunity to enhance the excellent relationship we enjoyed with Land O' Lakes, and at the same time show off our facility to some of the most discerning food service executives in the country.

We had several meetings with Larry Hokanson and his staff. They made it plain that they wanted the evening to be one that their guests would long remember.

The party was held on a beautiful evening in early summer. We converted what was then our cocktail lounge entertainment area into a room filled with hors d'oeuvres. We draped long tables with linen, terraced them, and arranged bouquets of flowers at various points along the tables.

We placed chafing dishes and ice carvings at appropriate places and filled them with items such as petite stuffed lobster tails, scallops parisienne, clams casino, oysters Rockefeller, jumbo gulf shrimp, and chilled crab claws. We arranged silver trays filled with creative hors d'oeuvres made with Land O' Lakes cheeses.

The tiered tables were over forty-feet in length. Two of the highlights were the Land O' Lakes symbol, the Indian maiden, sculptured from blocks of Land O' Lakes butter and cheese.

As the guests made their way through the hors d'oeuvres tables, strolling musicians provided a gentle unobtrusive musical background. The patio was set with cocktail tables. An oyster bar was set to the side. Two cooks were kept busy opening fresh oysters and clams.

The evening was picture perfect. The garden with its beautiful flowers and shrubs, the temperate summer breeze, the music . . . everyone was enjoying themselves.

Dinner was served in the Royal Oak main dining room. It was a double entree affair complete with appropriate wines. The first entree was fresh filet of sole. The second, roast U.S. prime rib eye. Between courses we served some special made Land O' Lakes sorbet.

A tomato stuffed with tiny peas and pearl onions was presented as one of the accompaniments to the roast rib eye.

At that time there was a small company near the restaurant that was growing tomatoes hydroponically. I went to the owner weeks in advance and explained that I needed perfectly sized tomatoes for this party. He promised to have them. I picked them up the morning of the party. They were perfectly sized, colored and ripened.

One of the guests was Mr. Sabes, an owner of the prestigious American Fruit Co. He called me over and asked, "Where did you get these tomatoes?" When I told him he took a pad and pen from his pocket and jotted the information down. He said, "I must have one of my people call on them." It was a subtle compliment.

When it was time for dessert we had several chafing dishes wheeled into the dining room and our staff prepared Bananas Foster. It was a festive finale to a remarkable evening. When the guests had departed I had an opportunity to visit with Larry Hokanson and his colleague, Andy Anderson.

They expressed their extreme gratitude over the way the evening had gone. I was ecstatic. The evening gave us a chance to put our best foot forward and it enhanced our reputation by quantum leaps.

Through the years we have done a lot of business with some of the people who saw our restaurant for the first time at that Land O' Lakes party.

* * *

The next major improvement we made was building a second garden. The room south of the bar area had been used as a cocktail lounge and late evening entertainment room. We were receiving ever more requests for private party and banquet space, and the entertainment room business was spotty at best.

We decided to convert the area to a dining room. The west wall of the room was windowed and the view was of a lawn area with several mature oaks in the background.

We wanted to create a more dramatic view from the dining room.

I called Ed Reed at the nursery and asked him to draw a plan. He proposed building a modest semicircular berm on a portion of the grassy area between the windows and the big oaks. Evergreens, ornamental trees and shrubs would be planted up and down the berm and flower beds would be positioned to give the most captivating effect.

We gave the go-ahead on the new garden. At the same time an automatic watering system was installed for the lawns and gardens surrounding the restaurant. We ran a contest to name the "new" dining room. The winning name, Oakview Terrace, seemed to describe the setting precisely. The room has been extremely popular both as a private dining room and as an addition to our main dining room on busy occasions.

* * *

After our fourth year we took a hard look at our financial position and our accomplishments. We were doing good business. We were paying our bills and meeting all of our financial obligations. We had made many improvements to the building and the grounds.

One reason we were able to do so much so quickly was that I was drawing a very nominal salary from Royal Oak. The bulk of Ruth's and my living expenses came from the installment sale of the Jax businesses.

The press had been very good to us. It seemed that every time we needed a boost, a newspaper, television program, or magazine would favor us with a kind review. We knew we had an excellent staff. We experienced extremely low turnover . . . far, far below industry averages.

Mark Satt, Diane Kozlak and I discussed some options. One of the ideas I brought forth was the possibility of setting up a profit sharing/pension plan for our people. Profit sharing was very rare indeed in our industry, but it seemed to me to be a good way to reward and keep loyal employees.

Both Mark and Diane showed interest in the idea so we went to a leading attorney in the field and discussed plans that would fit our situation. We ultimately set up a program.

I am proud of this for many reasons. Diane and Mark took a totally unselfish position in establishing the plan. As a small independent restaurant we broke some relatively new ground in our industry. I believe the staff has more than justified the faith we showed them by instituting the plan. They demonstrate repeatedly that they care about our guests, the business and each other.

Our turnover rate remains far below national, state and local averages. We also experience less breakage and less waste than comparably sized restaurants. Of course, there can be no profit sharing without profits, but we believe that, for us, profit sharing does not cost . . . it pays.

There is one down side with which we must contend. The Congress has changed the rules covering retirement plans on various occasions through the years. Each time they do this we must spend money on attorney and accountant fees to make sure we are in compliance with the law.

Attorneys and accountants are expensive and the bite they take from a small business and a modest plan such as ours is substantial. It seems that sometimes over-zealous legislation has the effect of throwing the baby out with the bath water.

I have often wondered why existing plans cannot be "grandfathered" so that small businesses would not have to waste time, energy and money keeping up with legislative changes.

* * *

One of the improvements we looked forward to making for years was a substantial addition to the main floor kitchen. Our walk-in coolers and food preparation area were located downstairs. Everything had to be brought up by dumb waiter or carried.

We knew that if we could get our coolers and prep area on the main floor we would be able to handle our product better and be much more efficient. We had ample space on our lot to accommodate an addition. So in 1983 we decided to tackle the project.

First, we decided what we wanted to include in the addition. Then we hired an architect to draw the plan so that everything would fit. We specified an expanded salad station, vegetable preparation area, meat-cutting area, additional reach-in coolers, walk-in coolers, three new sinks, dry storage room and a small private office for the chef.

We also provided space for our scale, mixer, an ice machine plus space for a new vertical cutter mixer, slow cooker oven, and a large baking oven. All new equipment was specified to be stainless steel where possible, even the exterior of the walk-in coolers.

The addition was designed to have easy-to-clean floors, walls and ceiling. The new loading dock would be outside the back door, and the chef's office had a window with a view of the dock and the property beyond.

We were spending roughly forty-thousand dollars a year to rent linen. Our plan called for us to convert the downstairs space that housed the present prep area to a laundry once we got the new kitchen operating.

Another problem we attacked at the same time was the shortage of make-up air. We designed a big new unit into our air handling system in the kitchen addition and were able to solve the negative air pressure problem for the entire building.

I told the architect we would not need a full basement under the new addition. (Once again I was trying to hold down costs.) When Ruth heard about this she reminded me that I almost goofed when I wasn't going to put a full basement under the new restrooms. She made a strong case for a full basement, citing storage for catering equipment, holiday decorations, extra china, glassware, linen and just plain growth. I relented and, of course, it turned out to be the right thing to do.

We began using the new addition in January of 1984. We often wonder how we got along without this space. We like to show people through our entire building. The kitchen and prep areas hold a fascination for those who are unfamiliar with commercial kitchens.

To this day people who make deliveries and see our kitchen for the first time tell us they are impressed by the stainless steel walk-in coolers and the bright clean appearance of the work areas.

By the summer of 1984 we had our new in-house laundry in operation. We purchased two commercial washer extractors and two commercial dryers. We bought "permanent press" linen, which was a blend of cotton and polyester.

It soon became apparent we should press our table linen. We had so much natural light pouring in through the dining room windows that every little wrinkle seemed magnified. We purchased a roller mangle and the problem was solved.

The in-house laundry saves us a lot of money. In addition to the savings versus a rental service, none of our silverware ever leaves the building mixed with soiled linen. When we used a linen service they periodically returned silverware that ended up in the laundry. With our present system it never leaves our premises. In just a few years the savings from the laundry paid for the entire kitchen addition.

* * *

In May of 1985 Mark Satt and I saw two pieces of equipment at the National Restaurant show in Chicago that we knew we had to have. One was a baking oven and the other a machine that could make some of the best gelato and sorbet imaginable.

Up to this time, we had purchased all of our bakery goods. The new oven opened up new opportunities for us. We began baking our own rolls, bread, croissants and muffins. The serving staff was enthusiastic about this new feature and delighted at informing the guests.

When the oven is in use, you are hit by the delectable aroma emanating from it as soon as you step inside the restaurant. In-house baking gives us an opportunity to be more creative and to present a fresher product.

The machine that helps us make gelato and sorbet was also quite expensive. It was more than half the cost of our first house. I suppose if we had looked at this type of expenditure from a strict cost effective or return on investment point of view, we would never have bought it. Surely, there are many good commercial ice cream companies to choose from on the market.

But here again, we believe there is an advantage to being able to say "we make our own" . . . particularly when you can present a superbly fresh product. We make our own gelato and sorbet several times each week. It's fresh and delicious and the serving staff likes to sell it because they can preface the recitation of the daily flavors with the phrase, "We make our own gelato and sorbet." That helps to sell.

* * *

As I looked forward to the start of our tenth year at Kozlak's Royal Oak, I wanted to come up with a classy anniversary promotion that we could run for the whole year. Ruth and I were driving from Naples, Florida to Minnesota, and we began tossing around ideas to promote the tenth anniversary.

The fabulous Ritz Carlton hotel had just opened in Naples and we had an opportunity to see it. We had met the night manager of the hotel, Minnesotan Harley Watson. Harley had been a hotelier for most of his working life. He had retired and was living in Hastings, Minnesota.

He and his wife visited Naples, Florida, and when Harley saw the nearly completed Ritz Carlton he decided he must come out of retirement to take a position at the beautiful new facility. We met him through mutual friends, restaurateurs Denny and Ann Hanson. Harley's wife stays in Minnesota during the winter season.

Harley's schedule at the new hotel was extremely demanding. He did, however, get an infrequent night off. On one of these rare occasions we had Harley and the Hansons for dinner as guests at our condo where we enjoyed a delightful evening.

As we were driving along, I mentioned to Ruth that it would be nice if we could offer a tenth anniversary prize that would include a stay at the new Ritz Carlton hotel in Naples. That did it. It sparked both of our imaginations. And before the day was out, we had what was to become our tenth anniversary promotion roughed out.

We hoped to be able to offer as a grand prize a ten-day stay at the Ritz Carlton in Naples, Florida. We envisioned a nearly year-long contest. Guests would be given an entry form to fill out whenever they visited the restaurant for luncheon, dinner or brunch.

Each Sunday at brunch we would have a drawing from the names of the people who had entered during the

131

previous week. The weekly winner would receive a twenty-five dollar Royal Oak gift certificate plus an invitation for two to a multi-course black tie dinner that would be held at Royal Oak on our anniversary date in November.

For entertainment at the dinner we would engage the eleven-piece Golden Strings, a group of accomplished violinists and accompanists who had performed for many years at the Radisson Hotel in Minneapolis. The finale at the dinner would be a drawing from the names of the weekly winners. The grand prize would be the trip for two to Naples with a ten-day stay at the Ritz.

Mark, Diane and Lynn liked the idea we had developed, but they were a bit concerned about the room cost at the hotel. At that time the least expensive room was two-hundred dollars a night in season. We thought we might be able to get a rate, so I called Harley Watson at the hotel. I told him what we were planning and asked if the hotel could participate to some extent.

He wanted to know if the hotel would be named on every entry . . . how we proposed to promote the contest . . . whether a room during the "shoulder" season would be acceptable. How many people we thought would participate.

I answered his questions and he said, "Let me take it to the general manager. I do know that the hotel can use this type of exposure. It was early December and I asked for a quick answer so we could start our promotion on January 1st, if we decided to go ahead.

I received a call from Harley a couple days later. He had visited with the general manager. Harley said, "The hotel will provide a room to your grand prize winner for ten consecutive days." He advised that a letter would follow. The letter arrived two days later.

It confirmed what Harley had told me. It further stipulated that the room would be a deluxe accommodation and that the hotel would have complementary flowers and champagne in the room when the lucky couple arrived.

We were delighted with the news. I wrote a letter to some of our restaurateur friends in the Naples area explaining our promotion. I received several replies. They expressed appreciation that we chose Naples and they included gift certificates to their restaurants for us to present to our winners.

The first letter I received was from Bierne Brown, owner of the Chef's Garden and Villa Pescatore restaurants. It included a generous gift certificate. Wow! Letters and certificates quickly followed from Farino's, The Rooftop, Witches Brew, Christopher's, St. George and the Dragon.

Some of the restaurateurs who sent certificates requested further information and literature on the promotion. We were delighted to share our ideas with them.

I designed and ordered our entry blanks. We would begin using them on New Year's Day. Our first weekly drawing would be on the first Sunday in January.

* * *

Diane, Mark and I discussed how we would promote the contest. We decided to promote it in a low key, and what we hoped would be a dignified manner. No splashy announcements or ads. Our basic objective was to say "thank you" to the people who had supported us through the years, and to add a little zest and suspense in the process.

We sent a letter to our credit customers and mailing list outlining the promotion. I had an attractive poster showing the Ritz and outlining the contest placed in the lobby. We made sure that staff (especially the servers) understood the promotion thoroughly so they could answer questions and help add to the excitement.

Otherwise, we decided to allow the word to spread gradually through the community.

Our entire year would focus on the Tenth Anniversary Dinner and drawing. We decided to freshen up the dining rooms before the big event. We made plans for new carpeting, new chairs for the main dining room, new wall coverings and a freshly painted interior.

Before we began that, there was one other problem I hoped to solve. We had been plagued from the beginning by a leaky roof in one part of the restaurant. Even though we rebuilt and replaced the entire roof before we opened in 1977 there was one area that was never reliably waterproof.

Naturally, it was in the main dining room. Repeated attempts to solve the problem met with only limited and temporary success. The problem was with a portion of the roof that was flat.

Flat roofs are often troublesome in severe northern climates. Ice and snow can cause problems that manifest themselves in the rainy season that follows. We had those problems. We also had three heating/air conditioning units on top of the flat roof.

The construction of our building is such that the flat roof was joined by a sloping roof that extended upward to the center of the building.

I began wondering if we could build a new roof from the peak of the sloping roof to cover the flat roof and our air conditioning units. I called in an architect and a structural engineer. We were able to build the new roof as I described by adding support posts on the outside of the building, to carry the extra weight.

The job turned out beautifully, and the posts are not visible from the dining room. The problem of leaks was solved. We encountered a new problem, however, when hot weather arrived.

The air conditioning units which had been adequate previously were no longer keeping the dining rooms comfortable. Once again, I called on my friend Jim Eldorado. He surveyed the problem and said, "Those roof-top air conditioning units are designed to be outside. The roof over them causes heat to build up and they can't perform properly. We have to fool them into thinking they are outside."

We added more vents from the roof to the outside and installed a fan to blow out the hot air between the two roofs when the temperature rises to a certain point. That solved the problem.

Our tenth anniversary promotion gained momentum throughout the year. We didn't experience any huge peaks or valleys, rather sustained moderate growth compared to previous years. We were enjoying our best year in the business.

As summer turned to autumn more and more guests talked about the grand prize drawing. In addition to ten days at the Ritz and air transportation for two we also included use of a rental car, the gift certificates at Naples area restaurants and golf at the challenging Pelican's Nest golf club.

New Brunswick
Lobster Bisque

Royal Oak House Salad

R.N. Phillips Vineyards
California
Chardonnay

Sauteed Boston Lemon Sole
Green Beans
Croissant

Black Currant Sorbet

Roast Minnesota Prime Rib Eye
Bordelaise Sauce
Petite Roasted Potatoes
Tomato filled with
Peas and Onions

Mill Creek Vineyards
California Gamay
Beaujolais
1984 Vintage
Estate Bottled

Cheesecake with
Raspberry Sauce

Flame Room Coffee

Entertainment:

The Golden Strings
featuring
Clif Brunzell

Many guests asked if they would be permitted to purchase a table at the anniversary dinner if they were not a weekly winner. We discussed this question at one of our meetings and decided we could open the dinner to sixty guests who would *not* be eligible for the grand prize.

We set the price for the dinner at one-hundred twenty-five dollars per couple. Many of our oldest and most loyal customers placed reservations as did many of our suppliers.

We thought it would be appropriate to have a "surprise prize" for those guests who were not eligible for the grand prize. Gene Foster, the general manager of the quaint and famous St. James' Hotel at Red Wing, Minnesota, gave us a Victorian Weekend for two for that purpose. This included a suite at the hotel plus dinner and brunch in their posh dining room.

By early autumn we had the menu set for the anniversary dinner. I contacted our wine supplier, Dan

Paustis, and asked him to select the appropriate wines to complement the dinner. Once he apprised me of his choices I hired a calligrapher to make up the souvenir menus.

We would have a menu rolled up and tied with a ribbon at each setting on the big night.

The dining rooms were now refurbished . . . the new chairs installed and the restaurant never looked better. We decided that we would have our holiday decorations installed and illuminate the gardens with small colored lights in the trees on the night of the anniversary dinner.

We also decided to install scores of tiny low voltage amber lights in the birch trees in front of the restaurant. Ruth and Lynn had ordered new custom-designed decorations for each dining room and everyone was anxious to see them.

One night in late September, as Ruth and I discussed the logistics connected with installing the holiday decorations, she stated that she wished we had a Christmas scene with lifelike figures in the garden. She mentioned that she had spotted a delightful scene of this type the previous winter outside a small art studio in Taylors Falls, Minnesota.

I suggested she contact the artists and ask if they would be able to do something for us at Royal Oak. Within the week Ruth and I were having lunch at Royal Oak with artists Mary and Darryl Wirkkula. It was their first visit to the restaurant.

And when they saw the garden area their imaginations moved into high gear. They were creative people. We decided to start with a theme that we could build on as the years go by.

We set a budget . . . the Wirkkulas gave us a plan and we approved it. The work was to be completed and installed by November 16th, the date of the anniversary party.

One would think that after forty-four years in the restaurant business a person would not get excited over one more dinner party. Wrong! I wanted our anniversary party to be perfect . . . something that those who were there would remember fondly for years to come.

The afternoon of the party everything fell into place. The holiday decorations were up. The lights were placed in the trees in the gardens. The flowers for the tables were delivered. Clif Brunzell, the leader of the Golden Strings, dropped in to position his special lighting and to check the amplifying equipment.

Mark Satt and his staff were busy in the kitchen and the pleasant cooking aromas became increasingly apparent. Darryl and Mary Wirkkula arrived with the figures they created and began positioning them. It was reminiscent of a Norman Rockwell scene. Mary and Ruth titled it "Decorating A Christmas Tree For The Woodland Animals".

In soft sculpture they had made three carolers. They also created a young lady with a babe in arms standing by, watching as the father leaned toward a Christmas tree with his young son on his shoulder.

The lad held an ornament in his hand and was reaching to place it on the tree. A soft sculpture dog was seen howling as the carolers sang. They also made several colorful elves that they placed on rocks, in trees, and other strategic places in the garden.

We spotlighted the carolers and the family. The scene turned out even better than we had hoped.

That evening Ruth and I arrived about an hour before the first guests. We watched the staff set up the dining room and assisted with final touches. The souvenir menu scrolls were set at each place:

Larry Malmerg and his trio were on hand to provide appropriate conversational music during the cocktail and dinner hours. They completed their tuning up procedure just before the first guests arrived.

The dining room filled rapidly. The guests looked extremely attractive. The ladies resplendent in beautiful dresses and gowns . . . the men in tuxedos. The mood was joyous. The dinner commenced on schedule and was served with artful precision . . . Our staff with the direction of Mark, Diane and Lynn did a superb job.

After dinner we served a complementary cordial. Then the house lights were dimmed and the Golden Strings led by virtuoso Clif Brunzel strode single file into the dining room playing their violins. They quickly fanned out throughout the room. For the next hour they captivated the crowd with their musical show.

When the entertainment concluded I took the microphone and explained how we would conduct the drawing for the "surprise prize" and the grand prize. The surprise prize winner (the Victorian weekend for two at the St. James Hotel) was drawn first and it was won by the Steve Schwieters. Steve was part of a group of three couples. They decided that they would pick a date and book three rooms at the St. James so they could enjoy the special weekend together.

The last order of business was to draw the name of the grand prize winner. The names of the eligible weekly winners were all in the tumbler. I called Harry Sadler from the audience. Harry had been a customer and a friend for as long as the Kozlak family had been in the restaurant business both at Jax and Kozlak's Royal Oak.

He was not eligible for the grand prize and he may have been the most senior person in attendance. We gave the tumbler an extra long spin and asked Harry to reach in and pick the winner. He selected the winning slip and handed it to me. I was astounded.

The winner was Kay Wilson. I announced the name and Kay and her husband, Mitch, came forward to accept the prize. They were a most attractive couple . . . both in their late twenties. They were likely the youngest couple there. Mitch stood about six-feet four-inches tall and looked like a movie star. Kay was also quite tall and very beautiful. Their excitement at winning was so genuine and spontaneous that the entire crowd quickly warmed to them and shared their joy.

As the crowd prepared to leave, Ruth and I were deluged with thanks and compliments from the guests. Time and time again people told us it was the finest dinner party they had ever attended . . . and this from many people who have traveled the world over.

In the days that followed we received many cards and letters of thanks and kind comments from people who were there. It was a night I will always remember as one of the highlights of my restaurant career.

Oh yes! I mentioned that I was astonished when the name of Kay Wilson was drawn as the winner. You see, her husband, Mitch, worked for us as a bus boy and waiter while he worked his way through college. Two of Mitch's brothers and one sister also worked at Royal Oak in our early years when they were going to school. His father built the Sandpiper . . . the restaurant which ultimately became

Kozlak's Royal Oak. Because of a number of bad breaks and unfortunate timing, the Wilson family had experienced many heartaches in the very building where we were enjoying a relative degree of success.

Kay and Mitch announced that they were expecting their first child, so the trip would be put off for a year. The Wilsons were popular winners. Perhaps there is poetic justice after all.

* * *

One week after the tenth anniversary dinner and drawing we held our tenth annual employees appreciation dinner. This too was a very special night. It gave us an opportunity to thank our staff for their splendid work and enjoy a sociable evening together. Once dinner was completed I gave a short "State of the Restaurant" report. This was followed by an analysis of our profit sharing plan by our investment account executive.

Next Diane and Mark presented gold pins to the people who had completed five years service. Also, attractive wrist watches were given to those who had been with us since 1977.

The remainder of the evening was devoted to dancing and good fellowship. I enjoy these yearly dinners with our staff and look forward to them with relish.

The tenth staff appreciation dinner seemed even more special than all that had gone before. I could feel the camaraderie and esprit de corps among our people. The next month they proved their dedication by efficiently serving the most guests we had ever seen at Royal Oak. It was our biggest month by far.

* * *

The restaurant business is a lot different today than it was when my parents started back in 1943. Their business was not subject to as many government regulations as is ours today. There was no such thing as tip reporting, F.I.C.A., tax on tips or sales tax.

The paperwork and license fees for federal, state, and local levels of government has increased many fold since those early days. There were no restaurant chains that provided competition in their market area.

General Mills and Pillsbury were primarily interested in flour, breakfast food and baking products. There were no Olive Gardens, Red Lobsters, Burger Kings, Bennigans, or T.G.I. Fridays. In order to compete with the corporate giants, we must attract and keep good people in our organization.

We have been fortunate in being able to do this. Every person that is hired is important personally to me and the job they perform is important to the success of the operation as a whole.

Let's meet some of them:

Jeanie Foshay has done waitress work for seventeen years. She is married and the mother of three children.

Jeanie: *"My first waitress job was at the lunch counter at Grant's department store. I also worked for Control Data for six years. We built computers. I was night foreman of our group.*

"I did waitress work at the Criterion (a fine St. Paul restaurant now located in Bloomington) for a year until it burned. I came to Kozlak's Royal Oak in 1979. I prefer waitress work over other jobs I have held.

"I like being among the people. I was always able to arrange my hours to accommodate our children. It is important to be home to get them off to school and to be there when they come home.

"They want to tell you about their experiences at school and the excitement of the day doesn't keep for them. With waitress work I could be with my children for these precious moments.

"The money is good . . . comparable to Control Data, but it was difficult to have people cover my job if the kids were sick for example.

"I don't need to work anymore. Bill (her husband) makes enough but I would go nuts if I was home all the time.

"It's like a family here. Everyone is concerned professionally and personally. If you are in a jam everyone is there to help. I've worked at places where the 'It's not my job' syndrome prevailed . . . to the detriment of the whole operation.

"I've learned a lot about people. I started working at a young age and was not at all worldly. I enjoy watching personalities. Lots of people ask for me . . . people from all

140

over the metro area.

"Yes, I have served many celebrities. However, three of the most memorable and most considerate were Senator Hubert Humphrey, Lorne Greene, and Governor Wendell Anderson."

Mark Azman: We have set aside a few minutes to visit before the start of the lunch hour. It is the holiday season. He was an impressive young man. In an earlier day he might have been described as "clean cut" . . . well-groomed . . . no nonsense . . . polite. He was wearing a Royal Oak tenure-year pin on the lapel of his waiter's jacket. When he was not away at school (Holy Cross at Worcester, Mass.) he lived with his parents in the prestigious and fashionable North Oaks community that is near the restaurant. He was an honor student in high school. He was a member of the student council and lettered in track.

Mark: *"My father sent me here for an interview five years ago. He wanted me to work and I wanted to work too. I was hired as a dishwasher. Later I did bus work and finally I became a waiter. Now I am a senior at Holy Cross majoring in economics.*

"The restaurant has provided me with lots of work and abundant spending money. I have steady work during the summer and at holiday breaks. I can walk right in. I don't have to worry about running around applying for a job.

"Economics has a lot to do with charts and graphs whereas restaurant work is a more personal, one-on-one relationship. I have learned how to deal with different people . . . fun folks as well as difficult folks. The work here has taught me responsibility. The schedule here is almost sacred. When you are scheduled you must be here. Waiting tables is political. You must be diplomatic. Some people are very demanding and others are satisfied and grateful for basic good service. Sometimes you must be like a chameleon from one table to the next. I am now more aware of how I present myself to others. I believe I am more understanding of others and more open-minded.

"The experience I have gained here has been invaluable . . . priceless . . . and will serve me well as I enter my chosen field."

Mark is now a practicing attorney in St. Cloud, Minnesota.

An Essay
on
Crisis Management

December was usually our busiest month at Kozlak's Royal Oak and December of 1989 was no exception. The month was extremely cold, but the snowfall was light, so it was easy for people to get around. We were enjoying our busiest holiday season on record.

Thursday, December 16th dawned cold and breezy. The outside temperature was well below zero but we were booked solid for both luncheon and dinner. Every table, booth, and private party area was booked for a 11-11:30 a.m. luncheon seating and again for another luncheon seating from 1-2 p.m. The dinner hours, which began at 4:30 p.m., were booked solid too.

At 11 a.m. I went into the cloakroom to help check coats. The restaurant was filling at a nice, even pace. At about 11:20 Diane came over to the checkroom and excitedly informed me that there was water coming through a portion of the ceiling in the main dining room. I took one look and headed for the chef's office to use the phone. Before I could reach the phone Diane was at my heels shouting, "Dad! Part of the ceiling fell down . . . there is water pouring in."

Without looking I realized a pipe from our sprinkler system had frozen and burst and I knew I had to get to the basement to shut off the main water valve. Water was pouring into our dining room at dozens of gallons per minute. I went through the dining room on my way to the basement and I could see that the portion of the false

142

ceiling that fell had landed in a traffic area where no one was seated.

As I raced down the stairs to shut off the main valve I passed server Sue Wendorf heading in the other direction. As we passed she called, "I'm going to rent some wet/dry pickup machines." I shut the water valve off and headed back to the dining room. What I saw was our entire staff trying desperately to soak up the water that had flooded the room.

Waiters, waitresses, busers, cooks, everyone was trying to soak up the watery mess as well as pick up the acoustical tiles and insulation that had come down. Every bar towel, rag, clean table cloth and napkin was pressed into the fray.

When the sprinkler pipe burst it set off the fire alarm at our nearby fire station and in minutes the firemen were on the scene. The fire chief thought he detected the odor of natural gas and he told me to evacuate the building. I got on the loud speaker system and asked everyone to leave. Two servers stepped in to help in the cloakroom. The evacuation was surprisingly swift and orderly. Diane called nearby competitors to see if they had room and relayed the information to our guests as they were leaving.

We quickly determined that we had no gas leak. The odor was merely from the stagnant water that was in the broken pipe. Our employees drifted back into the building and continued to clean up. I called my brother Bill at Jax Cafe and asked if he had space available for some of the groups we had booked for the evening. He told me what was available and we decided that if we couldn't get open we would have Jax Cafe as an option for our guests.

Next, I called our sprinkler company and asked that they get someone over quickly to repair the broken pipe. The supervisor/dispatcher at the sprinkler company is the son of our longtime employee Dotty Peil. Two pipefitters were at Royal Oak within the hour. Replacing the broken section took only a few minutes.

Bill called back to tell me that there was a man named Bill Fredlund who specialized in cleanup after fires, floods and other problems. It was now about 12 noon; I reached Fredlund just as he was leaving for lunch and explained our problem. He said he knew the restaurant and he sounded genuinely sympathetic. He said, "I will have about a dozen people coming to you from various parts of the metro area. They will be there within the hour and they will know what to do."

Chef Mark Satt contacted the health department and explained what had happened. They instructed Mark to throw out all the food that was on the salad bar because of possible contamination from the insulation. They also told us to carry out the broken ceiling and wet insulation without going through the kitchen.

By 12:30 Fredlund's crew began arriving. They had containers for the debris. They had more machines to extract water from the carpet. They used plastic to seal off the salad bar from the two 12' by 12' bays of the ceiling that were damaged so that our staff could sanitize the salad bar and get it ready for re-filling.

At 1 p.m. Diane came to me and said, "I suppose we had better start calling our reservations and help them make other arrangements for tonight." I told her to wait until 2 p.m.

I thought we had a chance to get the place back together.

I had our office contact our insurance company and let them know what happened. I called my friend Warren Hesselroth at H & B Company and explained that we needed two bays of our ceiling replaced. H & B installed the acoustical ceiling twelve years earlier and they knew what material was used.

Within minutes he called back to tell me he had the material and two installers would be in at midnight to do the job.

Next, I contacted our electrical contractor and asked him if he could install a system of heat tape on our sprinkler pipes so we wouldn't have to worry about a recurrence of the problem. He could . . . and did install the system a few days later.

I contacted our insulation company and made arrangements for them to reblow the insulation once the ceiling was re-installed.

I walked downstairs to the laundry and saw eight or nine waitresses readying our linens. Every piece in the dining room had to be stripped from the tables and rewashed as well as all the linen they had used to sop up the water from the carpeting. The kitchen too was a bee-hive of activity. All the salad bar items had to be freshly prepared. All the dishes and every side tray, piece of sil-ver and glassware that was in the dining room had to be rewashed. The busers and some of the servers busied themselves in the dining room wiping down the chairs and helping the Fredlund crew in any way they could. I have never seen such cooperation and helpful dedication in all my years in the business. Our staff was absolutely great.

At 2 p.m. I asked Fredlund's crew how long they might take to finish their job. They said they expected to be done by 4:30. Mark, Diane and I decided we would be open for the evening. I called Bill and informed him we expected to be operating by 5 p.m. and thanked him for his consideration and help.

We realized that none of our people had had any lunch. Our kitchen crew was so busy getting reorganized that we called a local pizza parlor and had them send over several pizzas. When they arrived everyone took a very short break and then went back at it.

By 4 p.m. Fredlund's crew had finished removing all the debris from the dining room and had the water ex-tracted from the carpet. They began stapling plastic over the two 12' by 12' open ceiling bays so that the cold air between the false ceiling and the roof would not enter the dining room. The dining room staff now began setting the room for the evening trade. The plastic on the ceiling of the two damaged bays made a stark and unsightly con-trast with the finished acoustical ceiling in the rest of the room. I remembered that we had balloons and helium on the premises because at Sunday brunch we have a col-ored balloon as part of each table's centerpiece.

I instructed the checkroom ladies to start filling red and green balloons with helium. At 4:45 p.m. the Fred-lund crew departed and we released roughly two- hun-dred red and green helium filled balloons to the plastic ceiling.

What was moments earlier an eyesore "hole" in the ceiling now became a festive mini attraction.

I left for home at 5 p.m. As I walked to my car guests were streaming toward the entrance from various points in the parking lot. The restaurant had a super busy night. Some of our staff worked a double shift because of the problems caused by the broken pipe. No one complained. Actually, I believe those of us who shared in the experience of that day developed a closer bond than ever before. We were fortunate to build a good esprit de corps with our staff over the years but this brush with adversity made it even better.

The next morning I arrived at the restaurant at 7 a.m. The two men from H & B Company were laying the last acoustical tiles into the suspended ceiling. They did a fine job and when they finished I treated them to a breakfast of steak and eggs. The next week we installed the heat tapes on the pipes. They come on automatically when the temperature between the ceiling and the roof drops below 40º. Next the insulation was reblown into the ceiling and our sprinkler system was reactivated.

The settlement with our insurance company also was amicable. We had business interruption coverage in addition to the standard coverages. Our adjuster was amazed that we only lost one day's luncheon business as a result of the problem. We submitted our bills and were paid promptly. Case closed!

PART
TEN

People
Passing
Through

The nature of the restaurant business (particularly those establishments that do considerable banquet business) is such that many part-time employees are needed. The trick is to build a strong and stable professional, full-time staff and augment them, as needed, with well trained "regular" part-time people.

Through the years we had scores of interesting people who helped us in the part-time capacity. Let's meet a few of them.

Stanley J. Fudro:

Stan is a veteran of World War II. When he was discharged he returned home to Northeast Minneapolis and enrolled at the University of Minnesota.

While he was a student there he worked as a bartender at Jax to supplement his income.

"I found bartending to be interesting work. It taught me a lot about how to deal with people. It helped me to sharpen my skills in how to relate to others. I learned how to speak differently to different people. It was valuable experience for the career path I chose. I gained a better understanding of the real world and the diversity of ideas and attitudes that exist."

Stan Fudro was elected to the Minnesota House of Representatives in 1956 and served twenty-four years in that body. IIe retired from the Legislature in 1980, having served longer than any other representative from his district in the history of the state. Stan also worked as a business agent for the Carpenter Union until retirement. He continues to be active in community affairs and remains one of Northeast Minneapolis' most popular citizens. His counsel is much sought after and respected.

* * *

Edward J. Gearty:

Ed served in the U.S. Navy from 1942-1948 (Pacific Theatre). He returned to the family homestead in North Minneapolis nurturing a dream to become a lawyer.

He attended St. Thomas College in St. Paul where he studied pre-law and was admitted to Georgetown Law School, Washington, D.C., in 1952.

"I went to Washington, D.C. to study but I had to work too. My friend Harry Leonard contacted our congressman (Roy Wier) and I was fortunate to get a job running an elevator.

"I did that from May through September when the congressman's patronage ran out. I placed an ad in the paper saying that I was a law student looking for part-time employment. I received a call from the owner of the Golden Parrot restaurant.

"I met with him and he offered me a job tending bar at his fine establishment. I worked there for three years. My schedule was such that I could attend class, study, and still earn some much needed money.

"I passed the District of Columbia bar in 1955 and returned to Minnesota. Then I began studying for the Minnesota bar exam. I stopped at Jax one afternoon and visited with Lefty. He mentioned that he was trying to find someone to work behind the bar for him so he could go to the Little World Series Baseball game that evening.

"I mentioned that I was an experienced bartender. I began work that evening and worked part-time at Jax for nearly two years. I liked the conversation and association with the patrons. I enjoyed the people I worked with . . . the atmosphere.

"Jax was a real social center that brimmed with conviviality. It was interesting to see the business deals that were conducted during the lunch hour. Business lunches then, as now, were really an extension of the workday.

"Shortly after I went to work as a special assistant attorney general, I concluded my bartender career."

Ed Gearty was elected to the Minnesota House of Representatives in 1962 and served in that body until elected to the state senate in 1970. He served in the senate until his voluntary retirement in 1980. He continues to practice law in Minneapolis.

* * *

Joe Sochacki and Walter Sochacki Jr.:

The family of Walter "Red" and Helen Sochacki was always very special to the Kozlaks. Red, a high school teacher and basketball coach, and his wife were originally from the nearby suburb of Columbia Heights.

They have been customers at Jax since their courting days. When they married and began raising their family Jax was the place they brought their children to celebrate birthdays and other special occasions. They started a tradition that has lasted for half a century.

Joseph, a tall and handsome redhead, was their oldest child. He became enamored *with* the restaurant business at a very early age. He told us that when he was old enough to work he wanted to work at Jax. Shortly after his fifteenth birthday he applied for a part-time job. He started as an assistant in the dishwashing department and over a period of time we gave him an opportunity to work in various departments in the restaurant. He excelled at every task and was extremely popular with the staff and guests.

He reflected the values his parents taught him. He was courteous, helpful, and hard working. Even as a young lad he possessed a fine presence. His carriage was what you might expect from the most practiced captain of a luxury liner. There was no doubt in anyone's mind that he was special and headed for big things.

During his senior year of high school he applied for admittance to Cornell University at Ithaca, New York . . . one of the nation's finest restaurant/hotel management schools. He was accepted and his parents dug in to meet the financial burden.

His mother went back to work. Joe worked at Jax during summer and holiday breaks. He wanted

149

experience and he got it. I recall parties in the one-hundred to three-hundred guest range where Joe would help behind the bar during the social hour, then proceed to the kitchen and help serve the dinner, and later be seen in his best suit performing maitre d' duties.

When he graduated from Cornell he took a job as assistant food and beverage manager at the Holiday Inn in St. Paul. He married Rose Marie and they began raising a family.

He became the food service manager at Dayton's department store in Minneapolis. His career was advancing and he was building a solid reputation. Next, he became the assistant manager at the prestigious Columbia Club in Indianapolis, Indiana.

The next opportunity for advancement that Joe accepted was the general manager's job at the lovely Golden Valley Country Club in suburban Minneapolis. He remained at Golden Valley until the Columbia Club offered him the job of general manager.

It was then back to Indianapolis for Joe, Rose Marie and the children. He had an outstanding job and his prospects for the future looked limitless . . . and then tragedy. Joe was struck down with incurable cancer. There was nothing the best doctors could do to save him. He was survived by Rose Marie and their three children. Joe Sochacki died at age thirty-four.

Walter Sochacki Jr. was three years younger than his brother Joe. He worked at Jax weekends and summers in the late 1950s. Walter has an engaging personality and a scintillating sense of humor. It is fun to be with Walter, but he also has a more serious side. Perhaps that is why he is so successful at his vocation.

Walter was ordained a Catholic priest in 1968. He is presently the pastor of St. Rose of Lima in Roseville, Minnesota. He is also responsible for the busy parish school (grades kindergarten through eight) plus additional duties at the chancery office in St. Paul.

Father Walt: *"It's been 40 years or more since I worked at Jax, but I can remember as though it was yesterday. I did various jobs: dishes, bussing, salad preparation, janitor. I remember Mr. Kozlak (Joe Sr.) coming in very early in the morning when I was doing janitor work. He* would go to the farmer's market as early as possible to purchase produce and bring it to Jax.

"We had a big fellow from Poland named Boleslaw who scrubbed the kitchen. He also had to wash, wax and machine buff the barroom floor. Mr. Kozlak would inspect the floor by getting on his hands and knees to make sure it was done properly. If he wasn't satisfied he made Boleslaw do it over after he clocked out. Boleslaw quickly learned to do the job properly the first time.

"Part of my job as janitor was to clean the rest rooms. When I step into the men's room at Jax now I think back to how I scrubbed those toilets.

"I started bussing when I was just fifteen. One of the things we had to do was pick the lobsters out of the tank when they were ordered. I was scared to death of them at first, but I learned to do it.

"We also netted the trout from the garden stream when customers selected them for dinner. The first time I fished trout one of the trout jumped out of the creel as I came through the dining room on my way to the kitchen. It flopped around on the carpet as I tried to pick it up. I was just a kid and terribly embarrassed.

"I really liked Lefty. When I did janitor work our shifts overlapped a bit and we had opportunities to visit. He was a pleasant person . . . always concerned about the customers and the restaurant. When I worked as a bus person I had an opportunity to observe Lefty and Jiggs (Bill Evans) when they tended bar. I often think back on how well they handled people. They would look them right in the eye and show interest and compassion.

"In a way they were father confessors. Their job at times became like mine today.

"Yes, I had one experience at work that shook me for a while. I was working in the kitchen and a supervisor who was there for a time told me to peel the potatoes that had been par-boiled so they could be made into hash browns.

"I was peeling away and a few minutes later he came at me with a blue streak of profane abuse telling me how stupid I was for taking too much of the potato with the peel. I felt terrible. All he had to do was show me what he wanted.

"There was a lesson learned in the way he treated

me. I decided I would never be that type of person.

"I still run into people I worked with at Jax. They have stopped me on the street downtown and asked, "Aren't you little Red?" I wish I could remember all their names, but after forty years . . .

"As a group, the folks I worked with at Jax were genuine people. Some may have seemed a bit crusty but I consider them the salt of the earth."

Jack: "Where did that expression come from?"

Father Walt: *"It's in the Bible. Matthew 5:13-16. "You are the salt of the earth and the light of the world.*

"One more item about Mr. and Mrs. Kozlak (Joe Sr. and Gertrude):

"In 1968 one-hundred dollars was a lot of money. On the occasion of my ordination they gave me a hundred dollars.

"I love my work . . . the priesthood . . . I am as excited and enthused about my job today as I was the day I began my studies."

* * *

Sandra Hillary: Waitress at Jax in 1960s

We were sitting in her office in City Hall in Minneapolis. She was serving her second term as a member of the Minneapolis City Council. Her appearance is flawless . . . her demeanor gracious and dignified. She is open and forthright about her life.

Her childhood was less than happy. The family was poor . . . her father was an alcoholic. She attended St. Joseph's school on the near Northside in Minneapolis.

Sandra: *"It was through some of the exceptional teachers I had there that I could first see past poverty and family problems to a possible better life. I was always a reader and this too broadened my horizons.*

"I began doing waitress work at age twenty-one and I worked in the restaurant industry for over twenty years. I was fortunate to work at up-scale establishments.

"The experience I gained was an education in itself. I was rubbing shoulders with the business, professional and labor leaders of the community. It elevated my awareness of other people and suggested new opportunities. The

152

income too was excellent and the hours were flexible. It was a terrific experience to learn that there are so many different people. On the job I felt like an independent contractor. The better job I did, the better the rewards.

"A restaurant has its own hierarchy. There are the customers, the management, cooks, bartenders, wait staff, bus persons, dishwashers. A good server must learn to work within that system to be successful. You must be a diplomat. This helped me develop people skills and is beneficial in my job today.

"I enjoyed the camaraderie among the employees. The way we helped each other. I liked working for independent, family-owned restaurants. The whole operation became an extension of my family . . . you counted on them.

"I once worked for a chain-operated restaurant and it wasn't the same . . . to me the feeling was cold. There was no interaction . . . you didn't feel fulfilled."

She talks easily about her past alcoholism. "I had a problem with alcohol for about five years. Twice when I was working at Little Jack's restaurant my employer helped get me to treatment. I haven't had a drink for over fifteen years."

Sandra's political career began in 1982 when she decided to run for office. The ward she represented is historically Democratic. More often than not the Democratic party endorsement is tantamount to election.

She challenged the Democratic endorsed incumbent in the primary election, citing his ineptness. She demonstrated her grasp of local issues to the electorate and scored a stunning upset victory.

Her years in office have been distinguished by her ability to focus on the livability of neighborhoods. She is vitally interested in programs such as the Coordinated Neighborhoods Action Plan where people share their problems and work at solving them. It is obvious that she loves her work.

Sandra: *"It was President Kennedy who sparked my interest in the political process. I wanted to get involved . . . I dreamed that I too could make a difference. For me to be here in this office and the way it happened* *seems almost that it was preordained.*

"*Today, my highest priorities are exceptional educational opportunities for the children of our city . . . clean, safe neighborhoods and being able to work effectively with the business community, county, and legislature so that these goals are achieved and maintained.*"

She was later elected to the Hennepin County Board.

* * *

Jim Haracz: (Worked at Jax 1956-1958)

Jim: "*I worked as a bus boy at Jax for nearly three years. I started when I was fifteen years-old. It was my first real job away from home. I was attending De LaSalle High School at the time.*

"*Wayne Fyle and I split the evening work early in the week and we worked together on weekends. I logged a little less than thirty hours a week. And between my paychecks from Jax and tips from the servers, I made eighty to eighty-five dollars a week.*

"*That was big money. Most of the other kids who worked at that age had paper routes or worked in grocery stores. They were lucky if they made fifty-five cents an hour.*

"*In 1956 I bought a 1950 Ford Coupe for two-hundred dollars. School let out at 2:30 p.m. On the days I worked I would hurry to get to Jax before 3 p.m. If I was lucky I could make it before the chef dismantled the steam table after lunch. I would then maybe get a Salisbury steak, short ribs or chicken and dumplings.*

"*The older waitresses like Rosie and Alta treated us particularly well. On busy nights they would slip us a couple extra dollars.*

"*In 1957 I bought a new Ford. It cost sixteen-hundred dollars. Here I was sixteen years-old with a brand new car. It was stripped down but it was new. And it was mine. In 1958 I traded the Ford for a new Chevrolet.*

"*And then a new ruling came in that said you had to be twenty-one to be a bus boy. I could not work at Jax. Joe Kozlak Jr. got me a job at Hypro Engineering. Wayne Fyle went to work in the kitchen and eventually became Jax chef.*

154

"I went to the University of Minnesota for two years. I worked for Standard Oil in their repackaging room. After college I worked for Emrich Baking company as a driver salesman. I did real well at Emrich and was one of their top salesmen. I also worked part-time tending bar at a couple places."

We were sitting at a little table at the back of the room. The sign outside reads Jimmy's Bar and Lounge. It is a misnomer. The building is small. There is, at most, room for sixty people to be seated. It is located on a corner in a quiet residential neighborhood in Northeast Minneapolis, two blocks from Jax.

It is 9:30 a.m. There are about a dozen men at the bar. Most are retirees. All but three are drinking coffee. They gather each day to discuss current events and to reminisce. It is like a club with no formal structure and no dues.

"In 1975 this place came up for sale so I mortgaged everything I had and bought it. I even had a name picked out ——.

"I like it here. We make all our drinks from scratch. No prepared mixes. I put in some food here too. We have ham, ham and cheese sandwiches, some pizza, chili, things like that. We get a few people for lunch and if people get hungry here at night they don't have to leave here to get some food.

"We have a Sunday 'brunch' here too. I pick up a couple hundred White Castle hamburgers every Sunday and we serve them free from 10 a.m. 'til noon. We heat them in the microwave. They cost me forty-two cents each, but we serve a lot of Bloody Marys and build good will. A lot of people stop in after church."

(Jimmy's is less than three blocks from two large churches: one Catholic, the other Russian Orthodox.)

"I sponsor twenty-four bowling teams, thirteen softball teams, two basketball teams, even two trap shoot teams. You have to make things happen to survive in this business today. You can't just open the door and expect people to come in. We also offer alcohol-free beers, wines and cocktails.

"Many people have a misconception about my type of

place. They think folks come here to get drunk. But that just isn't so. People come here to socialize. We are a social center and an authentic sports bar.

"Look: I have four television sets here, a VCR and some electronic equipment I haven't figured out how to use yet.

"Have we ever had people who overindulged? It has happened and we do not let them drive. We take them home. I had one lonely old gent from the neighborhood who was inclined to overindulge.

"I sat him down and told him we would only serve him if he came in sober and his limit would be two drinks. He could stay as long as he wished but two drinks a day was it. We are still good friends.

"I have been here seventeen years now, and everything is paid for. We have four children. One son works here with me. My wife and a daughter own and operate the "Forget Me Not" flower shop about a mile from here. We own some homes in this neighborhood as investments.

"I like this place . . . this business. I appreciate the independence I have; but most of all I enjoy the people. If I ever lose that feeling I will know it's time to leave."

PART
ELEVEN

Politics
and
Public Service

One spring day in 1968, I noticed an announcement in our suburban newspaper. The District 32B Democratic Farmer Labor club was to hold a meeting at Howard Johnson's restaurant in Columbia Heights, to discuss possible candidates for the state house of representatives in the fall election.

I had not been to a partisan political meeting for fourteen years. I maintained an interest in politics and government. But other than becoming an informed voter, I could not find the time to participate actively in the political process. I had free time the night of the meeting, so I attended. I went along with nothing particular in mind. I just wanted to see what was going on.

The legislature had been reapportioned before the previous election. The house district in which we lived consisted of the suburbs of St. Anthony (where we lived), Columbia Heights, Hilltop and part of Fridley. All except Hilltop are first-tier suburbs that border Northeast Minneapolis, where I had been born, and where our family was deeply rooted and well-known.

I saw a few people that I knew at the meeting. Among them were Jim McNulty, a long-time acquaintance and former mayor of St. Anthony, Bill Flaherty, a successful businessman and respected political activist, and Jim Durand, a high school classmate of mine whom I had not had much contact with since school. I met some people at the gathering whom I had heard of but had not known previously. Among them were Bruce Nawrocki (Mayor of Columbia Heights), Vivian Caesar (Mayor of Hilltop) and Charles Lefebvre, a postal employee who understood and enjoyed the scent of politics.

In the previous election the 32B seat in the house of representatives was won by Jack Meyer. There was no party designation in legislative races at that time but Meyer had caucused with the conservatives (Republicans) and the Democratic Farmer Labor Party (D.F.L.) wanted to recapture that seat.

The main topic of the meeting was to discuss possible candidates. I listened to the discussion and it appeared that Jim Durand wanted the blessing of the people at the meeting to be the endorsed candidate. This was not an endorsement convention but it appeared to me that if the group would reach a consensus on a potential candidate, that person would certainly have a leg up on the nomination.

The meeting was very open and several people questioned whether Jim Durand had the name recognition and the contacts to generate the financial support necessary for an effective campaign.

The meeting dragged on and it seemed they were not prepared to come out for Jim Durand at that meeting. It was getting late and I wanted to leave. I was recognized by the chair and said, "It is getting late and I must ask to be excused, but before I go I would just like to say that it seems to me that Jim Durand has carried water on both shoulders for party candidates in the past and if he wants your help now perhaps he should get it."

I left the meeting. When I got to the parking lot, and as I was about to enter my car, two men called to me. It was Jim McNulty and Bill Flaherty. They struck up a conversation and asked if I had ever thought about serving in the Legislature.

I told them I don't know how that would mesh with our business, so I better not think of it. Flaherty said, "Now Johnathan, we think you should consider it. You are well known in the community and we feel that you can win . . . and we will help you." I told them I would consider it, but I really thought I could not convince my business partner (brother Bill) and my wife that it was something I should do. Also, I had just spoken for Jim

Durand and I would not want to disappoint him. They said they would speak with Jim if I was interested in running so that there would be no conflict between us.

When I got home I discussed the events of the evening with Ruth. She said she thought I should run. She knew of my interest in the Legislature and she gave me every encouragement. The next day I discussed the possibility with brother Bill.

Although he wasn't particularly enthusiastic, he did understand that I had a desire to do some public service. He knew the Legislature was always interesting to me because of my educational background and our father's involvement. I felt that I had Bill's tacit approval.

Over the next few days I received phone calls from some of the people who had been at the 32B D.F.L. meeting, asking me to run and offering their help. Chuck Lefebvre's offer to help was particularly welcome because he knew the practical side of campaigning . . . how to build toward election day and how to marshall support.

The phone calls indicated to me that McNulty and Flaherty were drumming up support for me. And when they approached me again, I told them I would run if I had Jim Durand's support. They indicated this would be no problem and I assumed all was in order.

The date of the 32B endorsing convention was set. A couple days before it was to be held, I received word that Jim Durand was also going to seek the endorsement. I was more than a little surprised and tried to decide what to do.

Because I had not heard it from Jim, I decided to call him. When I reached him I said, "Jim, the endorsing convention is coming up and I am calling to ask you to make a seconding speech for me."

He fumbled for a moment and said, "I was planning to seek the endorsement too. We thought you should have to win it." I said, "I know you will do what you feel is right, but it seems to me that we will have a better chance of defeating the incumbent if we are united at the outset."

He thought for a moment and said, "O.K. Jack . . . I'll be glad to give a seconding speech to your nomination." From that moment on Jim Durand and his wife, Sally, were two of the most loyal and hardest working supporters a candidate ever had.

The endorsing convention was held and I was endorsed unanimously. I gave a short acceptance speech and the die was cast. I was in the swim and I knew it was going to be a difficult race to win.

I had pledges of support from many people, but organizing those pledges into an effective group was the challenge. Chuck Lefebvre and Jim Durand did a superb job of lining up people to assemble yard signs, distribute literature and erect signs.

One of the first people I turned to for expert advice was state Senator Harold Kalina. Harold and I grew up two blocks apart. We attended grade school and high school together and have been friends for our entire lives. I helped him during his first election campaign, and now he offered to help me. Harold was a student of campaign literature and his help in designing mine was invaluable.

Harold, Jim Rice and I designed my first piece of literature, well before filings for the office were open. Rice came up with the headline: *Return Effective Leadership.* It was a clever ploy. Whenever my opponent's friends objected to the slogan they also were advertising my candidacy.

One of the discussions we had when designing my literature was whether or not to use the phrase endorsed by D.F.L. and labor. Some thought it might not be appropriate because officially the office was "without party designation." I insisted on naming both the D.F.L. and labor because I had asked for their support and they tendered it.

The last thing we had to decide after the piece was composed was the color. Both Kalina and Rice wanted it done in red, white and blue. We were discussing shades of red and blue when it occurred to me that Anheuser Busch must have put some research into the colors on the Budweiser label. So when I took the copy to the printer I took along a bottle of Budweiser and asked him to duplicate the red and blue on the label.

Shortly after this I composed a letter that I would send to some of the people I knew outlining my candidacy and asking for their support. I included a card that they could sign indicating their willingness to help and in what manner. We held the letter until after I had filed and then mailed them. The response was most gratifying.

Before I filed I tried to visit every relative I had within

160

the district to inform them of my intentions and ask for their support. Every one of them gave me their blessing and worked for my election. I will always be grateful for the kindness my relatives showed me. I can think of few things worse than having close relatives' opposition in an election.

Filings for state officers opened on July 2nd, and it was decided that I should file on the very first day. Chuck Lefebvre contacted Peter Tema who was a good friend of Secretary of State Joseph Donovan. He asked if he could arrange to get a picture of me with the Secretary of State.

It was arranged and on July 2nd I filed. A picture was taken of Mr. Donovan and me. In the picture Donovan was pointing to a picture of my father in a 1921 vintage legislative manual.

The picture and accompanying story announcing my official entry into the race appeared prominently in the local press. The headline read: "Kozlak files for House Seat." A caption under the picture quoting Donovan read, "That's your dad," as he pointed to my father's picture.

Shortly after the announcement appeared in the paper Chuck Lefebvre said we had better get started on the door-to-door work. I planned to knock on as many doors in the district as possible to introduce myself and ask for support. LeFebvre had a map of the district blown up that we could color in as we completed canvassing a given area.

He devised a plan whereby we would cover the heavily trafficked streets first. As we went along we would ask for placement of lawn signs. It was best to get them on the more heavily traveled streets first.

When we got on to the less-traveled streets, the plan was to skip every other street. The reasoning was that when neighbors talked over the back fence they would mention being visited by the candidate. When the skipped streets were covered at a later date, the word would again spread that the candidate had visited the neighborhood.

Chuck and I started the door-to-door work on 29th Avenue in St. Anthony Village on a warm summer evening in mid-July. He took one side of the street and I the other. I would introduce myself as a neighbor who was running for the Legislature, hand over my election card and ask for their consideration when they went to the polls.

161

When the response was warm I would ask for permission to place one of my lawn signs at a later date. Lefebvre made a similar pitch and always said, "There's Jack across the street." If it was someone I knew or someone who showed interest, I would cross over and visit for a few moments.

When there was no one home I would write, "Sorry I missed you – Jack" on one of my cards and leave it in the door. My opponent picked up on this idea a few weeks later. He had some of his cards with the "Sorry I missed you" message printed on them. I never did that. I preferred to write the message out, and I think it had better effect.

Ruth and I had a little cabin at Balsam Lake, Wisconsin where we would take our family on my days off. Our next-door neighbors were Mr. and Mrs. Emil Anderson.

One Sunday shortly after I filed for office, I was sitting at a picnic table in our yard addressing envelopes. Emil Anderson walked over and said he had heard that I was making a bid for the Legislature. We visited for a few minutes and he asked, "Do you know a fellow named Wendell Anderson?" I told him I did not. Emil simply said, "You will."

Wendell Anderson was Emil's nephew. He was a state senator and would eventually become governor of Minnesota and then United States senator . . . but more on that later.

Emil Anderson was many years my senior and I had great admiration for him. He gave me a bit of advice that day that stuck. He told me that campaigning was tough and demanding work. He said, "You can't win sleeping."

All during the campaign I kept a full schedule at Jax. Some days when I was working a split shift at the restaurant, I would go home and try to take a short nap to rest up for the dinner hours. I would lay down and all I could think of was Emil's remark, "You can't win sleeping." I gave up trying to rest in the afternoons. Instead, when I was on a split shift, I would continue my door-to-door canvass of the district.

Through a stroke of luck I was able to obtain a telephone company cross-directory. This book gives the name and address of subscribers on a street-by-street

1968: Then United States Senator Walter Mondale and Jack pose for campaign picture.

1968: (L toR) Jane Muskie, Jack, Ruth, United States Senator Edmund Muskie, Eugene Stokowski (Congressional candidate), Ann Stokowski. Muskie had just finished being interviewed on Meet the Press, *then moderated by Lawrence Spivak.*

FOR LEGISLATURE . . .

TRAINED FOR PUBLIC SERVICE

Jack Kozlak by training and experience is well qualified to serve in the legislature. A lifelong resident of the area, a homeowner and business man (co-owner of Jax Cafe), Jack knows our people, our problems and brings valuable qualities of leadership to our legislative district.

* Holland and Holy Cross grade
* Graduate Edison High School
* Graduate St. Thomas College, Bachelor of Science degree (Political Science)
* Member St. Charles Borromeo Church
* Member Lions Club

* Member Chamber of Commerce
* Active participant in numerous civic projects
* Endorsed by D.F.L., Labor, Business, and Professional people

1968: Vice-President Humphrey and Jack pose for a picture to be used in Jack's campaign literature.

| | | DIANE | | MARK | MARY |
| LYNN | CAROL | JACK | | RUTH | PAUL |

April, 1970: United States Senator George McGovern, Ruth and Jack. Jack introduced McGovern at the Anoka Country Statesmen's Dinner.

Golf outing with United States Senator Edmund Muskie and Governor Wendell Anderson at North Oaks Country Club. Jack won a dollar from Muskie.

basis. Before I went into a neighborhood I would make a little crib sheet that gave the addresses and last names of the homes I was to visit. When people answered the door I could greet them as Mr. X or Mrs. Y and this made a very favorable impression. I don't believe my opponent ever caught on to this tactic.

I also made it a point to contact and pay courtesy calls on public officials of the communities that the district encompassed. I recall a visit I made to the home of Albert Kordiak. He was the chairman of the Anoka County Board of Commissioners and a popular and astute political figure over a long era.

We were about the same age, but Al had already served sixteen years on the county board. We visited for about a half-hour and the vibes were excellent. Finally, he told me that although he was a Democrat, he had made it a practice not to give his personal endorsement to candidates.

He told me he would help me by talking to people he thought he could influence in my behalf. But there would be no formal public endorsement. That was fine with me, and I always felt that he was true to his word. He did give me the names of some of his relatives to contact so that I would have the use of the Kordiak name on my literature.

In the final analysis a candidate must sell himself . . . endorsements may be beneficial but in a tough race with a hardworking incumbent opponent, such as I had, the challenger must go to the voters directly.

I also called on the former office holders and former candidates who lived in the district and asked for their support. It seems that former public officials are often left with a void in their lives when they are no longer in the limelight. By calling on these men and women who had served honorably in the past, I was able to gather much support and encouragement that I might never have otherwise gained.

Constituents such as former legislators George Murk and John Nordin consented to the use of their names on my literature. Former St. Anthony mayors Frank Madden and Jim McNulty did the same, as did former mayor Andrew Speculant of Columbia Heights, and Mayor Vivian Caesar of Hilltop, and former Anoka County Commissioner August Peterson.

167

My friend Peter Tema and I made a call on former representative John Nordin. Nordin had served in the house of representatives with my father back in the 1930s and had represented a large portion of what was now district 32B as recently as the 1965 session. He had an office in Isanti, a few miles north of the district.

When we walked in he said, "Let's go next door to the little restaurant and have a cup of coffee." As we went out the door he reached across his desk and removed the telephone receiver from the cradle. I asked him why he did that. He said, "If someone calls while I am out and they get the busy signal, they will figure I'm on the phone and call back."

I had a very special visit with John Nordin. He spoke of how he and my father worked together in the 1930s to promote the development of highways that went through their districts. He said, "I took care of Highway 65 (Central Avenue) and your dad took care of Highway 47 (University Avenue)." We hit it off in grand style.

He offered to run a display ad before the primary election in the Columbia Heights newspaper endorsing me. However, he said he wanted me to compose it. I got out a sheet of paper. As I began to write Mr. Nordin said, "Now don't use any big words or people will know I didn't write it."

The campaign heated up quickly. On a Saturday afternoon in late July, Lefebvre organized a group of about twenty volunteers to assemble lawn signs. These good folks gave about four hours of their time on their day off.

I stopped by to nail a few signs together and to thank everyone for their help. When I drove home that afternoon I drove by the home of our mayor, Duane Miedke. He lived a mere block away as the crow flies, and I noticed he had a crew of men assembling signs for my opponent.

The pace quickened in the local press as well. Some of my supporters wrote letters to the editor attacking my opponent's record for his vote on the sales tax issue. Minnesota had no sales tax until the 1967 Legislature passed it.

My opponent stated when campaigning in 1966 that he was opposed to a sales tax. Yet, once elected he voted for it. The sales tax was still a timely issue and many people were determined that Jack Mcycr would bc hcld accountable for his vote.

Part of the strategy of my campaign was to issue press releases outlining my position on various issues. Ed Kaspszak, a friend and most capable newspaperman, prepared the statements for me. This was a great help because it increased the time I could spend canvassing the neighborhoods.

As the pace quickened Ruth too became totally involved. Here she was with six growing children and loads of responsibility, but she made time to help with the campaign. Many evenings we would walk through the neighborhoods knocking on doors and asking for votes.

Ruth would take one side of the street and I the other. We would introduce ourselves and leave a piece of literature. And before departing I would say, "That's my wife, Ruth, across the street." Ruth would say, "There's Jack . . . we are working together." As we went along we would ask the people if they would like a lawn sign.

We always received the most favorable response when we were together. On some evenings our oldest son Mark, who was now old enough to drive a car, would meet us as we completed canvassing a street. He would take the addresses of the people who wanted lawn signs from us. Then he and a couple of his buddies or some of our younger children would help him install the signs.

The evening Ruth and I canvassed Main Street in Fridley was memorable. I had a lot of relatives living in the area and we were constantly being told by the homeowners, "I know your cousin Gene, or Rudy, or Helen, or Ann, etc."

The requests for lawn signs were incredible. Our sons, Mark and Paul, as well as daughters, Diane and Mary, were following along that evening installing signs. When we finished that evening, Main Street was virtually plastered with our signs.

From that day on many people whom I met for the first time said, "You're the person with all the signs."

I was fortunate to have so many capable people who volunteered their help. Bill Flaherty took on the job of campaign treasurer, and I never had to worry about that aspect of the campaign. He saw to it that all the necessary governmental forms were prepared and filed. He deposited the contributions and paid the bills. Bill Flaherty later performed the same task for State Attorney General Warren Spannaus.

Walter Logacz provided a big boost to the campaign. He was a Columbia Heights city councilman, a school teacher, and he was young and single. Consequently, he had some free time in the evenings, and he enjoyed doing the door-to-door work with me.

LeFebvre arranged for us to have a campaign headquarters. Ross Brown, an insurance agent with an office in Columbia Heights, gave us the use of a large room downstairs for our headquarters. Brown, too, was running for the Legislature in a district north of mine.

The year 1968 was a tumultuous one. In April, Martin Luther King was assassinated. In June, Robert Kennedy was killed on the night he won the California primary. The Vietnam war raged on, Americans saw the horror nightly on their television sets. The nation was deeply divided on the issue of our involvement.

The Democratic National Convention was held in Chicago in early August. Anti-war demonstrators clashed with the Chicago police as the nation watched on television. The Democratic party was splintered.

Hubert Humphrey came away with the nomination, but many experts questioned whether it had much value. Humphrey's popularity was at low ebb. Many polls showed Governor George Wallace of Alabama with more support than Humphrey at this juncture.

Humphrey and his running mate, Senator Edmund Muskie of Maine, left Chicago following the convention and went to Humphrey's home at Waverly, Minnesota, to sort things out and plan their campaign.

Early Sunday morning after the convention I received a call from Eugene Stokowski. Gene was a D.F.L. candidate for Congress and we were old friends. He said, "Did you know that Senator Muskie is going to be on *Meet The Press* later this morning at KSTP?" (a local NBC affiliate). I did not.

Gene wanted to know if I could arrange to get us in so we could meet Muskie and get a picture with him. I told him I would work on it, but advised him to proceed as if we had clearance.

We agreed that we would meet at the station with

170

our wives one-half hour before the show went on the air. Gene said he would try to contact Pete Marcus, a good professional photographer, and have him meet us there.

I really didn't know where to begin to gain access to *Meet The Press* and Muskie. However, I started by calling the home of Jerry Soderberg, an attorney, a D.F.L. activist and close friend of Vice President Humphrey.

He didn't know how to get us in but he suggested that I call Bruce Solmonson, the vice president's son-in-law. I called Solmonson and he directed me to call Wendell Anderson. Luckily, I reached him. I had still not met Wendell Anderson. I gave him my name and told him I was a neighbor of his Uncle Emil's at Balsam Lake. I informed him that Stokowski and I wanted to meet Senator Muskie and hoped to get a picture with him that we could use in our campaign literature.

He said that Muskie's coordinator was a gentleman named Nordy Hoffman. Anderson said he would call KSTP and speak to Hoffman, so we could meet the new vice presidential candidate. Time was short, so he told me to go directly to the television station and ask for Nordy Hoffman. He said he would have everything cleared before we got there . . . and he did.

Ruth and I met Gene and Ann Stokowski at KSTP. Nordy Hoffman greeted us and ushered us into a small side room where there were television monitors set up for us to watch the show.

There were no spectators other than Jane Muskie on the set itself. We had a few moments to visit with Hoffman so I mentioned that I had a very dear friend of Polish extraction who I thought would be delighted to speak with Senator Muskie.

I was thinking of Stanley Wasie. Wasie was a self-made man who achieved great financial success in the trucking business. Although he was basically non-political, I knew that he was extremely interested in advancing Polish Americans.

He had set up educational scholarships for worthy Polish American youngsters. And although he did not seek to draw attention to himself, he was becoming known for his philanthropy. Hoffman instructed me to give Mr. Wasie a call and tell him that Senator Muskie would telephone him when he was finished with *Meet The Press*.

I dialed Stanley Wasie's home and the phone rang and rang. Just when I was about to give up Mr. Wasie answered. He told me he had just come home from church and the phone was ringing as he entered the house. I explained that I was at KSTP and asked him if he would like to chat with Senator Muskie. He said, "You are kidding." I told him to watch *Meet The Press*, which was scheduled to begin momentarily. Then after the show Senator Muskie would call. Mr. Wasie was delighted.

Gene and Ann Stokowski, Nordy Hoffman, Ruth and I watched the show from the anteroom. Senator Muskie was questioned by Lawrence Spivak and the other reporters on the panel. He handled the situation masterfully. He seemed cool, calm and reassuring in spite of the problems he had encountered in Chicago. His demeanor helped set the focus on the days ahead rather than the past.

Nordy Hoffman was ecstatic with Muskie's performance. Immediately after the show Muskie came into the anteroom and our group met him for the first time. We had scarcely met when a call came through for Senator Muskie. It was Vice President Humphrey. He called to congratulate him on a superb job. When that call was completed I briefed Senator Muskie on Mr. Wasie, after which I dialed Wasie's number.

Stanley Hubbard Sr., the owner of KSTP, was also a friend of Wasie's, and he was in the room with us when I called Mr. Wasie. When Wasie answered Mr. Hubbard snatched the phone from my hand and said, "Stan, you damn fool . . . this call will cost you ten-thousand dollars." Wasie replied, "I don't care if it costs twenty-five thousand." With that I retrieved the phone and introduced Stanley Wasie to Edmund Muskie.

They chatted for several minutes and compared their backgrounds. Wasie said that his name was shortened from Wasiliewski. Muskie said his family name was originally Muskaciewicz. Mr. Wasie congratulated the senator for being on the ticket and told him he only wished the order was reversed.

He invited Mr. and Mrs. Muskie to visit him and his wife at their Lake Minnetonka home. Although the visit was not practical or possible at that time, they established a friendship that lasted as long as Mr. Wasie lived.

The Wasies were guests of the Muskies at their

172

Kennebunkport home and the Muskie's visited the Wasies in later years in Minnesota. Both men enjoyed golf and I had the pleasure of being with them on two occasions where we enjoyed an afternoon of golf followed by dinner with our spouses.

When Senator Muskie finished his conversation with Stan Wasie, we had an opportunity to visit with him and his wife, Jane. Peter Marcus, the photographer, arrived and the Muskies, Stokowskis and Kozlaks went back to the *Meet The Press* set where several pictures were taken. Lawrence Spivak, the moderator of *Meet The Press*, was still there, so we had an opportunity to meet him and the men who were on the panel.

It was an exciting morning. When we left the T.V. station Ann, Gene, Ruth and I went to our house where we relaxed and recounted our good fortune.

As the election season progressed I received much help from the Democratic Farmer Labor party. Warren Spannaus (later Minnesota's Attorney General) was the state party chairman. He organized issues seminars for the D.F.L. candidates. These seminars helped define the issues of the day and gave tips on how to communicate effectively with the voters.

Early on there was a Sunday morning breakfast meeting of the D.F.L. endorsed candidates at a downtown St. Paul hotel. It was an opportunity to meet our counterparts from throughout the state.

Senator Walter Mondale was at this meeting and all the candidates had a picture taken with him for use in campaign literature and press releases.

This was the first time I had met Mondale and he made a very favorable impression on me. We only visited for a few moments but he knew the district I proposed to represent and named many mutual friends. He said, "You should be able to win this election." He offered his help and encouragement. I ran into Walter Mondale intermittently over the years and he always remembered me and called me by my first name.

On another occasion, endorsed D.F.L. candidates had an opportunity to be pictured with Hubert Humphrey. A room was set aside at a St. Paul hotel. The vice presidential seal was hung on the wall that formed the backdrop. A United States flag and the Minnesota state flag were positioned so they would be seen in the picture.

Nearly two-hundred legislative candidates lined up to get a picture with the vice president. Even though we each had only a few seconds with Humphrey it was still a memorable experience. He had a kind word for everyone, and as I stepped away after our picture was snapped he said, "Give Rosie a hug for me."

As the primary election campaign progressed, supporters of my candidacy and those of my opponent's conducted a weekly letters-to-the-editor battle of their own in the local paper. This added spice to the campaign and heightened the involvement of more and more people. A few days before the primary election, the district's League of Women Voters conducted a candidates' meeting at the city hall in Columbia Heights.

Before the candidates' meeting I met at our headquarters with some of my campaign committee. They tried to anticipate questions that would come from the audience. We spent about an hour at this exercise and then proceeded to the meeting. It was my first public "debate" and I was a bit nervous, but I felt that my opponent showed more anxiety.

The moderator of the program explained the rules for the evening. Each candidate was to be given a specified number of minutes for an opening statement to be followed by rebuttal and then questions from the audience.

My opponent and I were sitting side-by-side facing the audience. When the moderator finished citing the format for the evening, she turned to us holding a coin in her hand and said, "We will toss a coin to see who speaks first." She barely got the last word out and I winked at the audience and said, "I don't gamble . . . let him call it."

With this, Jack Meyer got excited and pushed his chair back saying, "I don't gamble either." The audience howled. Finally, I said I would make an exception just this once to my aversion to gambling and call the toss.

We had a good exchange. I usually started my presentation with the old Will Rogers saw, "I am a member of no organized political party . . . I am a Democrat." If the opportunity presented itself I tried to work in a Magnus Johnson story. Magnus Johnson was a congressman and United State senator from Minnesota in the 1920s and 1930s and a member of the Farmer Labor party.

He was born in Europe and spoke with a thick Scandinavian accent. One day he was at a county fair where a huge crowd had gathered in a field to hear him speak. This happened before the days of good amplifying equipment. In order to be seen and heard, Magnus wanted to be able to stand above the crowd.

There was no stage built for him. But as luck would have it, there was a manure spreader close at hand. Magnus got up on the spreader and began his speech saying, "Ladies and gentlemen, I never thought I would see the day when I would be speaking from the Republican platform." Most people seemed to enjoy a bit of humor and it usually took the edge off the tense situations.

My opponent was a very thoughtful and serious person. However, if he had a sense of humor he didn't let it show. This may have hindered his rapport with undecided voters.

As primary election day approached, it looked like the vote would be close. Chuck Lefebvre said the primary vote would be light and he wanted me to finish a close second. I found it difficult to find any merit in finishing second but LeFebvre pointed out that a close second could be beneficial in keeping our volunteers working in my campaign rather than drifting off to other contests.

The last thing Ruth and I did on the night before the primary election was pay a courtesy call on William DeCoursey. DeCoursey was also in the race although he had not campaigned actively. We visited him at his home and wished him well. I told him that if I was eliminated from the general election I would support him. He countered by pledging to support me if he was not nominated.

On primary election day I was up early and stopped at several polling places to greet the workers. Ruth and I voted just before dinner time and then prepared our home for the reception we would have for many of our volunteers when they brought in the returns from their precincts.

We had a big board on the wall of our amusement room marked off for the returns from each precinct. The first returns we received after the polls closed were from St. Anthony. St. Anthony had voting machines so the results were available early. The news was not very good.

175

Meyer beat me bad in our own backyard. The vote was quite close in our home precinct, but in the one adjoining I got clobbered. LeFebvre said not to worry because the rest of the district would give us reason to celebrate. When all the returns were in I had won nine of fifteen precincts and was only one-hundred seventy-five votes behind the incumbent. The incumbent had garnered nearly fifty-two percent of the vote. Ours was a respectable showing, but we had plenty of work left to do and less than two months in which to do it.

We began the general election campaign by designing an attractive piece of literature titled Democratic Digest. It contained pictures of me with presidential candidate Hubert Humphrey, Senator Walter Mondale, and vice presidential candidate Edmund Muskie.

It contained endorsements and quotes by them. On the back was a brief resume of my qualifications plus a family picture and the names of nearly five-hundred citizens who endorsed my candidacy. It was an effective campaign tool, and as we moved toward the general election I thought I could sense our support gaining strength.

We got several breaks near the end of the campaign. The first came when someone in St. Anthony (probably the mayor at the time) enforced a sign ordinance of which we were not aware. There was an ordinance on the books that stated that all lawn signs must be placed back fifteen feet from the curb. I was not aware of it and neither were my volunteers. Also, most of the realtors in the area were unaware and thus in violation of the ordinance.

One afternoon a St. Anthony Village maintenance truck went through St. Anthony and began picking up all of our signs that were less than fifteen feet from the curb. Since we were unaware of the law, our signs were virtually wiped out. I was at work at the restaurant on this particular afternoon, when I heard stories of people chasing after the truck and demanding their signs be returned.

The village workmen were just doing their job as ordered, so there was really nothing else they could do.

Ruth received a call from one of our supporters who told her the truck was on her street collecting the signs. Ruth drove to the location and asked the workmen the nature of the problem. When they cited the ordinance, Ruth asked if we could have the rest of the day to reposition the

176

signs so they would be in compliance.

They said they were sorry but they had to follow their orders. They did tell Ruth where they were going to deposit the signs, so we were ultimately able to retrieve and reset them. The sign episode caused quite a flap in St. Anthony.

Our supporters resented the manner in which the situation was handled and blamed my opponent. Most undecided voters thought it to be poor sportsmanship on the part of the opposition. In fairness to Jack Meyer I still believe this episode was hatched by one of his overzealous supporters without his knowledge or approval. However, he never denounced it and that hurt him.

Less than two weeks before election day I received a call from Eileen Kuehn, who was a reporter for the local newspaper. She asked if she could accompany me on an evening when I went campaigning door-to-door. We met a couple evenings later and went to a street in St. Anthony that I had not yet covered.

I rang the doorbell and a lady answered. I introduced myself and she said, "Oh yes we plan to vote for you." Then she asked, "Would you stay a moment and meet my father?" She left the room and returned a few moments later with a little old man in tow.

She introduced me to her father, Paul Kubic. Mr. Kubic was ninety-five years old. When we were introduced he excitedly told me that it was because of my grandfather that he made it to the United States. He said, "When I arrived in Minneapolis I could only say two words . . . Stanley Kozlak."

He told how he found my grandfather's house and how my grandfather put him up and found employment for him. It was a moving experience for me to meet this man, and Eileen was recording much of what he said in her notebook. She also took a picture of Mr. Kubic and me. The article she wrote appeared in the last edition of the weekly local newspaper before the election.

Also included in the article was a picture of me with my feet up on my desk which showed a hole that I had worn through the sole of my shoe. This reminded many people of a similar picture of Adlai Stevenson taken during the 1956 presidential campaign.

Another reporter did a story on my opponent and both articles appeared in the same edition. I have included both

177

articles here so that you can judge for yourself what an impact they made on the election.

A few days before the election both Jack Meyer and I were invited to appear at a Columbia Heights Chamber of Commerce luncheon. We were both a bit campaign weary by this time but we made our pitches to the group with great enthusiasm. Meyer was a member of the Columbia Heights Chamber and he felt comfortable with the group.

He used this occasion to accuse me of distorting his record on the sales tax issue. We had repeatedly referred to a quote by him as published in the local newspaper in the previous campaign, where he said he would not vote for a sales tax.

At this luncheon he claimed he had only promised not to support a regressive tax bill. It was pretty good rhetoric before the Chamber of Commerce. But when he finished speaking and before he could sit down I stood up and said, "I have one question for Representative Meyer. Did you or did you not vote for final passage of the sales tax bill?" He swallowed hard and answered, "I did."

I could sense from the reaction of the crowd that I had scored big.

At that moment I actually felt sorry for Meyer, and I told him later that I really wished that it had not been necessary to do that to him.

The Saturday afternoon before election day Harold Kalina, Jim Rice and I got together to reassess the campaign. Rice said he wanted to predict the outcome. He took out a piece of paper and wrote a number on it. He said, "This is the number of votes I think you will win by." He folded the paper and handed it to me. "Don't look at it until all the votes are counted," he said.

On the last night before the election, state Senator Harold Kalina and I made a final door-to-door sweep in Fridley. It was a cool November night and at nearly every house people had their T.V.s tuned in to final election coverage. Hubert Humphrey's campaign had caught fire and as we went from house to house we could see people watching his final hours of campaigning.

We were getting good vibes as we met the folks in this neighborhood. Kalina said it reminded him of his first campaign when he upset an incumbent. He predicted I would win as we finished the evening and the campaign.

OLD SHOES – Jack Kozlak, DFL-endorsed candidate for legislative district 32B grinned ruefully as he propped his feet up after an evening of campaigning and was chided about the hole in his shoe.

Kozlak Campaign Resembles Reunion

by EILEEN KUENN

Every evening about six Jack Kozlak and his pretty, vivacious wife, Ruth, put on their walking shoes and begin ringing doorbells.

Kozlak takes one side of the street. His wife, the other.

THEY STOP at every house, knock on every door and spend a few minutes chatting about why Kozlak is seeking election to the state legislature.

Many of the residents in Columbia Heights and St. Anthony they know on a first name basis,

"Campaigning is pretty much like a giant-sized family reunion," Kozlak thinks. "We keep running into people we haven't seen for ages."

Some, they've never met, but mention of the name Kozlak brings back memories of another age.

"OFTEN WHEN I introduce myself, they remember me as that skinny Kozlak kid who played with their kids back in grade-school days," Kozlak explained.

And, mention of the name Kozlak turns back the clock a couple of generations for many of the older residents.

Like Paul Kubic, age 95, who lives at 3657 Roosevelt St. NE, St. Anthony, for example.

"IT'S ALL because of your grandfather that I'm here today," Kubic exclaimed excitedly as Kozlak introduced himself.

"He's the one who got me a steamship ticket to this country more than 63 years ago.

"I've never forgotten your grandfather … he even had me stay with him 'til I found a place to live," the spritely old man reminisced.

"So you're Kozlak's boy … well, I've got to get my shoes on and go vote this year."

THINGS LIKE that are what makes campaigning just a great experience, Kozlak believes.

And, incidents like the moving venture of one Columbia Heights family who moved into St. Anthony Village last week …

"The first thing they took out of the moving van was our lawn sign," Ruth smiled happily.

"I REMEMBER: – 95-year-old Paul Kubic, 3657 Roosevelt St. NE, St. Anthony, had no trouble recalling the Kozlaks. "Your grandfather made it possible for me to be here today … I'll never forget what he did for me …"

The Kozlaks figure putting up lawn signs is an important part of campaigning – and have staked more than 1400, so far.

They've made it a family affair.

FREQUENTLY THEIR children meet them at the end of a campaign block, take the list of homes which have volunteered to "host" a lawn sign and pound in the family banner before their parents are out of sight.

Often the evening campaign walk looks like shades of the Pied Piper as neighborhood children – sometimes half a dozen – follow them from block to block.

KOZLAK thinks that's a good sign.

"There's an old saying in politics that when kids start following you, you've got it made," Kozlak beamed.

Even though they sometimes find their opponent's sign on a front lawn, the Kozlaks aren't daunted.

Kozlak stops anywhere and rings the doorbell.

"THOUGHT I'D say hello," he says easily. "I didn't want you to think I was chicken.…"

"Surprisingly enough it's often enough to make people switch signs," Kozlak said happily.

"Often it's a case of people who didn't know who was running against the incumbent. And, when they find out that I am the DFL-endorsed candidate, well – they change their minds," Kozlak grinned.

KOZLAK THINKS this is the "most involved" campaign in the history of the Columbia Heights-St. Anthony district.

"There's almost total community involvement," Kozlak said. "The interest is tremendous."

The campaign day begins at 5:30 a.m. for Kozlak, who is co-owner of Jax cafe. It usually includes a full business day, two or three political coffee parties and some two hours of door-to-door canvassing.

"But I've never felt better in my life." Kozlak grinned after finishing one evening's jaunt through six city blocks.

"I'VE HAD my share of sore feet and I've lost 20 pounds, but I figured if I made it down to 175 it'd be a good campaign."

"He tips the scales at 174 right now," Ruth smiled proudly, "and I've even lost seven pounds."

"Just join the Kozlak Health Club," Jack replied. "Good way to keep in shape."

[Wednesday, Oct. 30, 1968]

179

Jack Meyer takes a few minutes out from his six-day-a-week campaign schedule to sink into a comfortable lounge chair at home.

Meyer Jogging Campaign Trail

By JEAN HASKELL

Most political candidates are running for office; Jack Meyer is jogging.

MEYER, incumbent candidate in state legislative district 32B, explained that jogging is a great timesaver for door-to-door politicking.

"On 40-foot lots, you can't get up any speed, but it really helps with the 100-foot lots," he observed.

In an interview late Saturday night, Meyer said some people may think it funny to see a man in a business suit with campaign literature in his hand, loping down a residential street.

He thinks, however, any amusement is worth the campaigning time saved.

"It would look funnier if I got defeated."

THERE ARE hazards for any politician on the campaign trail, Meyer noted.

He once jogged his way head-on into a low picket fence, cracked his shins, and fell flat on his face.

More than anything else, candidate Meyer fears breaking a leg or twisting an ankle.

"You can break an arm and still be O.K., but break a leg and you're sunk."

To jog six nights a week and cover 95 per cent of the district's homes, Meyer has to be in good physical shape.

"YOU HAVE to wear crepe soled shoes, or you'll be miserable," he advised.

His sturdy shoe soles are thinning a bit, but have so far managed to survive three months of primary and general election pavement-pounding.

Door-to-door politicking is something of a science. Candidates, for instance, have to acquire a commanding air with dogs.

Meyer was once bitten by a canine, but was saved by the thick bundle of cards in his hip pocket.

"It would be interesting," he noted, "to keep statistics on how many doorbells don't work."

ALTHOUGH he was once met at the door by a voter holding a butcher knife, most residents are friendly and congenial.

Since August, Meyer estimated only a half dozen persons have been "obnoxious."

About three-fourths of these persons are women, he remarked.

He does concede, however, that he meets many more women than men.

Women are at home most of the day and are usually the ones to answer the doorbell.

He finds it amusing to see a man engrossed with the television order his wife to answer the door.

THE PERSONS he meets are usually caught off guard and rarely can think of questions for him.

Of those who do, he said, the bulk of questions are about finances.

"They want to know where the money is coming from and where it's going," he said.

Earlier in the year, Meyer received more comments on civil disobedience, but now proposed gun legislation seems to have taken second place.

Misinformation abounds, Meyer discovered.

SOME VOTERS think he is running against U.S. Congressional candidate Clark MacGregor.

"How do you like it in Washington?" one citizen asked the state legislator. Meyer out of necessity has to repeat himself.

He fears he is beginning to sound like a tape recorder.

Despite the problems of a legislative candidate, Meyer is bearing up well.

"It's a grind, but I enjoy it."

[Oct 30, 1968]

180

It was now up to the voters. We had gone through almost five months of intensive campaigning and all we could do was await the decision.

Early in the morning of election day I stopped at a few polling places to greet the workers. At 8:30 a.m. I went to Chet's Shoe Store in Columbia Heights. When I walked in, Chet Latawiec, the owner, eyed me warily and said, "What are you doing walking around with a hole in your shoe?"

I explained that I had to cover a lot of ground and just couldn't take the time to buy a new pair until now. He fitted me with new shoes and said. "O.K., you earned your vote" and wished me well.

On election night we had a reception planned at Jax. Many of our volunteers began arriving shortly after the polls closed at 8 p.m. At 8:30 I received a call from my neighbor, Don Zander. He had the returns from St. Anthony, where I had not done well in the primary. He was very excited as he told me that I had won my own precinct and had come out of St. Anthony with nearly forty-eight percent of the vote.

From that point on everything was positive. We won big in Columbia Heights. And when all the votes were in, we had a margin of eleven-hundred fifty-nine votes. The final tally was Meyer, sixty-eight hundred twenty-four – Kozlak, seventy-nine hundred eighty-three.

There were more votes cast in our race in our district than were cast in the race for congress. This underscores how hotly our race was contested. Usually, the falloff in interest is from the other direction. We had outstanding community involvement in our race. On election day eighty percent of those registered went to the polls.

I remembered the slip of paper Jim Rice had given me. I opened it and saw the number eleven-hundred thirty-three. He had missed his prediction by a mere twenty-six votes.

After the election Ruth and I took a short vacation. It gave us an opportunity to unwind and begin planning for the days ahead. We also reflected on the campaign and compared our perceptions of the highlights as well as the disappointments.

The cliche persists that politics makes strange bedfellows. It is also true that you find out who your friends are. One disappointment we both felt was from a couple we had considered friends.

The gentleman and I were college classmates. When we graduated he started a business that provided a product we used every day at the restaurant. He asked for our account. And even though we did not make it a practice to replace a supplier who was providing satisfactory product and service, we let his company in and discharged his competition.

A couple years later he and his wife wanted to join a golf country club where Ruth and I were members. They asked us to sponsor them. We did and when they became members we made it a point to introduce them to our friends and acquaintances.

One evening during the campaign I was canvassing their neighborhood. When I came to their house it was the Mrs. who answered the door. I greeted her as an old friend and asked for her support. She said, "But we are Republicans."

It was an awkward situation and I was taken aback. She did not invite me in so I just smiled and said, "Try and mark your ballot in the right spot." That was it. A rebuff I had not expected. I tried not to let it bother me and pushed on to make new contacts and new friends.

* * *

The pleasant surprises far outnumbered any minor disappointments we may have experienced. One such surprise occurred not long after I filed for office. State Treasurer Val Bjornson and Mrs. Bjornson stopped in for dinner at Jax on an evening when I was at the podium. Bjornson, a Republican, was one of Minnesota's most popular public figures and one of the best Minnesota vote-getters with the possible exception of Hubert Humphrey.

He had only lost one election in a long and illustrious career, and that was when he challenged Hubert Humphrey for the U.S. Senate seat in 1954. Bjornson ran a much closer race with Humphrey than any other person who ever was matched with H.H.H. in a senate contest.

Bjornson was an occasional customer at Jax. Whereas I always recognized and acknowledged him, I really did not feel that I knew him well. Certainly, we had never discussed any political issues. On this particular evening he asked to see me at his table. When I approached the table he beckoned me to be seated. He said that he was aware that I was a candidate for the legislature. He told me he thought it would be a great experience for me. He also said that he thought I would make a good legislator if elected. He concluded by wishing me well and saying, "I will not do anything to hurt you."

I was surprised and honored by his thoughtfulness and kindness . . . but that was the kind of person Val Bjornson was.

From Dan Cohen's book "Undefeated."

"Even Hubert Humphrey told the story during the 1954 campaign about when he came home from campaigning one night. His young son was sitting in his lap and said, "Daddy, what are we going to do if you get beat in this election?" And he said, "Son, don't you worry about that. If I get defeated I'll be defeated by one of the greatest Americans who ever lived . . . Val Bjornson. And if Val Bjornson is elected to the U.S. Senate, you and I can go to sleep at night and not have to worry about government, or peace, or the economy, or whatever."

Yes, that was the kind of person Val Bjornson was. So rather than try to attack him in the 1954 election, Humphrey just loved him to death.

Several friends and acquaintances who supported me wanted lawn signs but they did not want to be associated with the D.F.L. They asked if I could give them signs without D.F.L. on them. I didn't think it would be right to have two different signs and we never did.

These supporters solved the problem themselves by painting out the white D.F.L. letters into the blue background on the sign.

* * *

One of our line cooks was a lady named Billie Lamon. She was a motivated and gifted cook and also a political activist. I was flattered when she asked to help in my campaign. She asked if she could put on a fund-raising dinner for me.

I was a bit wary because I didn't know if a dinner in a legislative race would draw. I also did not want to bring my campaign to Jax and thus mix it with our business. My objections did not stop Billie Lamon.

She went out and rented a hall. She hired the Doc Evans band. Doc Evans was to the Twin Cities what Pete Fountain and Al Hirt are to New Orleans.

She organized a publicity and ticket sales committee. They got tremendous press with pictures of Doc Evans together with some of our attractive lady volunteers. Billie and her friends prepared and served an outstanding buffet dinner. The evening was a huge success and she presented the finance committee with a check in excess of eight hundred dollars . . . a big help to our campaign at a critical time. Months later, when the House voted on a bill to provide equal pay for equal work to women, I couldn't help but think of Billie. I trust she was pleased with my vote.

* * *

A few days after the election, Lawrence Hall stopped in for lunch at Jax. I only knew him by reputation. He had served in the Minnesota House of Representatives for many years (some with my father) and had served several terms as speaker of the House. He was at that time chairman of the Metropolitan Airports Commission and also the chief lobbyist at the Legislature for the wholesale liquor dealers in Minnesota. He asked me to visit with him.

He said he thought I should get on the Regulated Industries Committee. I was really green and asked what that committee did. He told me that it had to do with utilities and other industries, including liquor.

I told him that I did not intend to go to the Capitol to be self-serving. He countered by saying the best place to kill bad bills was in committee. It was a busy day for me and that was about the extent of our conversation.

A day or two later every new legislator received a notice from the speaker, L.L. Duxbury, saying he wanted to meet with us one-on-one. He wanted to interview us, and thus gain background information which would be beneficial to him in making committee assignments.

Duxbury held his interviews in a room at the St. Paul Athletic Club. I was more than a little nervous as I sat waiting outside his door for my turn. The door was louvered and I couldn't help but hear some of the interview in progress.

The fellow concluding his interview, a D.F.L'er, patronizingly told Duxbury that he wasn't really a strong party man. I couldn't believe what I heard and then the door opened and it was my turn.

Speaker Duxbury put me at ease immediately. We talked about restaurants for a few minutes and found that we had mutual friends in the business. Duxbury said he liked restaurant people . . . that he found them friendly and outgoing. Then he said, "I think you would do well on the Regulated Industries Committee."

I told him I did not want to be on that committee because it dealt with liquor bills and I did not come to St. Paul to be self-serving. He asked me what I would do if he assigned me to that committee. I said, "I would respectfully ask to be removed." He smiled and asked, "And if I didn't?" I said, "I'm sorry but I just wouldn't go." Next, he asked what interested me. I told him I would like appropriations. He said, "Appropriations! They meet for two hours every day — that's a lot of work."

I explained that it was my understanding that the appropriations committee was the best way to learn the workings of state government. And then I said, "I came here expecting to work and work hard." The interview concluded in a light and friendly vein, but I didn't have a clue as to what committees I would have.

In early December we had a minority caucus and elected the leadership of our group. It was a good opportunity to meet and visit with my new colleagues. One of them, Representative Joseph Priferl, had served with my father in the 1941 session.

The knife and fork circuit got into gear about this time too. Ruth and I were invited to many functions sponsored by trade, labor, and professional associations. We tried to attend as many as possible. This helped us to build friendships with legislators on both sides of the aisle. These were exciting days for us . . . new friends, new experiences . . . even the mail was addressed to The Honorable Jack Kozlak. Ruth remained unimpressed and I still had to shovel the walk and take out the garbage.

The holiday season sped by and the day for the Legislature to convene drew ever closer. A few days before the start of the session I received a call from Rod Chalmers, the editor of the Sun Newspapers that serviced our area.

He asked if I would write a weekly column giving my thoughts on the Legislature. It was an excellent opportunity to gain exposure and I agreed to do it. I chose the title: *As I See It* for my offerings. The first column described my thoughts on the day I was sworn in as a member of the Minnesota House of Representatives.

All the political reporters from the daily press were on duty at the start of the session. Stan Fudro collared George McCormick of the Minneapolis Tribune and told him that my mother was in the gallery. Fudro explained that she had been there forty-eight years ago in 1921 to see my father sworn in as a first-term legislator.

McCormick had a photographer take a picture of my mother and me overlooking the House chambers from the gallery. The next morning the picture and the story took a prominent place on the second front page of the Minneapolis Tribune.

I recall stopping for gasoline at the neighborhood station the day that the picture and story ran. The gentleman that was working the pumps said, "Just imagine . . . one day on the job and all your colleagues know who you are."

I hadn't given it a thought but when I reached the Capitol I was amazed at how many people commented on the picture and the article.

Very early in the session I took a list of the names of the one-hundred thirty-five House members and had a box of fifty matches embossed with each member's name. We were able to make these up at the restaurant. And, of course, the restaurant's advertising with caricatures of Bill and I were on the inside of the cover.

When they were ready I had the pages put a box on each member's office desk. The response was terrific. Everyone appreciated the gesture. I made an impression that proved positive for me *and* the restaurant.

More than twenty years later I still run into people who received those matches and who tell me they have saved some of them. Many of the recipients, who were not previously acquainted with the restaurant, became loyal customers.

PART
TWELVE

Down to Business
at the
Legislature

The day committee assignments are announced is a day charged with excitement in the Legislature. Speaker Lloyd Duxbury interviewed each new House member a month before the session began to discuss their committee preferences and to get an idea of members' strengths and weaknesses. Members with seniority were requested to submit their preferences to the speaker by mail. He then set about the task of organizing committees and placing members on them.

The speaker's job in selecting committees is further complicated by the fact that time conflicts among committees must be avoided.

You could feel the tension as the chief clerk began to read off the committee titles and their membership. The blood pressure of nearly every legislator surely rose as they waited to learn where they would be placed.

Chief topic of discussion after this session among members was how they fared. I was placed on the prestigious appropriations committee, labor, highways, metropolitan and urban affairs, and county and township government. They were all quality committees and I could not have been more pleased.

Appropriations met for two hours each weekday morning. It was a quick study in how state government operates. Heads of every state and semi-state department make their case for funding. We heard from the president of the University of Minnesota and his minions; chancellor of the state college system as well as every constitutional officer. I cannot recall any one who came before us suggesting that their department or sphere of activity could be operated with less staff or less money. I found the process fascinating as one after another stated their case for increased funding over the previous biennium. The chairman of appropriations at that time was Richard Fitzsimons. He was a grain farmer from Argyle, Minnesota, population seven-hundred eighty-seven. He ran an excellent committee and I felt that his practical approach and clear thinking helped save the taxpayers millions of dollars without sacrificing essential services.

Fitzsimons placed me on the state departments' subcommittee and late in the session I was placed on the house/senate conference committee where we allocated millions of dollars to various state departments. It was a signal honor for me to serve on the conference committee first as a freshman and second as a member of the minority caucus.

The chairman of the conference committee was Senator Donald Sinclair. He was serving his sixth term as senator and the smooth manner in which he resolved the differences within the committee was masterful. When we got hung up on a difficult question he could move us away from the problem and on to areas where we could agree. Later we would go back to the points of disagreement and one by one they would be amicably resolved until our work was done. Senator Sinclair worked the conference committee hard. We had a deadline to meet and he made us all aware of it. We worked many nights and even long hours on Sunday and the job got done. Sinclair too was a farmer. He lived near the little town of Stephen (population eight-hundred sixty-three) in southwestern Minnesota. One could not observe Fitzsimons and Sinclair at that time without developing profound respect for these dedicated citizen legislators.

* * *

One day, late in the session, the weather turned

warm and it felt like summer was just around the corner. I dressed for work in a pair of checked black and white slacks, powder blue sport jacket with matching tie and black and white wing tip shoes. Traffic was exceptionally heavy that day and I was about five minutes late getting to the appropriations committee meeting. The meeting was already in progress when I entered the room. I could feel that all eyes were on me as I walked to my seat. Vice chairman Verne Long, a farmer from Pipestone, was conducting the meeting. He watched me approach my chair and just before I sat down he said, "there is a cold horse out there somewhere today." We all had a good laugh.

* * *

Early in the session Dave Roe, president of the Minnesota, A.F.L./C.I.O, came to me and asked if I would carry a bill that would make mace illegal except for use by police. Roe was walking a picket line in Mankato, Minnesota when someone sprayed him directly in the face with the substance. He explained how debilitating a whiff of mace could be, and even demonstrated it by spraying some in a saucer and then dampening a toothpick with it and dabbing it under my eye. It was a convincing argument for the strict control of the substance. I agreed to author the bill. He told me that Senator Wendell Anderson would introduce the bill in the senate.

I introduced the bill in the House, secured a hearing date before the appropriate committee and presented the case for the bill. The committee reported the bill out favorably, and it was placed on the docket for consideration by the entire House of Representatives.

When the bill came up I made the presentation for its passage. I was more than a little surprised when Representative Gary Flakne rose to comment on the bill. Flakne was a real insider with the majority, and had he chose to do so, I am convinced he could have killed the bill. He was a leader with the majority which had eighty-five votes, and I was a newcomer with the minority that had but fifty votes.

In his comments he cast a few doubts on the advisability of the bill and I thought he was about to argue to kill it. Ultimately, what he did do was offer an amendment that would extend the legal use of the substance to police and the national guard. When he finished I was recognized by the speaker and said, "I can understand the wisdom of that amendment." Everyone had a good laugh and when the votes were taken both the amendment and the bill passed handily.

The next day I went to the floor of the senate and sought out Senator Wendell Anderson. I told him that our bill was passed by the House and asked how he was progressing with it in the Senate. He seemed surprised that I had been able to get it passed in the House so quickly. He proceeded to tell me that he had not yet asked for a hearing on the bill and explained why he had not.

At that time Wendell Anderson had already served two terms in the House and was in the midst of his second term in the Senate. He was a former member of the U.S. Olympic hockey team, a lawyer, a member of an intelligence unit with the U.S. Army Reserve. He had served as an infantry officer when on active duty. Anderson was thirty-five years old and a Democrat. The politics of his situation was this: the conservative (Republican) majority in the Legislature was not anxious to let Wendell Anderson pass any legislation that they thought might advance his political career. They perceived him as a potential threat to run for statewide office and they knew that with his credentials and his name he would be a formidable candidate.

Anderson suggested that I present the bill to the appropriate Senate committee. He said, "It will be good experience for you." I agreed to give it my best effort.

The Senate committee I was to appear before was chaired by Senator Gordon Rosenmeier. He had been a senator for twenty-eight years and was unquestionably the most astute and most powerful legislator at the time. Most legislators who served with him and observed the skill with which he operated would consider him one of Minnesota's most influential legislators of the twentieth century.

As I sat on the sidelines in his committee waiting for my bill to be called, I was a little nervous and somewhat in awe as I watched him conduct the business of his committee.

Eventually, he called up my bill by its Senate file

number. I proceeded to the podium facing the committee and launched into my presentation. I had hardly begun when Senator Rosenmeier tapped his gavel and said "Just a moment here. Who are you?" I had neglected to introduce myself to the committee. I think Senator Rosenmeier could sense my embarrassment as I corrected my mistake and as the discussion of the bill ensued he could not have been more helpful or gracious. The bill, with Senator Rosenmeier's help, passed easily out of committee. The bill easily passed in the Senate and was eventually signed into law by Governor Harold Levander.

Shortly thereafter Representative John Salchert (a medical doctor) came to me and asked me to co-author a bill. The bill became known as the cytogenetics bill.

During the campaign of 1968, Representative Salchert was the point man for the D.F.L. minority in the House and he cut several radio ads that the Republicans considered highly inflammatory. He felt that the majority members would not let him pass a bill no matter what its merit, so he asked me to carry it in the House.

Perhaps the best way to describe the bill is to quote a news release that I issued on February 20, 1969.

NEWS RELEASE

Hearings began Wednesday on the cytogenetics bill in the Minnesota House.

Representative Jack Kozlak appeared with Representative John Salchert, M.D., in favor of the bill, of which they are authors.

The bill provides for a free laboratory to test for chromosome damage in cells of persons requesting tests. "The justification for this legislation can be seen in our mental hospitals today," said Kozlak. "Testing of parents can provide information as to the chances of their conceiving mentally retarded children. Testing of babies can tell us at an early age, whether or not the child will require specialized care.

"We have an opportunity to attack mental retardation at the very root of the problem," said Kozlak. "We've been attacking the problem after it occurs all these years. It's time to take the necessary steps in the direction of prevention.

"Thousands of people are suffering the effects of

ruined lives because of genetic damage. We can help change this situation."

Kozlak is a representative from district 32B (Columbia Heights, St. Anthony).

-30-

The "cytogenetics" bill contained an appropriation for forty-thousand dollars. As a member of both the appropriation committee and the state department sub-committee of appropriations, I was able to convince my colleagues of the advisability of passing the bill. Representative Salchert kept a low profile throughout the process and the bill became law. This is just a little example of how the legislative process sometimes works. The idea for the bill was Salchert's and yet because of the politics of the situation he did not receive the credit he deserved.

During the session I received a letter from Mrs. Tom (Elaine) Young. She was the mother of a retarded child and was active in the Minnesota Association for Retarded Children as it was then known. Her letter pointed out that transportation to school and activity centers for mentally retarded children had been overlooked. Her letter was heart rending as she described the situation where healthy children are bused to school and a retarded child in the same family must be left behind and wonder why.

I lined up some of my colleagues as co-authors and introduced a bill to provide transportation for mentally retarded persons to daytime activity centers. Following is one of the columns I wrote for the local newspaper addressing both the cytogenetics bill and the transportation bill.

AS I SEE IT
by Rep. Jack Kozlak
March 13, 1969

The problems faced by the mentally retarded are a major concern of all citizens. A number of beneficial programs have been initiated to attack these problems.

192

Unfortunately, the problem of transportation for the school age mentally retarded has been largely overlooked. While programs for the retarded are available, many parents cannot avail their children to them due to a lack of transportation funds.

Last week I was author of a bill to provide public transportation for mentally retarded persons attending daytime activity centers.

It has been observed that often one-third of the expenses involved in the treatment of mentally retarded individuals are associated with transportation to and from the center.

All children in Minnesota are supposed to be provided with a free education. The fact that some are retarded should not deny them this right.

Sometimes the most comprehensive and enlightened program devised to solve a problem cannot fully succeed until the seemingly insignificant contingencies are provided for. In this case, it is my aim to do all within my power to remove the stumbling blocks from the path of progress.

While treatment for the mentally retarded is essential, it is even more important that we take steps to prevent retardation. A bill, of which I am the author, to provide for free laboratory chromosome tests to detect damage in reproductive cells, would advance the cause of prevention.

The justification for this legislation can be seen in our mental hospitals today. Testing of parents can provide information as to the chances of their conceiving mentally retarded children. The results of this testing would enable the people involved to make an enlightened choice as to whether they should risk bearing children of their own, whether it would be better to adopt, or a myriad of other possibilities.

We have an opportunity to attack mental retardation at the very root of the problem. We've been attacking the problem after it occurs all these years. It's time to take the necessary steps in the direction of prevention.

Thousands of people are suffering the effects of ruined lives because of genetic damage. We can help change this situation now.

Our ultimate aim is to prevent mental retardation. Failing this, we must treat and train the retarded so that they can lead happy productive lives, and so they can *participate in our society to the fullest extent possible.*

-30-

The transportation bill for retarded children came up for discussion on the House floor at a particularly busy period in the session. When the clerk called the bill I was recognized by the speaker and merely said this. "The letter I hold in my hand can more eloquently express why I support this bill than any words I can devise. It comes from the mother of six children . . . five normal and one retarded." I then read Mrs. Young's letter. When I finished you could have heard a pin drop in the House chamber. Her letter had said it all. There was no need for further discussion . . . no questions . . . no dissent. The clerk called for the vote and the bill passed the house unanimously.

Ruth and I were later invited to a dinner sponsored by the Anoka County Association for Retarded Children Inc. where they presented me with a certificate of award and a pin in "Expressed Appreciation for valuable assistance given in behalf of mentally retarded children and adults." It was a gratifying experience to be so recognized.

The district I represented in the Legislature was unique in many ways. It was a metropolitan district and yet it encompassed all of three municipalities and part of a fourth. The district also lay in part in three important counties: Hennepin, which included the city of Minneapolis; Ramsey, which included the city of St. Paul; and Anoka, which was then one of Minnesota's fastest growing counties. Each one of these counties had its own caucus to discuss issues of special interest, and I made it a point to attend these meetings. In addition, there were often meetings with public officials of the municipalities as well as school superintendents and school board members. Add to this meetings and presentations by labor leaders, business and professional people, public employee leaders and interested citizens and you can quickly understand how busy a legislator can be during the session.

In the early weeks of the session, the House of Representatives usually adjourned from Friday afternoon until Monday. I was then able to work an evening shift at the restaurant on Friday and Saturday and also go in on

Sunday to line things up so brother Bill could have a day off. But as the session wore on, the legislative process took up every day of the week so I couldn't spend any time at Jax. Bill carried the load at the restaurant. It was an unusually busy and pressure-filled time for both of us.

As the session drew to a close, the pace at the Capitol grew ever more frantic. Bills sped through committees and the usual logjam began to build up on the house floor. Finally, the deadline for hearing bills in committee was reached and all the action switched to the daily sessions of the House. The race was now on to bring up all the bills that had cleared committee before time ran out on the session. The daily sessions began running into the night as bill after bill was brought up on the floor of the House for debate and a vote.

The final day/night of the session was almost unbelievable. By law the Legislature had to complete its work by midnight. Most of the bills that came up for passage late that night were non-controversial. They were being passed with virtual lightning speed. The clerk would read the title and number of the bill and in most instances there was no discussion. Many bills I feel were passed on blind faith. Of course, all the bills had survived the committee process but it was impossible to have a thorough knowledge of every bill and what it entailed. The only solace came in the hope that your colleagues acted diligently as your eyes and ears in the committees other than your own. At one point near the end of the session bills were being passed at a rate of one a minute. I thought of Bismarck's remark: "People who are fond of laws and sausages should never watch either being made."

No one made a move to slow the process because everyone had a bill or bills waiting to be called up for passage. If time ran out on your bill it would be dead for the session and the whole process would have to begin anew at the next session. I walked over to Representative Ed Gearty's desk and voiced my displeasure at the speed of the process. Gearty was serving his fourth term. He told me, "No matter what you may think . . . a lot of good legislation is being passed here."

With barely minutes to spare the conference committee bill for the state department's appropriations came to my desk for signature. It was necessary for those of us who served on the conference committee to sign it so it could be brought up for passage. The bill was passed moments later and at midnight, as prescribed by law, the 1969 session came to an end.

* * *

The 1969 session was a watershed session in many ways. It marked the end of biennial sessions. The liberals gained control of the house in the 1972 election and came close to gaining control in the Senate. The process seemed to begin whereby the traditional citizens Legislature began to be replaced by more and more career politicians and technocrats. As far as I know nearly every member of the 1969 Legislature had another occupation. Among others there were farmers, businessmen, labor leaders, attorneys, educators and doctors. These people formed a good mix of citizens from throughout the state. They passed laws with the knowledge that they would return to their communities to live among their neighbors with the results of their actions. I believe most legislators were motivated to serve by the simple desire to perform public service. The legislative salary of forty-eight hundred dollars per year was hardly a princely sum even in 1969.

There was very little staff for legislators at that time because the general consensus was that it wasn't necessary. We had four or five ladies in the steno pool for our caucus of fifty legislators during the session and they got the job done. When a constituent called their representative, they talked directly to the representative. They were not screened by an "aide" because there were none.

Our desks off the House floor were for the most part in a wide open unpartitioned room. We were able to communicate easily with our colleagues. With annual sessions came vastly increased staffing, private offices, more career "professional" lawmakers, plus increased salaries to reflect the "full-time" nature of the job.

Five members of the 1969 House of Representatives went on to serve in the United States Congress. They were Bill Frenzel, Richard Nolan, Arlan Stangeland, Martin Sabo (still there) and Arlen Erdahl.

I was favorably impressed by the people that I served with in the Legislature. For the most part, they were dedicated public servants by whom I believe the citizens of the state were well-served. Were there any legislators who tried to take advantage of their position of trust? There may have been a few. But they were very few in number; had no influence whatever with their colleagues and were quickly voted out of office.

There were some striking differences between the way the Minnesota House of Representatives was operated and the manner in which the United States House of Representatives operates. If you watch the U.S. House on CNN, you will notice that only on rare occasions are a large majority of the members actually in the House chamber when bills are being debated. Also, many times a member may be virtually alone and speaking for the record to a nearly deserted chamber.

The daily sessions of the Minnesota House always found nearly all the members in the chamber. If you could not be there you were required to obtain an excuse from the speaker. I recall an occasion when Congressman Clark McGregor addressed the Minnesota House and he commented on the vast difference in the member attendance at sessions between the U.S. and the Minnesota houses. He lamented the fact that the difference existed, citing reasons why he thought our system was better.

I managed to stay politically active after the Legislature adjourned in 1969. It wasn't long before political fund raising dinners were scheduled, and Ruth and I attended a few. Potential presidential candidates were already testing the waters, and I had an opportunity on separate occasions to meet Senator Fred Harris of Oklahoma and Senator Harold Hughes of Iowa. Senator Edmund Muskie also came to Minneapolis for an event, and I had an opportunity to visit with him and renew our acquaintance.

In April of 1970 I was asked to introduce Senator George McGovern, who was the featured speaker at our Anoka County Statesmen's Dinner. Ruth and I sat at the head table with the senator. I asked him what he would like me to highlight in the introduction and was surprised that he wanted particular attention called to his military service during World War II. McGovern went on to become the Democratic nominee for president in 1972.

I had occasion to meet him again. He was featured at a large dinner on the second floor at Jax. By this time he was being covered by all the United States news services plus the British, French and many others. When he rose to speak and all the media plugged in, our electrical service was blown out. McGovern spoke by candlelight and without amplification. Naturally, Bill and I felt terrible about the failure of the electricity, but McGovern seemed non-plussed. He later sent a kind letter actually joking about the incident.

On the statewide scene potential candidates for governor began stirring. The front-runners appeared to be state senators Nick Coleman, Wendell Anderson, and attorney David Graven. A meeting of legislators from North and Northeast Minneapolis and environs was held to discuss whom we should support as the D.F.L. candidate for governor. I listened intently to my colleagues and it became apparent that they favored Nick Coleman. Coleman was a fascinating character. He was the minority leader in the state Senate. He had a warm engaging personality, was razor sharp on the issues, and possessed a wit that he could use to charm a friend or totally disarm an adversary. I agreed to support Coleman at the state D.F.L. convention but I told my colleagues that I believed Wendell Anderson was more electable. Anderson had served in both the House and Senate. He was a former U.S. Olympic hockey star and the name Anderson is magic in Minnesota.

At this time I was also considering my own political future. Both Wendell Anderson and Nick Coleman wanted me to run for the state Senate and both offered to help me. U.S. Senator Walter Mondale also urged me to run for the state Senate. One day Columbia Heights Mayor Bruce Nawrocki and I went to a meeting together at the Nicollet Hotel and we ran into Mondale. Once again Mondale urged me to run for the Senate. I told him that Bruce was interested in the senate and Mondale said to us, "Jack, you run for the senate and Bruce you run for the House and you guys will broom in."

Some days later a meeting was held at Chuck Lefebvre's house where everyone that would have an interest in running for the Senate was invited. Former senator Vern Hoium said that he would be willing to run. Bruce

Nawrocki indicated his interest in the Senate and his dis-interest in running for the House. I indicated my willing-ness to run and by the time the meeting was over I felt that I had the support of everyone there.

When the meeting was over I returned to Jax and told brother Bill the result of the meeting. I could tell by his reaction that he wasn't too pleased at the prospect of my involvement in another long campaign, plus the possi-bility of me serving at least four years in the state Senate.

The next few days I did a lot of soul searching. I felt that Bill and I had a good partnership and I wanted it to continue. Our business at Jax was doing well and it was important that it continue to do well. Ruth and I had six young children . . . Bill's family was growing . . . and our widowed mother depended on the rent from the Jax property for her income. I was enjoying my fling in the political arena but I came to realize that I could not risk politics becoming more important than my responsibility to adequately provide for my family. I felt that I had to make a choice between a legislative career that would surely become more demanding and a restaurant career which was my best hope of continuing to provide a com-fortable living for my family.

I decided that I would finish my term as a state rep-resentative but I would not run for office again. I informed my family of my decision and really never looked back on it with any great regret.

I was a delegate to the state D.F.L. convention in Duluth that year and supported Nick Coleman's bid for the gubernatorial endorsement. At first it looked like a close race between Coleman and Wendell Anderson, but as each ballot was taken Anderson gained more votes. I stuck with Coleman until he decided to throw in the towel in favor of Anderson.

Once Anderson was nominated I did what I could to help him in his campaign. One day I received a call from Stan Wasie. He asked if I could set up a meeting for him with Anderson. They met for lunch at Jax, sat and visited all afternoon. Mr. Wasie really liked Wendy Anderson. He not only contributed generously to his campaign; he included Wendy and Mary Anderson in many of the social gathcrings that he and Mrs. Wasie hosted. Both Wasie and Anderson enjoyed golf, and I was fortunate to be included in various golf outings with them.

One of the things I wanted to do when I decided not to run for office was to help find a well qualified person to succeed me. Before I made any public announcement of my decision not to run I called on my friend Spencer Sokolowski. "Spike", as he was affectionately known, was practicing law in Columbia Heights. I stopped in at his office and informed him that I would not be running for re-election and asked him to consider running for the House. At first he acted a bit reluctant but I assured him that he would have plenty of help from the folks that worked in my campaign. I also explained what a gratifying experience it had been for me and finished by telling him that if he ran he would "never be sorry." Spike made the race and defeated the same person (Jack Meyer) that I had defeated two years earlier.

Wendell Anderson was elected governor and Hubert Humphrey was returned to the U.S. Senate in that election. Shortly thereafter, my brief legislative career came to an end.

PART

THIRTEEN

The Metropolitan Council

In November 1970 Wendell Anderson was elected governor of Minnesota. He took office in early January of 1971. Later that month he called me.

The governor said he wanted me to serve on the Metropolitan Council and asked if I would accept his appointment.

The opportunity to serve on the Metropolitan Council was considered a signal honor . . . however, one to which I neither aspired nor sought. The council was created in 1967 for the purpose of coordinating the planning and development of the seven-county Metropolitan area. The council consisted of fifteen members appointed by the governor. Governor Anderson had five seats to fill as he assumed office, and one of them was from the area in which I resided.

There were over one-hundred twenty municipalities in the metropolitan area in 1971 and the population was in excess of one-million eight-hundred thousand.

Council members included some of the most distinguished business, professional and political personalities in Minnesota. Council members Donald Dayton, George Pennock, Peter Gillette, Joseph Maun, Bob Hoffman, Jim Dorr and others were recognized nationally as leaders in their businesses and professions.

The council offcrcd an opportunity to be involved in community service without taking nearly as much time as

201

the Legislature. It seemed it would fit comfortably with my duties and obligations at the restaurant. When I accepted the governor's offer to serve, he said, "Please do not tell anyone that I am going to appoint you because I want to announce all five of my Metropolitan Council appointments at the same time." I assured him that I would keep mum on the subject.

Part of the appointment process that governors must adhere to is a stipulation that they consult with legislators from the council district before announcing an appointment. It seems the purpose of this is to show courtesy to the legislators and also to make sure the legislators have no serious objections to the governor's choice.

Some people who wanted to be appointed to the council began lobbying the legislators to intercede with the governor on their behalf. I didn't think too much of it until I received a call from my friend Bruce Nawrocki, the mayor of Columbia Heights. He informed me that he wanted the appointment . . . that he had spoken to several legislators soliciting their support . . . and asked me if I would call Tom Kelm, the governor's administrative assistant, and put in a good word for him.

What a predicament! I couldn't tell Nawrocki that I had been offered the appointment, so all I could do was agree to call Kelm.

When I reached Kelm I explained that I had promised Bruce Nawrocki that I would call to put in a plug for his appointment. I was fulfilling my promise to Nawrocki. Kelm knew that I was to be appointed so I think he got a chuckle out of the charade.

In the days that followed Nawrocki put a full court press on the legislators and even the local newspapers began mentioning Nawrocki as the likely appointee. At this point I called Governor Anderson and told him that I knew he was being pressured to appoint Nawrocki. If he wanted to change his mind and appoint Nawrocki it was O.K. with me. The governor said, "I want you in that position . . . If I had wanted anyone else I would have asked them."

Shortly thereafter the governor met with the district's legislators and informed them of his desire to appoint me. I was told later that this came as a surprise to nearly everyone there. Most of the legislators were people I had served with, and they concurred with the governor's decision.

Becoming a member of the Metropolitan Council was

very gratifying to me. Aside from an opportunity to serve with the people I mentioned previously, the new members that were appointed with me were outstanding individuals. Albert Hofstede, the bright young former mayor of Minneapolis, was appointed chairman and we were friends of long standing. Other appointees were Stanley Kegler, a vice president at the University of Minnesota, attorneys David Graven and Robert Hoffman and community activist Sam Reed.

Early on I noticed that an occasional legislator (usually one looking for some exposure from the press) would come to our meetings and after being introduced would rail at us as to why we should be elected instead of appointed. I believed that the council should be elected too, but it wasn't in the power of the council to make the change. These diatribes got to be downright annoying, so I suggested to my colleagues that we pass a resolution favoring an elected council. In that way we could get rid of the grandstanders from Capitol Hill by in effect saying, "We agree with you; now go and change the law." The resolution passed easily, and for as long as I was there we were not subjected to that type harangue again. At this writing the council is still appointive.

Perhaps the hottest and most controversial issue to come before the Metropolitan Council during my tenure was that of selecting a potential site, if a new major airport was to be built. The issue seemed to boil down to whether a new airport, if built, should go south into Dakota County or north to Anoka County.

It was imperative that the Metropolitan Airports Commission (MAC) and the Metropolitan Council (MC) work together on this issue because of the charge given these agencies by the Legislature. The MAC was created in 1943 to promote the public interest in air transportation; to increase air commerce and to develop the full potentialities of the metropolitan areas as aviation centers. The Metropolitan Council (created in 1967) responsibilities are in the areas of metropolitan planning, coordination of local and special units of government and in research and study.

MAC and MC seemed to be having problems on how to address the issue of a potential new airport location. Lawrence Hall, a former legislator and former speaker of the Minnesota House of Representatives, was chairman of the MAC. He was from St. Cloud, Minnesota, and an appointee of the governor. Hall was a very savvy person.

He served in the house of representatives with my father in the 1930s and early 1940s. He was a successful lawyer who understood fully the workings of government. He represented the wholesale liquor dealers very ably as a lobbyist at the Minnesota legislature.

I saw him occasionally at the Capitol during my tenure as a legislator and had a few opportunities to visit with him briefly.

One day Hall was at our Metropolitan Council office and we got on the subject of a new airport site. I asked him if he ever thought of a joint committee of MAC and MC members to study the issue and come up with a recommendation. He said he thought the idea might work, but he didn't really know Chairman Al Hofstede and he was a bit apprehensive about whom Hofstede might appoint to such a committee from the MC. I assured him that Al Hofstede was one of the most forthright individuals anyone could ever hope to know.

Not long thereafter Hofstede and Hall announced the formation of the Metropolitan Council/Metropolitan Airports Commission Committee that would work jointly to study and ultimately recommend whether a new major airport, when built, should be located north or south of the core cities. I was one of the MC members placed on the committee.

The process that the MC and MAC committee went through was very interesting, and we heard from air traffic experts . . . soils experts . . . citizens groups (both advocates and opponents of specific locations). We heard testimony from representatives of various airlines, trucking interests, mayors, state legislators, congressmen plus business and labor interests. The proposed location of a new major airport was a hot issue.

It was interesting to see how some peoples' pre-conceived notions of where the site should be were changed as the process progressed. I recall one meeting we had scheduled at a school in Farmington, a town that would have been affected by a southern site selection. I arrived early, and as I was walking in, my colleague Donald Dayton joined me. He said, "I always thought I favored a south location, but this is too far south."

Advocates of a northern site argued that the marginal soil in Anoka County made more sense for an airport than did the rich farmland in Dakota County. Business interests both north and south argued for their side.

I favored a northern site for many reasons not the least of which was my belief that the development to the south of the core cities was badly outpacing that to the north. Also I could not understand why public policy should condone and even encourage the commercial development of prime farm acreage when abundant alternative land was available.

I believe Councilman Stanley Kegler also came to the conclusion early on that the site selection should go north. His brilliant questioning of the experts giving testimony laid bare many myths that had previously placed the northern area in a bad light.

Congressman John Blatnik, whose district ran from the Canadian border all the way down into Anoka County, was extremely interested in the site selection process. He wanted the site to be in his district and he made no bones about it. He called me many times to monitor the process, as did his administrative assistant Jim Oberstar. Blatnik was a twenty-eight year veteran in the Congress, and was then chairman of the roads and bridges committee.

One day he called for an update, and after I filled him in on the situation, he said, "You and Stan Kegler make a great team and do a fine job . . . but if that airport goes south it will be the only major airport in the United States with dirt roads."

As the day of the vote on the issue approached, the heat was turned up. Stan Kegler, who was also a University of Minnesota vice president, told how he was approached by Donald Nyrop, who was then the head of Northwest Airlines. Nyrop favored a southern site and everyone was aware of that.

Kegler was in his office and the phone rang. He picked it up and said, "Kegler." A young lady said, "Would you hold the line for a minute for Donald Nyrop?" Kegler said, "yes." He then looked at his watch, waited for one whole minute and because no one came on the line he hung up. A few minutes later the phone rang again and the same young lady said, "We must have been cut off. Would you hold again for Mr. Nyrop?" Kegler said. "We were not cut off. You asked me to wait for a minute and I did. Now if Mr. Nyrop wishes to speak with me tell him to pick up the phone and dial my number and I will be here. It's simple." With that Kegler hung up once more. Shortly the phone rang again. Kegler answered,"Kegler." The voice on the other end said, "This is Don Nyrop and I get the feeling you are a miserable so and so." Kegler and Nyrop both laughed at their rather bizarre meeting.

Nyrop then asked Kegler to join him for lunch sometime before the vote was taken. Kegler declined, saying, "If I were to have lunch with everyone who wanted to have lunch with me before the vote . . . I would be doing nothing but having lunch."

On the day the vote was to be taken, the council chamber was charged with excitement. I don't think anyone knew for sure which way the vote would go. Chairman Hofstede gave a final summation of the issue and then called the roll. The vote was nine to five in favor of a northern site. Hofstede who was not obligated to do so then asked to be recorded in favor of the northern site. The final vote became ten-to-five in favor of the north.

I was surprised by the margin of the vote and also pleased to see that among others Donald Dayton, a person for whom I had the utmost respect and admiration, voted for the north.

Twenty plus years have gone by since the day that vote was taken. There is no new major airport in the Minneapolis/St. Paul metro area. The population projection of four million people by the year 2000 that we were fed will not be met. At this writing the metro area population hovers around two million two-hundred thousand. The "old" airport continues to suffice and will probably do so for many years to come.

The issue of a new major airport continues to provide employment for countless airport experts, urban planners and assorted bureaucrats. The subject continues to surface for more debate and study. I don't know of any one of the people that participated in the work that was conducted in the 1970s being called upon to help enlighten the class of the 1990s. This is not meant as an indictment of the system, but merely an observation from which you may draw your own conclusions.

* * *

The question of a new or major renovation of an existing sports facility for the metro area was bandied about for many years. The issue seemed to be in limbo when I asked Chairman Hofstede if he would appoint a committee to look into the situation. Hofstede selected the committee and named me the chairman.

The committee held hearings where we listened to representatives from the University of Minnesota, Minnesota Twins, Minnesota Vikings and various interested citizens. Early on I had a meeting with Max Winter, who was then the head of the Minnesota Vikings organization.

Among other things, we discussed the possibility of the Vikings playing at a renovated Memorial Stadium. Winter seemed receptive to the idea. When I asked him about the handling of concessions, he said that his only concern was that they be professionally managed. Winter knew that Memorial Stadium could accommodate several thousand more people than their "home" at Metropolitan Stadium. Memorial Stadium was also designed for football, so it provided much better site lines for football than did the Met, which was primarily a baseball facility.

The University of Minnesota began a study on the feasibility of remodeling Memorial Stadium. Our committee visited Kansas City and New Orleans to gather information on how they structured the building of their new sports facilities.

Kansas City had recently built a stadium for its baseball team plus a stadium for its football team. The stadiums were beautiful and the projects were accomplished through responsible leadership from a broad range of the community. Both major league baseball and football were prospering.

In New Orleans we saw the Super Dome as it was being built. It was gigantic . . . built to seat eighty-thousand fans. We met with Mayor Moon Landreau to get his insights on the Super Dome. He took us on a tour of the project. I climbed to the top row of the structure. The seats had not yet been installed. From that vantage point big semi-tractor trailers on the floor of the building looked like toys. We went back to Mayor Landreau's office, where he answered our questions. I asked him why they decided to build such a huge facility. He explained, "You have to understand Louisiana politics." He told us how the project started as a city/parish (county) project. Then the state became involved because the governor wanted it big enough for "all the people."

At this point they had no tenant for any major league team, and the debt service on the structure was approaching thirty-thousand dollars per day. When Landreau was asked about this he said, "Well, we think the second deck at the Tulane University may be unsafe so our inspectors will check it out." Someone asked, "And if it's safe?" Landreau winked, smiled and said. "I guess we'll have to blow the damned thing up."

Moon Landreau was a fascinating character and, in the context of Louisiana politics, a successful mover and shaker. He later became the head of the federal department of Housing and Urban Development.

The results of the engineering study at Memorial Stadium at the U. of M. were disappointing. The old "brickyard" was at the point where it would not have been prudent to try to update it. The possibility of building a new stadium at the university that could be shared by professional teams was virtually out of the question, at the time. Money constraints, as well as Big Ten Conference rules, prohibited such arrangements.

In retrospect, I think our committee made a contribution because our hearings became part of the public record, and we succeeded in bringing the issue back into the limelight.The final result was that business interests and political leaders eventually came together to set the stage for the construction of the H.H.H. Metrodome in downtown Minneapolis.

* * *

The Metropolitan Council was an interesting experience, but it did not hold the same fascination for me as did the Legislature and the legislative process. What I enjoyed most was the opportunity to work with people like George Pennock, Donald Dayton, Mike Borgelt, Stan Kegler, Dave Graven, Pete Gillette and all my other colleagues. Many of the councilpersons at that time were executives from big corporations or big institutions. As a small businessperson I was in the habit of doing virtually everything possible in our business by myself or with my partner. By example, my colleagues at the council showed me how to make better use of staff and how to delegate responsibility. I believe these lessons helped me throughout my business career.

I served about four years on the Metropolitan Council. I decided to resign so that I could concentrate fully on my duties at the restaurant. Ruth and I had four children in college at this time, and our financial obligations were significant, to say the least. I enjoyed my years of public service, but I really had my fill of the process and thought it was time to move on.

PART
FOURTEEN

The Minnesota
Restaurant Association

Shortly after I resigned from the Metropolitan Council, I received a call from Bjarne Amundsen. Bjarne was in the process of "going through the chairs" at the Minnesota Restaurant Association and he asked me to become a member of the board of directors. I wasn't really very interested, but Bjarne was persistent and above all a great salesman for the association. He convinced me to attend a meeting of the board, and it wasn't long before I became an involved board member.

Soon after an issue involving the restaurant industry came up at the Legislature. I was asked to make a presentation for our position before the House labor committee. I made my presentation and actually surprised myself at how well it was received. Carl Nide, a labor leader from St. Paul, complimented me on my testimony. This was gratifying to me because we were on opposing sides of the issue and my position prevailed.

After the committee meeting I walked over to the Senate side and went on to the Senate floor. As a former legislator I was entitled to this privilege. Senator Nick Coleman, the Senate minority leader, spotted me and motioned me to come to his desk. He knew that I was interested in the affairs of the hospitality industry and he said, "Jack, I think you should know that your industry is not being very well-represented over here."

It was 1975 and at that time the executive director of the restaurant, hotel, and resort associations tried to handle the lobbying duties at the Legislature in addition to all the other duties that his job entailed. The Legislature was now meeting annually and the flood of legislation made it seem imperative to me that our associations hire a professional to monitor pending legislation and to lobby for our interests.

I brought this up at our next board meeting and our restaurant board suggested that we set up a small committee to meet with a similar group from the hotel and resort boards.

We met at the old Nicollet Hotel and, as a representative from the restaurant association and a former legislator, I pointed out the importance of having a professional specialist to handle our affairs at the state Capitol. I cited Senator Coleman's remark that we were not being very well-represented and in the light of some setbacks our industry had suffered in recent years, the committee was receptive to change.

They asked me if there was anyone whom I could recommend for the job. I pointed out that in my judgment it should be a former legislator . . . one who recently retired from the Legislature voluntarily, and one who was respected on both sides of the aisle. There were three or four whom I thought could do a good job and would probably be interested, but my first choice was former representative Tom Newcome.

The reason I favored Newcome was that I served with him in the Legislature and was impressed by his sense of fairness. He practiced law in St. Paul but he seemed to retain a small-town folksy demeanor that would set well with many out-state lawmakers. Finally, I recalled how he stood up against the majority of his own caucus in defending a report of his elections committee. At issue was calling for special elections for campaign improprieties involving two legislative races. One involved a liberal (Democrat); the other a conservative (Republican). Newcome and his committee submitted a report and recommendation to the House that both races should be re-run. What followed was an exercise in raw political power by leaders of the conservative majority of which Newcome was a member. The leadership of the conservatives succeeded in separating the two races and forced the Democrats to run a special election while exonerating the conservative. It was not one of the conservative majority's finest hours. They embarrassed Newcome (one of their own) to gain a dubious advantage. To his credit and testimony to his character, Newcome stood steadfast to his position against his caucus colleagues.

Our association hired Newcome as our lobbyist in 1976, and he has represented us for nearly twenty years as of this writing. I have often thought as government becomes more complex and more intrusive that our association would be even better served by having two lobbyists. Ideally, I would like one man and one woman – both former legislators and one from each political party. Recently, the associations hired a legislative specialist to work with Newcome. The results have been most positive.

Bjarne Amundsen became president of the Minnesota Restaurant Association in 1977 and held the job for a record three years. Bjarne and his son operated two Norsemen restaurants . . . one in Cokato and another in St. Bonifacius, Minnesota. The situation with the restaurant association during Bjarne's tenure required hands-on supervision by the president and Bjarne provided it.

The biggest revenue source for the restaurant, hotel, and resort associations was the annual Upper Midwest Hospitality or U.P.S. show that was sponsored jointly by the three associations. The show was held annually at the Minneapolis Auditorium and suppliers to the industry purchased space at the show to display their wares. When Bjarne became president there was danger of the associations and the U.P.S. show splitting apart, but Bjarne was able to keep the three groups together and created a foundation that allowed the associations and the show to grow and prosper.

During his tenure as president it became necessary to hire a new executive director for the associations and Bjarne took the lead in finding the right person for the job. After a lengthy search, he recommended Arnold Hewes.

Hewes came from Milwaukee, where he was executive director of the Metropolitan Milwaukee Association of Commerce.

It wasn't long before the associations took on a more progressive and more professional aura. Hewes recommended a full-time well-compensated staffer to sell memberships. The board agreed and memberships began to climb. The associations began to offer more seminars and enhanced communications. There were more and more reasons for businesses to join their association. Hewes also showed great skill in public relations and in his ability to deal with the media.

It was a gratifying and exciting time for me to be on the board. In 1979 I began the process of going through the chairs and in 1982 I began serving the first of two terms as president of the Minnesota Restaurant Association.

By the time I became president, the association had become a smooth running entity. This was due to the fine work performed by my predecessors, Bjarne Amundsen, Denny Hanson, and Margaret Cambray, together with executive director Arnold Hewes and his staff. It was actually a joy to conduct the meetings. The agenda was set, printed and timed. Hewes and his staff always had everything organized so that the meetings could proceed on schedule and be concluded in a timely manner. Our association had some fine accomplishments during my tenure as president. In 1982 the U.P.S. show had four-hundred forty-eight booths and twelve-thousand registered attendees.

Walter Conti was president of the National Restaurant Association and he came to Minneapolis for the show. He spoke at one of our seminars and was interviewed on our dominant radio station, WCCO, by Howard Viken. Conti also received good press in the Minneapolis and St. Paul daily papers, thus adding stature to our show and associations.

We also printed and distributed fifty-thousand copies of a restaurant dining guide. Our membership development and retention soared under the direction of chairman Don Hernke. We were able to increase the state tourism budget by 6.2 million dollars annually . . . our lobbyist (I prefer to call him our information officer) helped immeasurably to bring this about.

We did take a licking on one issue when the law was changed to require employers to become responsible for tip reporting. More paperwork . . . more government intrusion. Our association did one of the finest jobs in the nation of informing our members about the new tip reporting law and developed materials on the subject for our members that received national acclaim.

The year 1983 was a banner one. The U.P.S. show increased by one-hundred booths and now occupied both floors of the Minneapolis Auditorium and became one of the largest regional shows of its kind in America. The association offered still more seminars. The dining guide became available with twenty-five thousand copies in January and soon there was demand for twenty-five thousand more. In November the association marked its fiftieth anniversary with a gala celebration. Joe Lee, president of the National Restaurant Association, and president of General Mills restaurant group, attended and gave an address.

Among the many accomplishments while I was active on the Minnesota Restaurant Board, was the job that our association performed in developing alcohol awareness seminars. It deserves special mention. These seminars educated people in the industry on what their special responsibilities were in the service of beverage alcohol. It taught servers how to recognize a person who was over-indulging . . . how to dissuade someone from drinking too much . . . presented charts to show what level of consumption was within a safe limit for people. In short, it was a study in the responsible service of beverage alcohol. The seminars were well-received and well-attended and several local governmental units even offered reduction in liquor licensing fees for operators who sent their employees to the seminars.

I kept active in the Minnesota Restaurant Association until Ruth and I became Florida residents in 1986. Our son-in-law, Mark Satt, has served as a member of the board of directors of the Minnesota Restaurant Association for eight years. At age 40, Mark was named the association president over the largest part of an association that has grown to be the largest trade organization in Minnesota, with upwards of three-thousand members.

Editor's Note:
In October, 1993, Jack Kozlak was honored as an inductee to the "Midwest Hall of Fame" during the Midwest Food and Beverage Expo in St. Paul. He was one of five in the food and beverage industry singled out for fifty or more years of distinguished service in the hospitality industry. Others inducted were Arthur Palmer of the Lowell Inn, Stillwater, Minnesota; Clayton Montepetit, Griggs Cooper & Co., wholesale beverage distributor; John Rauchnot, Rustic Hut, Hudson, Wisconsin and Jeanne Hall of the Anderson House, Wabasha, Minnesota.

PART
FIFTEEN

The National
Restaurant Association

In late 1979 it was announced that Marcel Frederick, our representative on the board of directors of the National Restaurant Association, was about to complete nine years of service as a board member and according to the bylaws would not be eligible for re-election. I thought that Bjarne Amundsen would be the logical choice to succeed Frederick. Bjarne had worked longer and harder than anyone else for our state association and it seemed only fitting that he should be honored with a directorship on the National Restaurant Association board. I didn't give it another thought until Bjarne came to me one day and asked if I would like to be recommended for election to the N.R.A. board. I couldn't believe it and told him so. Bjarne explained that for personal reasons he did not choose to serve on the national board but would support me for the job if I wanted it.

At the time Bjarne was still working hard as president of the Minnesota Restaurant Association and was deeply involved in promoting the U.P.S. show. He also had some problems with his heart and thus decided he had enough to do without taking on another job.

I discussed the possibility of serving on the N.R.A. board with Ruth and my partners (daughter Diane and Mark Satt) and all were very supportive. With the blessing of Bjarne Amundsen, our Minnesota Association board voted to nominate me as their candidate to the N.R.A. board at the election to be held in May of 1980. I was interviewed by the N.R.A. screening committee and was subsequently elected to my first three-year term at the N.R.A. convention held at McCormick Place in Chicago in May of 1980.

The National Restaurant Association Board is very large. There are nearly sixty directors on the board, plus two international exchange directors each from Mexico, Japan, and Canada. There are twenty-plus past presidents who may attend the three board meetings each year. There are also seventy-plus honorary directors who are eligible to attend the meetings. Usually about fifteen to twenty-five honorary members will be in attendance at each meeting.

The opportunity to serve on the N.R.A. board was for me a great honor. It gave me the opportunity to meet and work with many of the national leaders of the restaurant industry. Ruth and I got to know legends such as Jerry Berns from New York's Club 21, Anthony Athanas of Boston's Pier IV, Dave Cowart of Morrison's, Pat O'Malley of Canteen Corporation and Chicago's leading booster . . . and their spouses. We also made friends with many of the nation's independent operators, such as the Millers from Gatlinburg, the Impeciatos from Atlanta, the Kawas from Omaha, the Balestreris from Monterey and many, many more.

The board of directors meets three times each year. Meetings are held in May, September, and January. The May meeting is always held in Chicago in conjunction with the huge National Restaurant Association trade show at McCormick Place. The September meeting is held in the nation's Capitol and dovetails with an N.R.A. sponsored public affairs conference. This gives the board members, as well as rank and file members of the association, an opportunity to visit with their representatives of the House and Senate in the elected official's office; or at an association sponsored reception honoring the legislators, or both. The January meeting is almost always held in a warm part of the continental United States.

When I first came on the board, only the May meeting was held in the same city (Chicago) every year. The other meetings were held at various places throughout the country and always at first-rate hotels or resorts. We met at the St. Francis Hotel in San Francisco; the Boca

Raton Hotel and Club in Florida; the Homestead in West Virginia; the Hershey Hotel in Hershey, Pennsylvania, and the Hyatt Hotel on Maui to mention just a few. The accommodations were always superb and the meetings plus the social aspects of the gatherings helped develop a true esprit de corps among the board family. Each board member paid for transportation and lodging for themselves and their spouses. The association picked up the tab for two or three receptions or dinners during the course of the meetings. Ruth and I budgeted roughly six-thousand dollars a year to cover our costs in conjunction with the board activities.

In 1979 the association moved its national headquarters from Chicago to Washington, D.C. Shortly thereafter they purchased a building near the nation's Capitol where operations are now conducted. The shift to the nation's Capitol underscores how important it is for an industry such as the restaurant industry to be in constant touch with the workings of the federal government. It seems to be a constant struggle to keep abreast of the machinations of overzealous bureaucrats, regulators and politicians. One of the more valuable services provided by the N.R.A. for its members is the job performed by its government relations staff. These folks are in touch with the activities on Capitol hill relevant to our industry. They work diligently at the direction of the board to diffuse harmful legislation and conversely to advance legislation that is beneficial to the survival or promotion of our businesses.

Some of the issues that the board dealt with during my tenure, in addition to a myriad of other proposed government regulations were: tip reporting; the business marketing meal deduction (referred to by our adversaries as the three-martini luncheon); targeted job tax credit; entry level wage legislation (minimum wage); and legislation vis-à-vis the federal government and the various state governments.

Every board member is a member of the government relations committee and this bodes well for a free flow of ideas and information on a nationwide scale.

It is also the business of the National Restaurant Association to provide services to its members that will render them more professional, competitive and profitable restaurateurs. Through the years a tremendous resource

216

center has been developed with publications for everything from employer/employee relations to recipes . . . customer relations . . . promotional ideas . . . proper food handling . . . sanitation . . . proper service and numerous other topics and subjects.

I was named to a task force to develop an industry-wide alcohol awareness program. We worked for several months with the staff and came up with a comprehensive set of visual and printed aids to help both servers and management provide responsible service of beverage alcohol. Part of the program was designed to show the consumer how to know their limits as well as educating the server to recognize signs of overindulgence and how to deal with the problem. This program was distributed throughout the country and has been a resounding success.

In 1983 president Joe Lee named me an exchange director to the Canadian Restaurant and Food Services Association. This was considered a real plum and I was surprised and honored to be so favored. The C.R.F.A. met three times a year. The April meeting was in Toronto in conjunction with their Host Ex trade show; the January meeting was held in Ottawa, the nation's Capitol, and the autumn meeting moved from place to place. I was an exchange director for two years and at the completion of my term Ruth and I were invited to an extra meeting by the Canadians, where they presented me with a momento/award.

The Canadian board was much smaller than our board so it was easy to get acquainted. Ruth and I made many friends and thoroughly enjoyed all our meetings with the Canadians. The meetings were held at deluxe hotels and the social gatherings that followed were always superb, although in most instances more casual than those of the N.R.A. Toronto and Ottawa are beautiful cities that we had an opportunity to explore and on other occasions we visited Calgary, Lake Louise, Banff and Winnipeg.

Our last meeting as a C.R.F.A. director was at the venerable Algonquin at St. John, New Brunswick. On the last night of our meeting our hosts had a farewell party at the seashore where we enjoyed steamed live lobsters, good music and stimulating conversation. It was a memorable ending to a most pleasant episode in our lives.

The C.R.F.A. meetings strongly resembled those of the N.R.A. Their dealings and problems with their government were much like our own, although it seemed that their government was even more intrusive than ours. The tax structure that they had to live with was burdensome in the eighties, and I understand that it is considerably more so at this writing.

At the time of my stint on the C.R.F.A. board it seemed to me that the Canadians were doing a much better job of gaining members than was the N.R.A. Their executive director, Doug Needham, and their membership director had developed policies and incentives that were getting outstanding results. I relayed what I learned to our own membership director. This is one of the ways in which our exchange system was beneficial.

The thought often occurred to me during our meetings that as we discussed our mutual problems, particularly concerning our respective governments, that their bureaucrats and our bureaucrats were probably meeting somewhere trying to figure out how to further regulate our industry or how to extract more revenue from us. It never seemed to get any easier.

Chicago, 1983: National Restaurant Association President John Dankos presents Jack a commemorative plate to mark his second term as president of the Minnesota Restaurant Association. Ruth received a rose.

219

*Canadian Restaurant and Foodservices Association circa 1984.
(L to R) Peter Golf, Jack, member of Parliament Bill Gottselig,
M.P. George Minaker.*

*United States Senator Howard Baker and Jack circa 1984 at a
National Restaurant Association Board of Directors meeting.*

PART SIXTEEN

Hennessy Traveler

In early 1985 I was offered the opportunity to represent the National Restaurant Association as a Hennessy Traveler. The Hennessy Air Force Award program grew out of one of the recommendations of the Hoover Commission, which was established by President Eisenhower. One of the task groups was charged with making improvements to troop feeding programs. Among other recommendations the task group suggested that services initiate a competition among food service operations that would identify and reward the best ones. The Air Force was the first to implement the recommendation and establish a program that became known as the Hennessy Award Program.

The program was named in honor of John Hennessy, who was a member of the task group. Hennessy was one of America's most capable and respected hotel and restaurant executives. He began his career as a hotel freight elevator operator and worked his way up to become vice president of Hilton . . . then the largest hotel corporation in the world. During World War II President Roosevelt appointed Hennessy chairman of the War Food Committee, where he developed food service systems capable of sustaining millions of military personnel involved in the war effort.

The Hennessy Trophy competition began in 1957 and over the years has become a highly sought after, prestigious award. The primary civilian sponsoring association for the competition is the National Restaurant Association together with support from the Society of Food Service Managers Association and the Food Service Executives Association.

*"The John L. Hennessy trophy is an annual
award presented to the Air Force installation, in
the single and multiple facility categories, having
the best food service program in the United
States Air Force. The award is based on the
entire scope of an installation's food service program, exhibiting excellence in management effec-
tiveness, force readiness support, food quality,
employee and customer relations, resource conservation, training, and safety awareness.*

*"The Hennessy Trophy Awards Program
was established to:*

- *"Promote excellence in customer service
  and meal quality throughout Air Force food
  service by recognizing outstanding dining
  facility operations and management.*

- *"Inspire high morale, motivation, mission
  support, and a professional image through
  pride and spirited competition.*

*"The annual Hennessy Trophy Awards Pro-
gram reflects the dedication, pride, and fellowship of the civilian food service industry and the
Air Force in improving the Air Force way of life.
The Hennessy program also allows the sharing of
valuable information between the travelers, who
are recognized leaders in the civilian food service
industry, and base-level food service personnel.
Achieving success in the Hennessy competition is
the reflection of pride, commitment, and motivation to be the best. The tools of success include
superior customer service, astute management,
command support of food service operations, and
the attitude on behalf of the base to excel and
become a winner."*

My involvement as a Hennessy Traveler began with
an orientation session in Washington, D.C. The orientation was an all-day affair at Andrews Air Force Base. We
met with Colonel Pickering and his staff where our duties
and our mission was outlined. We met our travel com-
panions also. Our team coordinator representing the Air
Force was Captain Michael Filan. The representative

from the Foodservice Managers Association was Mrs. Deanna Hormel. She was then manager of food service operations for the Hallmark Company in Kansas City, Missouri.

Following our orientation session we had an opportunity to visit Air Force One which was at Andrews. We met the crew that handled the food service on the plane and were presented with some souvenirs such as coasters, cocktail napkins and pictures. That evening we were treated to a fine dinner with our Air Force hosts where we further discussed our pending trip. The next morning we returned to our respective homes. Our team of Hormel, Filan and Kozlak would not meet again until we were met at the airport in Austin, Texas by our hosts from Bergstrom Air Base. It was there that our job as evaluators began. The trip lasted thirty-nine days and we traveled in the neighborhood of fifty-five thousand miles.

It should be pointed out here that as evaluators Deanna Hormel and I were given the equivalent rank of brigadier general. At every base we were treated with the utmost courtesy and given V.I.P. accommodations.

Our team was driven from the airport at Austin to Bergstrom Air Base where we were then escorted to our quarters. All three of us were given beautiful suites complete with living room, dinette, bedroom and kitchen. There was a car for each of us at our door. This proved to be totally unnecessary because we were escorted wherever we had to go. On our first night in Texas we were honored at a dinner reception at one of Austin's finest clubs by the chamber of commerce. We were given the red carpet treatment and presented with plaques making us honorary citizens of Austin.

The next morning we began our evaluation at Bergstrom. Captain Filan, Deanna Hormel and I each kept notes on what we saw and what we ate. We monitored all three meals in the cafeteria as well as checked record-keeping procedures, sanitation in the kitchen and servers' efficiency. We also did evaluations of the flight kitchen at midnight. Each evening when our work was completed Filan, Hormel and I would compare notes and score the facility on the 1038 form that was provided. The procedure was similar at each base.

At each base there was a briefing by the commanding

officer that gave us insights into the base mission, and this was always of great interest. Also, at every base there was a dinner or a reception in our honor attended by the top brass and these were generally delightful affairs.

At Bergstrom they put on an air show for us, showing the capabilities of the F15. We also had an opportunity to try our hand at flying an F15 simulator. When our work was completed we departed Bergstrom on an Air Force plane and were flown to Goodfellow Air Force Base near San Angelo, Texas.

Goodfellow was an installation of the U.S.A.F. Air Training Command. The primary mission there was to provide training in cryptologic skills to students of all U.S. military components. While there Filan, Hormel, and I were interviewed on a local television talk show. It was an interesting experience near the end of our stay there. When we returned to the base following the show, the base and wing commanders hosted an outdoor barbecue for us at Colonel Carr's home. It was my first encounter with fajitas and they were great.

Our next stop was Colorado Springs, Colorado. We were to evaluate the Granite Inn dining facility within Cheyenne Mountain, but our living quarters were at nearby Peterson Air Base.

The Cold War was still very much alive when we visited Norad in Cheyenne Mountain. The base mission there was to provide warning and assessment of ballistic missile attack of the North American Continent, and to provide space surveillance to detect, track, identify and catalog earth orbiting satellites, furnishing reliable warning of atmospheric attack.

Security at the mountain was intense. The necessity for tight security also posed some unique problems for the food service operation, but in spite of that the Granite Inn was exceptional.

We had a full-scale tour and briefing of all that went on at the mountain and it was fascinating. Everything that was orbiting in space was being tracked there, some five-thousand articles, even an astronaut's glove that was "lost" in space. At the time the facility was built within the mountain it may have been capable of withstanding a nuclear attack. The buildings within the hollowed out mountain were built on huge springs. The "mountain" contained a self-sufficient water and electrical power supply as well as a food supply that could last for weeks in case of an emergency or an attack. This incredible facility was built in the 1950s for little more than sixty-million dollars.

The next stop in our travels was the U.S. Air Force Academy at Colorado Springs, where we evaluated the airmen's dining hall. Mr. Jose Fernandez was the food service officer in charge. He had won the Hennessy Award on two previous occasions and it was easy to see why. The facility was squeaky clean and the food was excellent. As we interviewed the young students, we received innumerable positive remarks on the quality, quantity and diversity of menus. One day as we were doing an evaluation I was stopped by a young lady student, Ms. Moran, who asked me if I was from Kozlak's Royal Oak Restaurant in Minnesota. She then proceeded to tell me that her parents treated her to dinner there following her high school graduation.

I was so impressed with the Air Force Academy and Cheyenne Mountain that I took my son-in-law, Chef Mark Satt, to see the facilities later that year. We developed a friendship with Jose Fernandez and he in turn visited our restaurant on a trip to Minnesota the next year.

From Colorado Springs the Air Force transported us in a small aircraft, I think it was a C12, to Castle Air Base at Merced, California. It was the roughest flight any of us on board had ever experienced. The pilot informed us that even the commercial pilots were having difficulty until they could get to forty-two thousand feet. It seemed that we bounced around for hours unable to see a thing until the pilot succeeded in getting us above the clouds for a few minutes and the flight smoothed out. All too soon it was time to begin our descent and once again we were bounced and tossed about. We landed at night on the very edge of a severe electrical storm. We were met by Chief of Services, Lieutenant Colonel Bobak and taken to his home for dinner. It was gratifying to be back on terra firma but the ground felt like it was moving for a long time after that flight.

Evaluating was now becoming routine for us. We observed breakfast, lunch and dinner meals plus food service at their crash kitchen and flight kitchen. We also attended a food service training class as well as a birthday meal celebration. This was then a new innovation where service personnel were honored when their birthday came within that month.

During our three-day stay at Castle we were treated to a tour of the Gallo Winery at Merced. This facility was truly state of the art. From the quality control in the production of the wine to the packaging . . . storage . . . shipment . . . even bottle making, it was incredible. We were told that Gallo owned or had under contract vineyards that totaled in acreage more land than the entire state of Rhode Island. Someone pointed out Julio Gallo as we made our way through the complex, so I went over and introduced myself to him and we posed together for a picture.

Next stop was to be McClellan Air Force Base at Sacramento. We were flown there by a young lady pilot. The sky was clear and the air was calm and we enjoyed a beautiful though brief flight. Once again we performed our evaluation over a three-day period and happily we had a couple days of rest and relaxation built into our itinerary before we were to fly to Alaska.

Willie Jefferson, the food service officer, took us on a tour of Sacramento where we saw the rejuvenated riverfront, railway museum, state Capitol and other points of interest. From there we headed to San Francisco with a brief stop at former N.R.A. president Bob Power's Nut Tree complex.

We had two full days to enjoy and explore San Francisco, and we made good use of the opportunity. Finally, it was time to depart for Alaska. We were to fly Alaska Airlines to Anchorage. When we got to the San Francisco airport it became apparent that Alaska Airlines was involved in a labor dispute. The machinists union had the place covered with pickets announcing that they were on strike. We checked at the counter and were told that our flight was to leave as scheduled. After checking my bags I went over to the insurance counter and purchased a sizable policy and mailed it to Ruth. The flight to Anchorage with a brief stop in Seattle was uneventful and pleasant.

We arrived at mid-afternoon at Anchorage International Airport and were transported in staff cars to Elmendorf Air Force Base. We each were assigned a suite in a "chateau" building. The suites were complete with kitchen, living room, dining room, bath and bedroom. I was told that President Reagan had occupied the suite that I was in on a previous visit. After giving us some time to get settled, we were taken to a theater where we viewed an "Alaska Experience" film. The film was in essence an orientation for us to the vastness and wonders of the state of Alaska. Next, we were taken to the Tower Club where we enjoyed a delightful dinner in the company of Colonels Hodge, Sprick, Ardis and their wives.

Sunday, March 17 was a day for sight-seeing so after breakfast and church we were driven to Alyeska Ski Resort where we had an opportunity to enjoy the scenery and visit their specialty shops. From there it was on to Portage Glacier . . . more beautiful scenery everywhere we looked.

We returned to our quarters in time to freshen up for a cocktail reception at the home of Lieutenant General Bruce Brown, Commander of the Alaskan Air Command, and his wife, Claudyne.

Before I started on the Hennessy trip I decided to buy a kelly green sport coat to wear at some of the warm weather stops along the way. The invitation to the Browns read "Civilian Informal" and since it was St. Patrick's Day I wore my green coat. I was particularly interested in meeting General Brown because I noticed in his biography that he was born in White Bear Lake, Minnesota, a suburb of St. Paul, and that he spent his formative years there. (It was customary for Hennessy Travelers to receive biographical sketches of the top brass at each base and they in turn received information on us).

When Mrs. Hormel, Captain Filan and I arrived at General Brown's house the first thing he said was, "Where is Jack?" He knew I was from Minnesota and also had a restaurant very near his home town. When we met and he saw my green coat he seemed truly surprised. He said, "To think that you were going on a thirty-nine day trip and would think far enough ahead to take a green coat for St. Patrick's Day is amazing." The General enjoyed recounting his early days in Minnesota. His time in elementary school . . . his first paper route . . . his family life. He also had a keen sense of history and delighted us with the story of his current residence. It was here that President Nixon met Emperor Hirohito. The house had recently been placed on the national historic registry and was in the process of being restored. We all enjoyed a very special evening in the company of the Browns.

Early the next morning we received a command briefing in advance of our flight to Shemya. Present at our briefing in addition to General Brown were sixteen colonels, one captain and two master sergeants. Of primary interest to us as Hennessy Travelers was what we could learn of Shemya itself. What follows is a thumbnail sketch:

SHEMYA: *The island is roughly two miles by four miles.*

The temperature ranges as high as sixty-three degrees during the summer and as low as seven degrees in the winter. August is the warmest month with an average maximum in the low fifties and a minimum in the forties. The coldest month is February with an average daily maximum of thirty-three degrees and an average minimum of twenty-eight degrees.

Shemya is the next to the last in the Aleutian Chain of U.S. islands. It is about one-thousand five-hundred miles from Anchorage: three-thousand miles from Seattle; two-hundred fifty miles from the nearest Russian island and roughly four-hundred fifty miles from the Russian mainland.

Shemya Air Force Base, sometimes referred to as "The Black Pearl" or "The Rock", is the most westerly of AAC's bases. The Command's 5073d Air Base Group provides base support to various tenant units assigned to other Air Force commands, primarily the Strategic Air Command.

The once uninhabited island was first occupied by military forces on the twenty-eighth of May 1943 during the final days of the battle to retake nearby Attu from the Japanese.

Shemya was originally intended as a B-29 base for the bombing of Japan. The present day ten-thousand foot runway and Birchwood hangars were constructed to accommodate the bomber. However, the Joint Chiefs of Staff decided to employ the B-29s from China and the

Mariana Islands in the central Pacific. Shemya, instead, became the home of the 29th Bomber Group whose B-24s flew bomber and photo reconnaissance missions against the northern Kurile Islands while its B-25s, based on Attu, attacked Japanese shipping in the North Pacific. The Group was inactivated in October 1945, and replaced by the 343rd Fighter Group. The latter was inactivated on the fifteenth of August 1946.

Air Force activities were reduced after World War II and for a time the Air Force considered transferring the island to the Civil Aeronautics Authority, the forerunner of the Federal Aviation Administration. However, the Air Force decided to retain Shemya because its location provided an ideal refueling stop on the Great Circle Route, particularly during the Korean War. The 5021st Air Base Squadron (AAC) provided base support.

Following the Korean War, Shemya was declared surplus and the base was inactivated on the first of July 1954. The facilities were turned over to the Civil Aeronautics Authority in 1955. They were then leased to Northwest Orient Airlines who remained on the island until 1961.

The Air Force resumed operations on Shemya in 1958 in support of various Air Force and Army strategic intelligence collection activities. Shemya also continued to support the Great Circle Route. The 5040th Air Base Squadron (AAC) was activated on the fifteenth of July 1958 to provide base support. The squadron was redesignated the 5072nd Air Base Squadron on the first of October 1962, and upgraded to a group on the fifteenth of October 1974, in recognition of the number and complexities of the tenant units it supported.

Shemya was redesignated from an Air Force Station to an Air Force Base on the twenty-first of June 1968.

Shemya Air Force Base has been the scene of two major earthquakes. The first, measuring 7.75 on the Richter scale, occurred on the third of February 1965. It was followed by severe aftershocks and a tidal wave. Damage, however, was limited to cracks in the taxiways. The other earthquake, measuring 7.5 on the Richter scale, occurred on the first of February 1975 with a high degree of damage to the runways and hangars. Communications were disrupted for a short period of time.

We flew to Shemya via Reeve Aleutian Airways. The aircraft carried very few passengers but every bit of remaining space was converted for cargo. Shemya from the air looks like little more than a speck but the experienced pilot had no difficulty in bringing the aircraft in safely even in what proved to be near gale force winds.

Our quarters here were austere compared to what we had experienced, although we each had a small room which proved to be adequate for our three-day visit. On our first evening we were served dinner at the consolidated open mess. The entree was fresh king crab legs and we all agreed that we had never had crab legs that were that delicious.

The main dining facility on Shemya is the Blue Fox Inn. The facility was named after a mangy looking fox that inhabits the island. The dining room was pleasant enough, but there was little else on the island except that dining room for full meals and many of the young folks who were stationed there quickly became tired of it. The island had a gymnasium and a bowling facility for recreation and of course there was fishing available, but it was hardly a place where most healthy young adults would choose to be. There were no real trees on the island but if you looked hard you could find a small occasional wild flower.

Hormel, Filan, and I completed our evaluation and found time to explore the tiny island. There remained evidence of the Russian influence there that predated U.S. ownership. We saw a small Russian cemetery and remnants of a Russian Orthodox church. The Pacific Ocean and the Bering Sea also met in that part of the world and many believe that is what accounts for the huge waves that crash together offshore.

Shemya was interesting, but three full days were enough for us. We couldn't help but feel a bit sorry for the young service people who were there for six months, a year, or even longer.

There were a couple airmen on board our flight back to Anchorage. They had completed their tour of duty on Shemya and couldn't wait to leave. You could see the expectation on their faces as the jet thundered down Shemya's runway and when the wheels left the ground they let out a whoop and a holler that told the whole story.

From Anchorage we were scheduled for a 12:55 a.m. flight to Honolulu. Our flight was very late and we spent most of the night in the airport at Anchorage. I don't remember what time we got airborne, but we didn't arrive in Honolulu until nearly 9:30 a.m. We had no sleep and were hoping we could have a few hours rest.

We were met at the airport by a lieutenant colonel and a captain. They were aware that our flight was very late, but they had planned that we take a walking tour of the Waikiki area and we couldn't dissuade them. Tired as we were, we trudged along with them until they decided it was time to head to Hickam Field.

The welcome there was impressive. As we entered the gate we saw our names in huge letters on a welcoming sign board. Our quarters too were impressive. The units we occupied were similar to that afforded President Marcos on his last stay in the United States.

The dining facilities at Hickam had a distinct Hawaiian flavor. The dining hall was the Hale Aina Inn and the flight kitchen was the Hale Aina Mokulele. Menus reflected the abundance of fresh fruits and vegetables available in Hawaii, and table decorations usually included fresh flowers. Our evaluation went along very well and when our work was completed we had a couple days to relax before the flight across the Pacific and the continent.

Captain Filan and I had an opportunity to play a round of golf at the course at Hickam. We also had a tour of Pearl Harbor and a visit to the U.S.S. Arizona shrine. On our last night we treated ourselves to dinner at the beach front restaurant at the Royal Hawaiian Hotel where we could look across the water for a perfect view of Diamondhead.

The next day we made the long flight all the way to Fort Meade, Maryland, which is located between Baltimore and Washington, D.C. We no sooner arrived than we found ourselves at a reception in our honor. After thirty days this lifestyle was becoming routine. During the next three days we did our inspections and evaluation. We also found time for an evening junket to Baltimore where we had an opportunity to see the newly-renovated waterfront community with its plethora of shops and restaurants.

From Fort Meade we were transported to National Airport in Washington, D.C. for a flight to Kennedy Airport in New York.

From Kennedy we were to fly to Heathrow in London. We always flew in coach class when on commercial airlines, and that is how we were scheduled for our flight to London. When we arrived at the gate to board, the lady at the desk asked if we would step aside and wait until we were called. The aircraft was being boarded and it seemed to us there could not be much room remaining. Captain Filan went to the desk a second time and the lady in charge said not to worry . . . we would be called. Finally, when it seemed there was no one left but the three of us we were called to board. It was then that we were told that we had been upgraded to first class. What a treat! We had a delicious dinner . . . fine wine . . . a mellow cordial...plus room to stretch out and enjoy some sleep before our morning arrival in London.

At London's Heathrow Airport we were met by Chief of Services at R.A.F. Fairford, Captain Mary Wood and Food Service Superintendent Ronald Montcalm. We were transported by van to R.A.F. Fairford which is some sixty miles from London. Fairford is located in the Cotswolds, one of the most beautiful parts of England with quiet out-of-the way villages and hamlets that have remained essentially unchanged for centuries.

R.A.F. Fairford was opened by the Royal Air Force in January 1944. In 1951 it was handed over to the U.S. Air Force. In 1964 R.A.F. Fairford was transferred back to R.A.F. control.

The U.S. Air Force returned to Fairford in 1979 when the 7020th Air Base Group, a U.S. Air Force in Europe unit, was designated and activated. In September 1979, the KC-135 Stratotankers arrived and the 11th Strategic Group, Strategic Air Command assumed control of tanker operations. When we were at R.A.F. Fairford in 1985 the mission was: Refuel AWACS Planes in the Persian Gulf.

The main food service facility at R.A.F. Fairford was the Falcon Arms Dining Facility. We found it to be an older, extremely well-cared-for and well-maintained facility. The mix of personnel from the U.S. and England appeared to work well together. The net result was a smooth running, well-coordinated operation. R.A.F. Fairford scored second in our evaluation . . . slightly behind the winner: Cheyenne Mountain.

Before we left England we were taken on a tour of the Cotswold area and managed to spend a whole day and one night in London. We did many of the touristy things: St. Paul's Cathedral, Westminster Abby; Tower of London, to name a few. I took Captain Filan and Mrs. Hormel to see Smithfield Market where most of the lamb, beef, pork, chickens, etc. are processed and distributed. We also visited Herrod's Department Store, the Scotch Shop, and Fortnum and Masons Store, where the clerks wear full dress cutaways. We finished our day in London with dinner at the Wig and Pen Club, which is located, as might be expected, in the section where journalists and barristers often frequent. The Wig and Pen was operated by a gentleman named Dick Brennan. Brennan earned a great deal of notoriety as the chef on the voyage of the Mayflower II to America in the 1960s.

Our flight back to the United States brought us to Atlanta where we landed in mid-afternoon on a pleasant day in early April. Mrs. Hormel went on to Kansas City; Captain Filan returned to Tyndal Air Force Base, and I flew on to Southwest Florida Regional Airport, where Ruth met me. After thirty-nine days we were together once more at our home in Naples.

Our team met again in May at the Hennessy Awards dinner which was held at the Hyatt Regency Hotel in Chicago. The personnel from the Granite Inn at Cheyenne Mountain were presented the winner's trophy. The runner-up was the Falcon Arms at R.A.F. Fairford and several of the staff from both facilities were treated to the trip to Chicago for the festivities. I addressed the crowd of some three-hundred fifty people in attendance with an account of our trip complete with a slide presentation of many of the highlights. The National Restaurant Association, working together with the Air Force, made sure that the awards dinner was an event that everyone in attendance would long remember.

Following the dinner our team was invited to a meeting of the Hennessy Travelers Association, which is the alumni group, and installed as members in good standing of the association.

The Air Force also asked each "traveler" from the civilian sector to submit a report with our observations and recommendations. What follows is what I sent to the Air Force:

The thirty-nine day trip that took our Hennessy team to ten Air Force dining facilities was my first encounter with military feeding. My work in food service has been primarily with the operation and ownership of "fine dining" restaurants in the Twin City area of Minneapolis/St. Paul, Minnesota. These restaurants seat from one-hundred fifty to six-hundred guests and offer extensive menus serving luncheon, dinner, breakfast to groups and Sunday brunch.

This will be a chronicle of my impressions of Air Force dining facilities as I saw them . . . at the time I saw them. Some of my conclusions and/or suggestions may be wide of the mark but if one or two are useful perhaps the effort will have been worthwhile.

I was greatly impressed by the emphasis placed on cleanliness in the facilities we inspected. Everyone knew we were coming and all the facilities looked good, but the procedures developed by some of the units were truly outstanding.

One facility had cleaning procedures framed and posted by each piece of equipment telling exactly how the job should be done right down to the precise amount and type of cleaning agent to be used. Another listed exact specifications, time of day, day of week, number of times each month etc. for cleaning of hoods, restrooms, walls, ceilings, etc. These duties were delegated and the individuals responsible signed off when the job was completed.

The "clean as you go" idea seemed to be well-accepted at nearly every place I saw and the result was that the floors and work tables almost always looked good.

Equipment: One of the categories on the 1038 form that I paid particular attention to was the minor maintenance reporting repairs. One item that seemed to crop up repeatedly for repairs at certain facilities was the dish washing machine. Upon questioning I learned that the dish machine contract is usually given to the lowest bidder. After seeing the number of repairs logged to the low bid machines I question whether initial price of the machine is reason enough to award a contract. (Most of these machines cost thousands of dollars). Perhaps service calls on various pieces of equipment should be evaluated by the center to help determine which manufactured product gives the best service. Companies that supply chemicals for dish machines (Econ Lab, Dubois etc.) may have data available to help in making a more enlightened choice of equipment. These companies do minor servicing of machines all over the country and are usually willing to share their knowledge. "The cheapest is not always best, but the best is always the cheapest."

Energy Conservation: I noticed many signs and notices posted calling attention to energy conservation. At some places lights were shut off when areas were unoccupied and many were careful to turn off ovens and grills when not needed. I was surprised to learn that in most, if not all, instances the energy consumption of the dining facilities is not metered separately from the rest of the base. Dining facilities and kitchens are big users of energy and it seems to me the best way to know how you are doing in conserving energy is to be able to know how much energy you are using each month. In the private sector the operator gets a bill each month and that bill can be compared to previous months and is also an incentive to reduce the use of unnecessary energy. Perhaps energy consumption could be significantly reduced in many Air Force dining facilities if the amount used was monitored and metered and converted to civilian dollar costs to create a greater awareness.

I also noticed several facilities were very

short of "make up" air. This usually results in significant heat/cold loss and is costly as well as uncomfortable.

At Shemya the food warehouses were located about as far from the kitchen as possible. We were told that new warehouses were to be built. Surely they will be built closer to the dining facility but we noticed that the dry storage warehouse was separate from the frozen warehouse. The dry storage warehouse was heated to keep certain canned goods from freezing. When we entered the frozen food warehouse we noticed that the building, although uninsulated, was warmer than the dry storage facility just because of the heat supplied by the compressors. Suggestion: Perhaps one large warehouse could be built for both dry and frozen storage whereby the heat from the compressors could be utilized to keep the dry materials at the desired temperature. With proper insulation and louvers to allow excess heat to escape this should provide significant energy savings.

The remarks that follow are impressions that I received and I submit them not only as a person involved in food service, but also as a citizen and taxpayer.

I was surprised that the use of outside contractors was so widespread. It seemed to me that the "full" contract system lent itself to significant duplication of effort and added costs.

It also concerned me to think that if the contract system is brought to its ultimate conclusion in food service the Air Force could become dependent on outsiders and subject to many of the risks that operators run in the private sector such as job actions and work slowdowns. In some of the contracts it appeared that pay scales and benefits were much higher in many categories than those in the private sector. It seems to me that if some supplementary civilian help is necessary the hiring and supervision of such personnel might be best handled by qualified military people, thus eliminating the need for another layer of management as typified by the contractor system.

Most contractor management people I talked with like the present system and cite the competitive bidding process, by which they are selected; but that process does not seem competitive in the same sense as that which exists in the private sector. They do not seem to have great capital investment in dining hall and kitchen equipment to say nothing of HVAC and many other big ticket items. Also the contractors enjoy the protection of the S.B.A. provision and in some instances "set asides" which shelter minority operators.

This is not to be interpreted to mean that the job of serving the customers is not being done acceptably because for the most part it is . . . but I think that an impartial study by qualified persons should begin to research the possibility of a more self-sufficient, highly-motivated and more independent Air Force food service system. For all the improvements that have been made in military food service in recent years I think the aforementioned objectives could be reached by some attitude shifts; an even greater emphasis to professionalize food service work and some good public relations work to elevate the perception of food service work to a much higher level.

Some obstacles to these procedures that presently exist seem to be: 1) the perception that food service is somehow not as important as other work in the Air Force; 2) I visited with some young people who were sent into food service because, "I got into trouble;" 3) Others I visited with, who truly liked food service, lamented the "Palace Balance" system which they felt directed them away from a career preference into areas of lesser interest to them; 4) Still others felt that sufficient opportunities to increase their culinary skills were lacking, and almost always no matter how good some of the Air

Force personnel were (and many were outstanding) the feeling that their efforts were not viewed with proper respect seemed to come through; 5) The Air Force personnel in charge of supervising a crew and providing proper service also seemed strapped for qualified people on many occasions and seemed in constant anxiety over who would be pulled out of their operation next by "Palace Balance". It appeared that the system tended to discourage supervisors and lowered morale in the work force when they see the best in food service pulled away by "Palace Balance".

I think an independent study of Air Force food service should address the possibility of recruiting young men and women for careers in food service. There are scores of schools throughout the U.S. today where young people are paying tuition to learn the skills that will give them entry to food service careers. It seems that the Air Force could develop a program that would attract many of these people.

The study could also explore the means of professionalizing and glamorizing food service and increasing the image and status of food service people. Thought could be given to providing interested people with aptitude, specialized training at some of our good culinary and hotel management schools. Explore the possibility of creating a military culinary and billeting school that would enjoy comparable stature with West Point, Annapolis, or the Air Force Academy. The school could offer courses in subjects that would further professionalize other work performed by services such as mortuary, etc.

In conjunction with this effort, explore the possibility of providing more creativity and imagination to be used by cooks . . . perhaps rewards for ideas that are accepted into the worldwide menu system.

Explore the possibility of allowing more people to come up through the ranks to high positions in the services. If food service held out the possibility and probability of gaining general officer status it might help accomplish the afore-mentioned attitude shift.

Remember Napoleon's admonishment, "An army travels on its stomach." Perhaps it will travel best if the food delivery system is self-sufficient, properly trained and accorded a greater degree of importance.

Knute Rockne, the great football coach saw the need for psychological equity among his players. When his "four horsemen" were getting all the headlines and accolades and it began to go to their head . . . he had them scrimmage behind the second team line. The first team line played defense and an important object lesson was struck home. Everyone soon learned that it is the team effort that is important and that the glamorous backfield lost its luster without top notch support from the line.

Nit Picking:

The following are some items that caught my attention and might bear mentioning.

1. At one base only margarine was offered as a spread. When I asked why there was no butter I was informed that they use it when it is "free" but otherwise it was, "too expensive." This surprised and puzzled me. It seems to me that both butter and margarine could be used so that the dairy farmers' product would always be available. Also it seems like good public relations to try to use as many wholesome products as possible that our farmers produce.

2. At many bases vegetables were extremely overcooked and became mushy. Perhaps this problem should be addressed and some changes made in either cooking instructions . . . holding procedures, or both.

3. Everyone had a different idea on what constituted acceptable garnish. Perhaps some guidelines and publications could go out to the cooks. Whereas we saw many creative garnishes that complemented the food and were edible, there were others that showed a lack of training and direction. (Such as four grapefruit

halves . . . one in each corner of a pan of hot grits).

4. At one base we were told an entirely new dining and kitchen facility was being designed. This was a contract operated facility. I asked the contractor that if he were building a new facility . . . did he have any ideas for increased efficiency. His response was, among other things, that he thought much greater efficiency could be achieved with considerably less space. I asked if anyone had contacted him for his ideas and observations. The answer was, "No." I think good communications are generally good policy and perhaps it would be beneficial to consult with people such as the aforementioned contractor when designing a new facility. Some subtle regional difference may come to the fore and thus help the planning and construction process.

5. The military has a unique opportunity to introduce popular regional foods into the system and could conceivably do an even better job than they are now doing. Consider wild rice from the Great Lakes states. Wild rice was once only an expensive gourmet item. Even today only a small percentage of Americans are familiar with this delicious food. Some years ago a system of planting and cultivating wild rice was developed and now the possibility of expanded markets and relatively inexpensive wild rice are limitless. The military could help develop these markets and thus help some of our less prosperous states by introducing this and similar items into the system when the opportunity presents itself.

6. At some point in the future might it be possible to devise a system whereby foods in the region of the base could be more easily purchased when fresh and abundant, such as fruits and vegetables? Could good old-fashioned ham with the bone in be brought into the system when convenient in place of the less desirable canned variety? Could local fresh fish be a possibility when close at hand rather than the

240

frozen and often pre-breaded variety?

In conclusion: The hospitality and courtesy we received as Hennessy Travelers will always be remembered and probably never matched. It was an outstanding learning experience. I saw parts of the "Lower Forty-Eight" that I might never have otherwise visited. The trip to Shemya was particularly interesting because I know that relatively few civilians have made it. I also read the book "The 1000 Mile War", an account of the Japanese presence in the Aleutians during WW II while on the trip.

Fairford too will hold a special place in my memory because of the opportunity to see a foreign country and observe how well our people interact with their British counterparts.

Most of all, the fun was in getting to meet and visit with so many fine folks. From Bergstrom to Shemya; from Hickam to Fairford . . . from the greenest airmen to the most seasoned generals, they all made us welcome and helped to make the Hennessy trip an experience of a lifetime.

In early 1986 I decided not to accept a third three-year term as a National Restaurant Association director. Ruth and I were changing our domicile to Naples, Florida and although I was still active in the operation of Kozlak's Royal Oak Restaurant I did not think it would be fair for me to represent Minnesota when our legal residence was elsewhere.

Before I retired as an active board member, there was one point that I wanted to make with the existing board.

It seemed apparent to me that our board was not truly representative of our industry. I do not want anyone to think for one moment that there were board members who were not dedicated to promoting our industry. The board was truly solid in that respect. What concerned me was the manner in which we were perceived. For example, each year the association would invite a few congressmen to the National Restaurant convention in Chicago. It was a good opportunity for the legislators to get a feel for the size and scope of our industry when they walked the floor and saw the number of vendors at McCormick Place. It also gave the board an opportunity to express our concerns to them in a somewhat informal setting. Following one of these sessions I visited with one of the congressmen with whom I had served, when we were both members of the Minnesota House of Representatives. He asked me why, in an industry as diverse as ours, that our board was so heavily white male. It was a poignant question . . . and one that gave me much food for thought. Later, I had an opportunity to visit with a black congressman from Texas who was at our convention and I asked him how he perceived our board as representatives of our industry. He in effect told me that we were seen as the "fat cats" of the restaurant business.

At that time the board did not reflect the ethnic, gender, or racial diversity that made up our industry. It seemed to me that we might have more success in dealing with Congress if the board was more representative of the industry as a whole. I mentioned earlier that it cost us about six-thousand dollars per year to attend the board meetings and it seemed obvious to me that we didn't have any representation from the thousands of small operators because they probably could not afford it. Thus, we were not able to have proper input from a huge segment of the industry, plus we may not have been presenting the industry in its best light from a public relations or lobbying standpoint.

I discussed the situation with some of my colleagues and we devised a proposal that would have made it possible for future board members to be partially reimbursed for expenses in conjunction with board meetings. It was our feeling that we would be able to get a broader, more representative group of people on the board if membership became more affordable. I felt it was logical for me to make the case for this proposal because I was going off the board and could in no way be seen as being self-serving on the issue.

On the night before the issue was to come before the board for a vote, it became apparent that lobbying against the proposal was under way by some of the association's past presidents. We brought the measure up for a vote the next day and it was spiritedly debated. The opponents contended that "not one better person" would come to the board if the proposal was adopted. We proponents made the point that this was an attempt to make the association more representative of the industry as a whole.

When the vote was taken our proposal was narrowly defeated. Naturally, those of us who worked for its passage were disappointed but the system does work . . . often times in strange ways. In the years that have followed the board has achieved more ethnic, gender and racial balance, much of it due to the sensitivity of the nominating committees. In 1994 the National Restaurant Association elected its first black president, Herman Cain. Mr. Cain proved to be the right person at the right time in the right place for the association. His service was not merely distinguished . . . it was brilliant!

Honorary Directors

Life as an honorary director of the National Restaurant Association continues to be interesting. Ruth and I attend an occasional meeting where we have an opportunity to renew old friendships and acquaintances. I am kept informed of the business of the association by virtue of the correspondence that goes to all directors. If so motivated, honorary directors may speak out on issues at the board meetings and I have done this as well.

Early in 1993 Ruth received a call for me from the Association Corporate Secretary, LaVerne Warlick. The 1993 Hennessy trip was soon to begin and the gentleman who was scheduled to make the trip became ill. LaVerne was in the process of calling three or four former Hennessy Travelers to see if someone would make the trip on such short notice. I was on an errand when the call came and when I returned Ruth gave me the message. Ruth knew how much I enjoyed the first Hennessy trip and she encouraged me to go again. I called LaVerne and was informed that the trip was mine. My passport was still valid so there were no problems.

My second Hennessy trip was twenty-five days. Our team of four were: Ute Rainer-Schmitt representing the International Food Service Executives Association; Captain Gary Snapp and C.M. Sargeant George Miller. Our trip lasted twenty-five days and our evaluations were done at Davis Mothan AFB at Tucson, Arizona; Hill Air Force Base at Ogden, Utah; Peterson Air Force Base at Colorado Springs; Keesler Air Force Base at Biloxi, Mississippi and Chicksands Air Force Base, England.

The second Hennessy trip was much like the first, although it seemed to me that the dining rooms were even more posh than I remembered in 1985, and the quality of the food and service appeared slightly improved. I think that most veterans would be amazed by the improvements in food service that have taken place in the Air Force since the inception of the Hennessy Awards program. I will always be grateful for having had the opportunity to participate as a representative of the National Restaurant Association in such an interesting and worthwhile endeavor.

Mrs. Hormel, Captain Filan and Jack during television interview at San Angelo, Texas.

February, 1985: Typical welcome accorded Hennessy Travelers. (L to R): Jack, Deanna Hormel, Captain Filan.

1985: Mr. Cecil Sala, president of International Food Service Executive Association, Sacramento Chapter, presents plaque to Hennessy Evaluators Hormel, Filan and Kozlak.

(Above) 1985: Jack with preppie Mary Moran of Shoreview, Minnesota, at the U.S. Air Force Academy. She told Jack that her parents took her to Kozlak's Royal Oak on her eighteenth birthday. She had "pheasant under glass."

(Right) Jack near Bedford, England, at a Royal Oak restaurant 1993.

PART
SEVENTEEN

Odds and Ends

It was in the morning much before the time when we began serving lunch. A little old man from the neighborhood walked in the door and stepped up to the bar and looked across at the cigar display. The least expensive cigar we had at that time was twenty cents.

Bill was at the reservation desk. As soon as he spotted the man he walked behind the bar and asked if he could help him. The man held up a dime and asked in his best Slavic accent, "Mister, do you got cigar for dime?" Bill thought he would be nice to the old timer so he said, "Sure," and reached back to pick out a cigar. As he did this, the old gent whipped out a dollar and said, "I'll take ten" . . . and he did.

* * *

In the early 1960s a petite lady named Mary Conley Majewski joined our staff as waitress. She had spent most of her life in Boston and had a pronounced and delightful accent associated with that area.

Mary had done waitress work in her native city before she moved to Minneapolis. Her resume included a couple of very fine restaurants plus the prestigious Harvard Club where she had served and came to know the famous Kennedy family. Mary was always pleasant with guests and many people made it a point to ask for her station.

At Jax the waitress station at the main bar is approximately in the center. There are stools on each side of the waitress station where people can sit and relax while they wait for a table.

It was the summer of 1963 and Mary stepped up to the waitress station at the bar and placed an order. On the two bar stools to her left were two men who were discussing the Kennedy family. They were exchanging disparaging remarks about President Kennedy, his brothers, his father and the rest of the clan. Mary could not help but overhear the conversation. I noticed that she was shifting her weight from one foot to another as she listened. I could tell a rage was building within her. I was within earshot of the men too and Mary knew it. She fidgeted as she contemplated what she was about to do, but finally she could stand it no longer.

As she removed her tray from the bar she turned to the men and said, "Don't knock 'em if you don't know 'em." Years later she told me she thought she would be discharged for what she said. As it turned out the men admired her spunk and wanted to know more about Mary's background. They not only were good customers, but eventually they became part of Mary's "fan club". Mary worked at Jax until her retirement in 1985.

* * *

One night after the rush, Lefty motioned to me from behind the bar. I stepped up to the bar and he asked me if I had heard of a new drink called the Bishop's Hat. I had not, so Lefty said, "I'll make one so you can try it."

First, he took part of a lime and cut it into a shape that resembled a bishop's hat. Next, he took a cordial glass and filled it with our most expensive cognac. He placed a sugar cube over the top of the glass and put the lime hat on top of the sugar cube. He placed a cocktail napkin in front of me with a flourish and carefully set the drink on top of it.

I looked at the glass with the sugar cube and lime on top and frankly I was puzzled. I asked Lefty, "How do you drink it?" He said, "Like this." He removed the sugar cube and lime from the top of the glass with one hand and in a flash poured the contents of the glass through his lips with the other!

* * *

It was mid-afternoon on a weekday. Two men who I knew quite well had finished a late lunch and decided to take a booth across from the bar to have an after-dinner drink. They had a couple and as I walked by they asked me to sit and visit.

I sat in the booth facing the front door. Somehow the conversation got on politics. These men were very conservative and on this afternoon they were verbally bashing Senator Hubert Humphrey. It seems almost unbelievable but as they were talking the front door opened and in came Hubert Humphrey.

He walked down the aisle toward the dining room and as he started past where I was sitting the man next to me spotted him and said in the most unflattering manner possible, "Sen-a-tor Humph-rey." The senator whirled around and as he smiled and extended his hand he said, "That's right . . . and the best one you ever had too." I introduced the senator to the men and excused myself. Humphrey sat, visited, and joked with them for several minutes. In typical Humphrey style he not only neutralized two detractors but made two new friends.

* * *

In the summer of 1960 the Minnesota A.F.L.-C.I.O. convention was to be held in Rochester. Dave Roe, who was the president of the Minneapolis building trades union, announced that he was going to run for the job to head the Minnesota A.F.L.-C.I.O.

A few days before the convention we received a call for a luncheon reservation from Dave. He said, "By the way . . . no matches." He was telling us that he didn't need any more match covers with his name printed on them. It was and still is the practice at Jax, and Royal Oak, to print the name of the person who places a reservation on match covers and have one at each place setting.

Just for fun I told the young lady who printed the match covers to print some saying "NO MATCHES FOR DAVE ROE". When Dave sat down with his group and saw the match covers he got a big kick out of it. One of the people in his group picked up on the idea and suggested that they have several hundred printed to pass out to the convention delegates. A match book with the message "No Matches For Dave Roe" made a catchy election card.

We got the matches ready that very afternoon and they went with Dave and his supporters to Rochester. Oh yes . . . he won his election and held the post until he retired . . . and our advertisement was on the inside of the match covers.

* * *

249

One afternoon Rosie completed the luncheon shift and decided to go to the supermarket. She went home and picked up her little dog "Tiger" and took him along for the ride. Tiger was an all-American dog. No fancy pedigree or papers but he was cute just the same. And Rosie loved him.

Rosie had Tiger stay in the car while she shopped and when her shopping was completed they returned home. About an hour later a lady called and said, "I saw your little dog in your car at the supermarket and I was able to track you by calling the automobile license bureau. I gave them your license number and they gave me your name."

She told Rosie that her female dog resembled Rosie's and she would like very much to mate the two dogs. "Would that be O.K.?" she asked. Rosie said, "Just a minute . . . I'll ask Tiger." When Rosie returned to the phone she reported that Tiger was agreeable. They had a good chuckle and set a date for the "wedding".

* * *

Father James Namie was an assistant at Immaculate Conception church in Columbia Heights when I was running for the Legislature in 1968. He was young and energetic. Everyone in town liked him. About a week before election day he stopped in for dinner at Jax with his pastor. Father Namie got me aside as they were about to leave and he said, "You are going to win this election." I asked him how he knew. He said, "The big boys downtown are betting on you."

* * *

It was our first spring season at Royal Oak. Bob Sappa was doing some carpentry work on the planter boxes that frame the front entry. His tool truck was parked under the canopy a few feet from where he was working. The bumper sticker on the back of the truck said, "Polish men are superior lovers."

An elegant older woman came out of the restaurant and as she started toward the parking lot she spotted the bumper sticker. She adjusted her mink stole, turned to Bob, nodded toward the bumper sticker and asked, "Where did you buy that?" Bob answered with mock indignation, "I don't know lady, I didn't buy it . . . my wife put it there."

* * *

It was the holiday season in 1963. I had the day shift so I was able to leave work shortly after 5 p.m. As I drove through our neighborhood I noticed most families had their Christmas trees up and lighted.

In those days of cheap and abundant energy most people in our area decorated the exterior of their homes and lighted outside trees too. Our neighborhood was particularly beautiful this time of year, and people from all over the Twin Cities would drive by to see the lights. It was a fairyland scene. And as I drove into our driveway I felt that I was really getting into the spirit of the season. I entered the kitchen and I could hear a minor disturbance taking place in the living room. I decided to investigate.

It seems that five and one-half-year-old Paul had come home with his pockets bulging with Christmas tree light bulbs. Ruth had been questioning him and Paul admitted that he had taken them from the trees at the Johnson's house directly across the street.

Ruth was pointing out to him in no uncertain terms that what he had done was stealing pure and simple. She told him that was totally unacceptable behavior and would not be tolerated.

Each time Ruth made a point, Paul's wide brown eyes became wider. And then the clincher from Ruth: "You will walk across the street and ring the Johnson's doorbell. When Mrs. Johnson comes to the door you will hand her the light bulbs and tell her you are sorry and that you will never do such a thing again . . . and I will be watching you from this window!"

Paul knew he was in deep trouble, but always the angle shooter, he asked, "Can't we just mail them?"

* * *

One of the most colorful characters in the Twin Cities was Monsignor John Dunphy. He was born in Ireland and his delightful brogue stayed with him for his entire life. John Dunphy was ordained in 1900. In 1925 he became dean of students at St. Thomas College. He held that position for thirty years. It was at St. Thomas that he earned the nickname "The King". Stories about "The King" are legion. He was of medium height but powerfully built. It was said that he could have made it as a professional fighter. Many a student in his dean days learned that he

251

relished mixing it up when reason failed.

He became pastor of the Ascension Church in North Minneapolis in 1955, and became an occasional visitor at Jax. He was quite old by this time, but his build was still formidable, and his reputation as "The King" never diminished.

One evening when Lefty was at the podium Monsignor Dunphy approached him and asked, "What is your name?" The reply was, "Lefty." The King barked, "Lefty! What kind of a name is that? What is your real name?" Half-frightened, he answered, "Ladislaus Tomczyk, Sir." The King snapped, "Hmmm, Tomczyk, Tomczyk. Would that be Polish?" Lefty, a bit shaken, replied, "Yes, Monsignor." The King thrust out his chin and proclaimed, "Don't anyone say anything bad about the Poles while I'm around."

* * *

In early October of 1983, Ruth and I visited Jack Miller and his wife, Jo, in Gatlinburg, Tennessee. Jack and I became acquainted as members of the board of directors of the National Restaurant Association.

On a crisp clear October day the Millers drove us through the colorful Smoky Mountains to Ashville, North Carolina, so we could tour the famous Vanderbilt mansion. As we walked back to our host's car upon completion of the tour, I noticed an automobile with Minnesota license plates parked nearby.

Just for a lark I took out one of my business cards and slipped it under the windshield wiper. Several months later I stopped at Jax of Golden Valley. Lenny Daniels, the bar manager, called me over and said he had something to show me.

It was the business card I placed under the windshield wiper at the Vanderbilt mansion parking lot. The card had been retrieved by a gentleman named Quentin Fiala. He brought it to Lenny.

Who was Quentin Fiala? Lenny Daniels' brother-in-law.

* * *

Today it is not uncommon for mail carriers to keep mace-like sprays with them as they walk their routes. They use these substances to repel aggressive and unfriendly dogs.

252

We had a mailman customer who had an even better idea. He asked our dishwasher to save him the steak bones that came back to the kitchen. He would carry a few with him each day. When he met a new dog he presented it with a nice bone. He never spent a dime on chemical dog repellents.

During twenty years in the postal service he never got bit.

* * *

In 1986, the Minnesota Restaurant Association invited National Restaurant Association president Ted Balestreri to participate in our Upper Midwest Hospitality trade show, held in February at the Minneapolis Convention Center. (Balestreri and his partner Bert Cutino own the famous Sardine Factory restaurant located on historic Cannery Row in Monterey, California.)

To honor Ted, I organized a special dinner at Royal Oak on a Sunday evening following the U.P.S. show. It was an opportunity for our Minnesota Association board members and their spouses to enjoy an evening visiting with the charismatic Balestreri in a relaxed atmosphere.

The centennial year of the St. Paul Winter Carnival was 1986. The centerpiece of the carnival was the fantastic ice palace that was constructed near Lake Phalen. It cost over a million dollars to build and was an attraction par excellence. The ice palace was lighted both internally and externally. Huge crowds inched their way past in the evening for an opportunity to see this amazing spectacle.

We wanted Ted to see the ice palace but time constraints prohibited us from taking the time to drive him there . . . Not to worry . . . Bill Naegele arranged to have a helicopter land at Royal Oak and fly Ted over the palace for a spectacular birds-eye view.

At the conclusion of his presidential year Balestreri addressed the crowd at the annual meeting of the N.R.A. in Chicago. He recounted his experience as president, citing the many states he had visited and extolled the hospitality he had received at every stop. He concluded his talk with this: "All in all, it was a fabulous year and the experience of a lifetime. But I have to tell you this . . . Only Minnesota folks have their own air force."

253

PART
EIGHTEEN

A Time to Work...A Time to Retire

After nearly fifty years in the restaurant business I was ready to retire. I had sold my interest in the business at Jax a few years earlier to my brother, Bill. Now son-in-law Mark Satt and our daughter, Diane, were ready and capable of owning and operating Kozlak's Royal Oak. Ruth and I reached an agreement with them whereby they became sole owners of the business and we began our retirement.

One of the questions I get from friends of mine who retired from family businesses is, "Do you still go to the restaurant often to see how they are doing?" The answer is that I do not. I would not have left the business had I not thought that Mark and Diane were ready to go it alone. I made up my mind that I would not interfere or try to second-guess them. Have they made any mistakes? Perhaps . . . but I made my share too and it is still a good way to learn.

I have heard many of my fellow retirees say things like, "I can't stay away" or "I have to know what's going on and be involved." I can understand that it may be difficult to let go of a business or businesses that you may have started or worked for years to develop but I believe it makes for better relationships all the way around to simply get out of the way when you retire.

The Joy of Retirement

Retirement does take a little getting used to. At first I missed the routine and even some of the pressure that goes with the work. It does get easier as time goes by, however, and the adjustment period does not last long.

The restaurant business is very demanding and through the working years our social life was very limited. Now that we have plenty of time our social calendar is abundantly full and we are thoroughly enjoying this freedom.

Jax and Kozlak's Royal Oak today

I enjoy visiting Jax. It is a vintage restaurant characterized by enduring excellence, appeal, and historic value. Jax is impeccably maintained and has managed to maintain its customer base over seven decades. There is some staff there whom I hired twenty and even twenty-five years ago and I love to schmooze with them. The beautiful woodwork in the dining rooms . . . the patio garden . . . trout stream . . . the art work all contribute to make Jax unique. Brother Bill and his wife, Kathy, now have their son Bill Jr. with them in the business, so it appears that the tradition of the Kozlak family at Jax will live on.

Kozlak's Royal Oak Restaurant is a jewel. The spacious grounds and the gardens become more beautiful each year as they mature. The dining rooms, lounge and kitchen all reflect the fact that the entire facility is receiving tender loving care. There is a relaxed air of professionalism among the staff. You get the feeling that they enjoy their work and they value each other. There are still some staff members there who opened with us in 1977, and there are many more who have completed at least ten-years service.

Many of the policies and projects that we began years ago have been kept in force and continue to bear fruit. Organized tours of the restaurant are available for school children. They get to see the entire facility and then have an opportunity to question the chef and manager. They are sent away with a generous serving of Royal Oak ice cream.

Each year there is a dinner party for the staff and their spouses or friends and service awards are presented. There is a gold pin for five years . . . a watch for ten . . . and a personalized gift for fifteen-years service.

Each year there is also a gift for student employees who graduate from school.

Both our daughter, Diane and our son-in-law, Mark Satt, have worked hard for the restaurant industry as well as their own restaurant. The Minnesota Chapter of the National Association of Women Business Owners has named Diane their Woman of the Year and Mark Satt was named the president of the Minnesota Restaurant Association in 1996.

Our youngest daughter, Carol Braun, is currently catering manager at the restaurant in addition to performing some office and other manager duties. Carol is the perfect utility person, having had experience at nearly every job in the restaurant.

Our son, Mark, is in real estate sales and was recently featured in Minneapolis/St. Paul magazine for his work in upgrading a central city neighborhood. Daughter Mary, her husband, Dr. Paul Myers, and their three children, live in Neenah, Wisconsin, where Paul is a neonatologist at the Theda Clark hospital.

Daughter Lynn Satt is busy with her two children and also works in the local school system.

Our youngest son, Paul, is married, has two sons and is busy designing and selling restaurant fixtures and equipment. He has done many projects in Minnesota and Wisconsin and has even done work in Germany and Kuwait.

So that concludes the profile of our family. Stay tuned for the next generation.

PART
NINETEEN

Favorite Recipes

Through the years we employed many interesting people who worked as bartenders or mixologists at our restaurants. I have already alluded to John Scovil, Phil Harris, Walter "Lefty" Tomczyk, Bill "Jiggs" Evans and Len Daniels. There were many more and they all contributed in their own way. Some of the folks that come to mind from Jax and Jax of Golden Valley are Steve Fellegy, Pete Warian, George Hauck, Fred Zajac, Steve Warian and Nick Totino.

At Kozlak's Royal Oak, Frank Locascio, Linda Zumwalde, Janet Greenwood, Dick Dippel, Jackie Entsminger, John Jonson and Jan Greger served with distinction. Perhaps, the senior member of the group is Lowell "Joe" Peterson. Joe went to work as a bartender at the famous Charlie's Cafe Exceptionale in Minneapolis in 1936 and stayed until the restaurant closed in 1983. Joe came to work at Kozlak's Royal Oak a few years ago and works part-time during the day when he feels fit. He is an inspiration to all the staff and still one of the most capable and best recognized barmen in the Twin Cities area.

Joe and I were reminiscing one day and we began discussing how drinks were made back in the 1930s, '40s, and '50s. During World War II, American whiskey and imported scotch were in short supply, but rum was plentiful. The liquor wholesalers set up buying allotments whereby retailers were in effect required to buy rum if they wanted enough whiskey and scotch to satisfy their customer demands. The result was a plethora of rum drinks brought forth by creative barmen. I refer to barmen because women did not tend bar in the Twin Cities at that time.

I thought it would be interesting to put down some "old time" drink recipes. So what follows is the way it was done a generation or two ago. The drinks that required shaking were accomplished by the bartender. There were no Waring blenders available. And when power mixers came on line, many restaurants were slow to buy them. In fact, Charlie's was one of the last restaurants to use power mixers. Evidently, owner Charlie Saunders liked the sight and sound of the bartenders shaking those cocktails in front of the guests. And I must admit, it did provide an element of charm to the procedure.

Consider what follows as a trip to yesteryear. When the recipe calls for a shaker glass, it means placing the ingredients into a container and then placing a larger container over it rather tightly. The next step is to pick up the containers with both hands and shake them vigorously. When shaken well, strain the mixture into the appropriate glass. Garnish and serve. Let's begin with a few rum drinks that gained popularity during World War II.

CUBA LIBRE

> *Juice ½ lime*
> *Drop rind in glass*
> *2 oz. Imported Rum*
> *2 cubes of ice*
> *Fill glass with cola*

Use 10 oz. glass and stir well

CUBAN SPECIAL COCKTAIL

> *½ oz. pineapple juice*
> *Juice ½ lime*
> *1 oz. Imported Rum*
> *½ tsp. Curaçao*

Shake well with cracked ice and strain into 3 oz. cocktail glass. Decorate with stick of pineapple and a cherry.

DAIQUIRI COCKTAIL

Juice one lime
1 tsp. powdered sugar
1½ oz. Imported Rum

Shake well with cracked ice and strain into 3 oz. cocktail glass.

BACARDI COCKTAIL

1½ oz. Bacardi rum
Juice ½ lime
½ tsp. Grenadine

Shake well with cracked ice and strain into 3 oz. cocktail glass. (In later years, both Bacardi and Daiquiri were garnished with a filbert.)

♈ ♈ ♈

Cream drinks experienced a spurt in popularity at the end of World War II. I list three that I recall being very popular in the late '40s and through the '50s.

BRANDY ALEXANDER

1 oz. Creme de Cacao
1 oz. brandy
1 oz. sweet cream

Shake well with cracked ice and strain into 4 oz. cocktail glass.

GRASSHOPPER

¾ oz. Creme de Menthe (green)
¾ oz. Creme de Cacao (white)
¾ oz. sweet cream

Shake well with cracked ice and strain into 3 oz. cocktail glass.

PINK SQUIRREL

1 oz. Creme de Almond liqueur
½ oz. Creme de Cacao (white)
½ oz. light cream

Shake well with cracked ice and strain into 3 oz. cocktail glass.

♆ ♆ ♆

One drink that was extremely popular in years gone by still has some fans today:

OLD FASHIONED COCKTAIL

½ lump of sugar
2 dashes bitters

Add enough water to cover sugar and muddle. One cube of ice. Two ounces of whiskey. Use old fashioned glass. Stir well. Add a slice of orange and a cherry. Serve with a stirring rod.

♆ ♆ ♆

Bartender Phil Harris had a lot of fun entertaining people at the bar at Jax with this "cocktail."

THE GHOST COCKTAIL

*Place a piece of turkish towel in the bottom
    of a mixing shaker.*
*Make sure the guests do not see that turkish
    towel. In full view of the guests add
    cracked ice.*
*Next add 1 oz. of lemon juice; 1 oz. of sugar
    water and 2 oz. of Grenadine.*
*Shake vigorously and have a 3 oz. cocktail
    glass set up in front of the guest who is
    expecting the drink. When you try to
    strain the mixture into the cocktail glass,
    nothing will come out of the shaker. The
    turkish towel absorbs all the liquid and
    the guest is mystified. Thus the name:
    Ghost Cocktail.*

♉ ♉ ♉

The following drinks in this section are provided by
my good friend, Lowell "Joe" Peterson. Some of the drinks
call for extra fine sugar or a lump of sugar, which you
seldom see at the bar these days. You may also notice
how some of the recipes have changed . . . the Martini
being the most notable.

Joe's recipe for Tom and Jerry Batter is superb and I
thank him for sharing it. It is a classic and in this day of
pre-mixes and preservatives, it is refreshing to be able to
pass it on.

BRONX COCKTAIL

*1 oz. dry gin
½ oz. dry vermouth
Juice ¼ orange*

Shake well with cracked ice and strain into 3 oz. cocktail
glass.

261

BRANDY MILK PUNCH

1 T. Extra-Fine Bar or Dessert Sugar
1½ oz. brandy
¼ oz. Meyers Dark Jamaica rum
3 oz. milk
1 whole egg

Put all ingredients in shaker glass. Fill with cracked ice
and shake long and vigorously. Strain into chilled 11 oz.
glass. Dust top with nutmeg.

GIN RICKEY AND GIN BUCK

½ fresh lime
1½ oz. gin

Squeeze lime into an old fashioned glass. Place lime in
glass. Fill glass with ice cubes. For Gin Rickey, fill with
chilled soda or sparkling water. For Gin Buck, fill with
chilled ginger ale.

ORANGE CASTLE

¾ oz. Cointreau
¾ oz. white Creme de Cacao
½ oz. fresh lemon juice
¾ oz. cream

Put ingredients in a shaker glass. Fill with cracked ice
and shake. Strain into a chilled 5½ oz. cocktail glass.

SIDE CAR

¾ oz. Cointreau
1½ oz. brandy
¾ oz. fresh lemon juice

Put ingredients in shaker glass. Fill with cracked ice.
Shake well. Rim a chilled 5½ oz. cocktail glass with sugar

262

and strain contents into it. Note: Use light rum instead of brandy and you have a "Between the Sheets" or a Boston style Side Car.

SAZERAC COCKTAIL

Pernod
1½ oz. bourbon or rye
1 sugar lump
Peychaud bitters

Pour a dash of pernod into a chilled old fashioned or low ball glass. Swirl it around so that the glass is well coated. Throw the excess pernod away. Place sugar lump in glass, add a dash of Peychaud bitters and a dash of water. Muddle bitters and sugar thoroughly. Pour in bourbon or rye and fill glass with water. Twist a lemon peel over it and drop lemon peel in.

MARTINI

The original martini was 1 part dry vermouth, 2 parts dry gin and a dash of orange bitters. In Europe, the ratio was equal parts of dry vermouth and gin.

MANHATTAN

The original Manhattan was 1 part of sweet vermouth, 2 parts bourbon and a dash of Angostura Bitters. A twist of orange peel was optional.

TOM & JERRY BATTER

1 qt. whole eggs
1 qt. frozen sugared egg yolks
4 lb. bar or dessert sugar

Thaw frozen egg yolks. Put eggs, egg yolks and sugar in a large mixing bowl. Place mixing bowl in a shallow pan of

263

boiling water. Stir constantly with a wire whisk until mixture is a hot syrupy mixture. Remove from heat and put bowl on mixing machine, using a large wire beater. Mix at a number two speed for about 25-30 minutes. To make drink: Heat mug and spoon. Add 1 oz. brandy, 1 dash of Myers Dark Jamaican Rum. Ladle a large spoon of batter in mug. Pour boiling water down side of mug until batter rises to top of mug. Dust with nutmeg. (Note: On all hot drinks, *do not over pour on liquor.* It will spoil the drink. While heating mixture, stir constantly. And do not take your eyes off it or you may wind up with an omelet.

♈ ♈ ♈

What follows are a few of the food recipes that have stood the test of time at our restaurants. We trust you will enjoy them but as you do remember there is nothing that takes the place of dining at a fine restaurant. (The following recipes are in portions designed primarily for multiple restaurant patrons. They may be expanded or reduced to portions that suit your individual situation.)

HUNTERS' SOUP

This soup is served at the Royal Oak Hunters' dinners and has received rave reviews.

> *1 lb. navy beans*
> *1 lb. split peas*
> *1 lb. black turtle beans*
> *1 C. white rice*
> *1 C. diced carrots*
> *1 C. diced onions*
> *1 C. diced celery*
> *½ C. red peppers, diced*
> *½ C. green peppers, diced*
> *½ C. ham, diced*
> *½ C. turkey, diced*
> *1 whole diced: tomato or canned tomato*
> *8 chicken bouillon cubes*

PREVIOUS EVENING: Place navy beans and split peas in large kettle. Cover with cold water. Quantity of water should be two inches above the beans. Soak overnight.

Place black turtle beans in large kettle. Cover with cold water. Quantity of water should be two inches above the beans. Soak overnight. Drain beans and peas (keep separate).

In separate pots, place navy beans/split peas and black turtle beans. Cover with water. Add 1 cup white rice to navy bean/split pea pot. Put 4 bouillon cubes in each pot and bring each pot to boil. Turn down heat and let simmer until beans and peas are fully cooked. Add more chicken bouillon and water, if needed.

Sauté all vegetables in butter or margarine.

Drain turtle beans when they are finished.

Mix navy beans, split peas and rice mixture with turtle beans. Add sautéed vegetables.

The starch from the rice and beans should thicken the soup. If too thick, add chicken broth to thin down. Season with salt and pepper to taste.

COQUILLE SAINT-JACQUES SAUCE

This recipe was used at the Cape Cod dinners at Jax.

2 C. heavy cream
1 T. chopped shallots
½ T. black pepper
5 T. chicken base or bouillon
½ C. brandy
½ bunch green onions, chopped
1 C. sliced mushrooms
1½ lb. scallops
Melted butter
Parmesan cheese
Garlic croutons, crushed
Salt and pepper to taste, if needed

SAUCE: Combine heavy cream, shallots, black pepper, chicken base and bring to boil. Heat brandy and reduce to ⅛ cup. Add to sauce. Sauté mushrooms and green onions in a separate pan until tender. Add to sauce. If necessary, you may thicken sauce with a roux.

PROCEDURE: Sauté 6 oz. of scallops in melted butter. Cook thoroughly. Drain butter from pan and add 2 to 3 ounces of prepared sauce. Mix and heat thoroughly. Place in ramekin and top with parmesan cheese and crushed croutons. Brown under broiler. Serve.

CLAM CHOWDER

This recipe, with minor variations, is served at both Jax and Kozlak's Royal Oak.

> ½ lb. butter
> 1 lb. flour
> ½ stalk celery, diced
> 1 green pepper, diced
> ½ onion, diced
> 23 oz. clam juice
> 23 oz. clams, chopped
> 1 qt. hot water mixed with 4 ounces
>   clam base and 2 ounces chicken base
> 2 lb. cubed potatoes (cooked)
> ⅓ T. cayenne pepper
> ⅓ T. white pepper
> ⅓ T. ground thyme
> 2 oz. sherry wine
> 1½ C. Half & Half
> 2 C. milk

PROCEDURE: In stock pot, melt butter. Add diced vegetables (celery, green pepper, onion) - cook until tender. Add flour to make roux. Cook roux for 5-7 minutes. Stir constantly so roux does not brown or burn. Add clam juice, chopped clams, and water mixture. Stir in seasonings. Simmer soup until it thickens. Add milk and half & half. Add potatoes. Heat soup to simmer, stirring constantly. Add sherry wine and serve.

KOREAN CHICKEN SALAD

This item makes a popular luncheon item. Served at Kozlak's Royal Oak.

3 lb. boneless chicken breast

MARINADE:
4 T. soy sauce
2 T. oil
2 T. sherry or white wine
½ tsp. ground ginger
½ tsp. cinnamon
2 cloves garlic, finely chopped

Skin chicken breasts and cut in half. Make marinade and thoroughly coat chicken pieces. Place chicken in shallow roasting pan and pour remainder of marinade over top. Bake uncovered at 400 degrees for 40 minutes, turning once. Cool and slice.

SALAD VEGETABLES:
2 C. iceberg lettuce, shredded
1 C. cucumber, thinly sliced
1 C. carrots, thinly sliced
⅔ C. green onions, chopped
1 C. bean sprouts
¾ C. slivered almonds, toasted and salted
2 T. sesame seeds, toasted

DRESSING:
COMBINE:
4 tsp. dry mustard
4 tsp. salt
4 tsp. Tabasco sauce
4 C. corn oil or sesame oil
¾ C. lemon juice

Toss salad vegetables, dressing, almonds and sesame seeds. Arrange plate. Put some chicken slices on top in a fan shape.

TOMATO-PESTO SOUP

We have had many requests for this soup.

INGREDIENTS:
1 qt. diced tomatoes
1 qt. tomato puree
2 C. heavy whipping cream
1 T. ground marjoram
¾ T. ground rosemary
1½ T. ground thyme
1 T. onion powder
3 T. sugar
1½ C. fresh Parmesan cheese
salt and pepper to taste

PESTO INGREDIENTS:
2 C. fresh basil
1 T. chopped garlic
½ T. grated Parmesan cheese
2 T. olive oil
3 T. pine nuts
salt and pepper to taste

METHOD: Prepare Pesto: Combine all ingredients, except olive oil. Place in food processor. While running, add olive oil slowly. Season with salt and pepper to taste. Set aside. In a heavy sauce pan or stock pot, combine diced tomatoes and tomato puree. Bring to a simmer. Add all herbs and spices and continue to simmer for 45 minutes. Add Pesto and bring back to simmer. Whisk in Parmesan cheese. Carefully incorporate cream to soup. NOTE: The acidity of the tomato products, the heavy cream and fresh Parmesan cheese make this soup sensitive to extreme heat. Go slowly. Reheat slowly. Garnish with fresh Parmesan cheese.

GREEN BEAN SALAD

This recipe was developed by Pete Kalina and is much requested.

> *1- 6 lb. 5 oz. can Blue Lake*
> *cut green beans*
> *½ onion, diced very fine*
> *mayonnaise*
> *salt*
> *lemon juice, (dash) bacon crumbled*

Place green beans in colander and rinse with hot water. Allow green beans to drain 1-1½ hours. In mixing bowl, place drained green beans and add onion and enough mayonnaise to bind. Season to taste with salt and add lemon juice. Mix well. Cover and refrigerate 24 hours. When serving, garnish top of salad with crumbled bacon. At Kozlak's Royal Oak we make our own mayonnaise and dressings. If you do not make your own mayonnaise, use a heavy mayonnaise that is light on vinegar.

POLISH COTTAGE CHEESE CAKE
(SEROWIEC)

This was served at Jax Polish Nights. Ruth also made some for a group of home economists at a party hosted by General Mills.

> *3 lb. dry cottage cheese or dry ricotta*
> *2 C. sugar*
> *½ C. flour*
> *1 tsp. salt*
> *1 C. rich cream*
> *12 medium eggs*
> *1 tsp. vanilla*
> *1 lb. graham crackers*
> *1 tsp. cinnamon*
> *½ C. sugar*
> *¼ C. butter, melted*

Force cheese through colander. Sift sugar with flour and

salt, add to cheese and mix. Beat egg yolks and add to cheese mixture. Add cream and vanilla and mix. Beat egg whites until stiff but not dry and fold into mixture. Roll graham crackers fine, add cinnamon, ½ cup sugar and melted butter. Save ½ cup of the crumbs for the top of the cake. Butter a 9/13" pan generously, line with cracker crumb mixture. Pour in cheese mixture. Sprinkle the top with the ½ cup crumb mixture. Bake 325 degrees for 1 hour - center will sink from edges. Test with toothpick to see if cake is done.

MRS. K'S WILD RICE SALAD

This recipe makes a delightful luncheon dish at Royal Oak.

> 1 C. wild rice (cooked)
> 6 green onions, minced
> 1 C. yellow raisins
> 1 C. cooked ham, minced
> 1 C. toasted pecan halves
> olive oil
> rice wine vinegar

Mix first 4 ingredients. Combine olive oil and rice wine vinegar to make dressing (approximately 2 parts olive oil to 1 part rice wine vinegar). Coat mixed ingredients with dressing to taste. Just before serving, toss with 1 cup toasted pecan halves.

KOZLAK'S ROYAL OAK HOUSE SALAD

FOUR SALADS:
1 head romaine lettuce
⅓ C. grated Parmesan cheese
⅗ C. fresh shredded Parmesan cheese
Homemade garlic croutons
Royal Oak House dressing

ROYAL OAK HOUSE DRESSING:
½ gal. heavy mayonnaise
¼ C. garlic juice
½ T. garlic salt
1 T. garlic powder
½ pint Half & Half
½ C. sugar
⅛ C. lemon juice

DRESSING PROCEDURE: Combine all ingredients in a large mixing bowl and mix well. (Make sure the sugar dissolved in the dressing.) At Kozlak's Royal Oak, we make our own mayonnaise using whole eggs, oil, vinegar and seasonings. At times, we find it necessary to adjust this recipe with added amounts of sugar and/or lemon juice.

TO PREPARE ROYAL OAK HOUSE SALAD: Carefully wash romaine. Dry leaves gently and thoroughly. If you leave moisture on them, it will thin down the salad dressing and give you a limp salad. If you clean the romaine in advance, spread the leaves out on an absorbent towel. Roll them up very loosely and put on the bottom shelf of your refrigerator to crisp. When ready to serve, break the leaves into bite-size pieces and place in a large mixing bowl. Toss the romaine with just enough of the grated Parmesan cheese to lightly coat the romaine leaves. Mix the romaine with enough house dressing to coat the romaine leaves. Do not use more dressing than necessary. Serve salad immediately in chilled salad bowls. Top with fresh shredded Parmesan cheese and your homemade garlic croutons. NOTE: Recipe will yield more dressing than is required for four salads.

CHUTNEY CHEESE SPREAD

This is a much appreciated item on the Royal Oak salad bar. Recipe courtesy of Helen Rose.

8 oz. softened cream cheese
4 C. sliced almonds
1½ tsp. curry powder
¾ tsp. dry mustard
1 - 16 oz. jar Indian Major Gray's chutney

Place all ingredients in a large mixing bowl and mix thoroughly. Refrigerate and serve.

BEEF TIPS

This recipe has been a favorite at Jax for years on the Friday luncheon menu.

½ C. red wine
1 lb. tenderloin beef tips or stew meat
1 T. tomato paste
1 oz. honey
½ C. sliced mushrooms
2 C. beef stock
1 C. flour
1 C. butter
salt and pepper

Brown beef in 10 in. skillet. Add red wine, bring to simmer and reduce until beef is cooked halfway. Remove beef but reserve juices in pan. Reduce to simmer and wisk in honey and tomato paste. In a separate pan, prepare the roux by melting butter and adding equal part of flour. Stir often to incorporate and also not to burn. Consistency of roux should be that of wet sand. Wisk in roux a little at a time to the boiling stock. Add roux until desired consistency, reduce to simmer. Now add reserved beef, mushrooms and salt and pepper to taste. Simmer for 10 minutes. Serve with rice or buttered noodles.

At Jax, you may net your trout from the garden stream and the trout are sped to the kitchen for preparation. The following trout recipes are extremely popular at Jax.

TROUT PARMESAN

4 trout, 12 oz. each, boned and butterflied
4 eggs, beaten
½ lb. Parmesan cheese, grated
salt
pepper
peanut or vegetable oil for deep frying
2 C. milk
4 T. flour
4 T. butter
capers

Dip trout into beaten eggs. Place half of the grated cheese on waxed paper. Press trout into the cheese to coat heavily. Salt and pepper generously. Deep-fry in peanut or vegetable oil until they are crisp.

To make sauce, heat milk to the boiling point and blend in flour and butter. Stir over low heat until thick. Add remaining cheese and the capers, and blend thoroughly. Pour over the fish before serving. Makes 4 servings.

WHOLE BAKED TROUT WITH MUSHROOMS

3 T. butter
3 T. vegetable oil
6 C. (about 12 oz.) sliced, mixed fresh wild mush-
*   rooms (Portobello, Crimini, stemmed Shiitake)*
1½ C. chopped onion
1 large celery stock, chopped
3 T. fresh parsley, minced
1½ tsp. dried thyme
3 oz. prosciutto, thinly sliced and chopped
4 whole trout (about 12 oz. ea.) cleaned
*   and boned*
2 T. fresh lemon juice
¼ C. butter (½ stick), melted

Melt 3 tablespoons butter with oil in heavy large skillet over medium heat. Add mushrooms, onion, celery, parsley and thyme. Cook until mushrooms brown and all liquid evaporates, stirring frequently, about 20 minutes. Remove from heat. Stir in prosciutto, season to taste with salt and pepper and cool. (Filling can be prepared 1 day ahead. Cover and refrigerate.)

Preheat oven to 350 degrees. Butter large baking sheet. Open fish as for book, drizzle with lemon juice and sprinkle with salt and pepper. Spoon filling over 1 side of each fish, dividing equally. Fold second side over, enclosing filling. Place stuffed fish on prepared sheet and brush outside of fish with butter. Bake until cooked through – about 30 minutes. Serve on platter. Yield 4 servings.

TROUT ITALIANO

4 - 8 oz. rainbow trout, boned
¼ C. black olives, sliced
2 T. Parmesan cheese, grated
Italian bread crumbs
Marinara sauce

ITALIAN BREAD CRUMBS:
¼ loaf white bread, crust trimmed
1 tsp. oregano
1 tsp. basil
1 tsp. parsley, chopped

Place all ingredients in Cuisanart and chop until very finely chopped.

MARINARA SAUCE:
¼ *C. olive oil*
½ *C. carrots, celery and onions,*
  chopped fine
1 *C. chicken stock*
1 *C. tomato paste*
1 *clove garlic, chopped fine*
1 *C. tomatoes, seeded and diced*
1 *tsp. basil*
½ *tsp. thyme*
1 *tsp. rosemary*
¼ *C. Parmesan cheese, grated*
1 *tsp. Worcestershire sauce*
½ *tsp. Tabasco sauce*
1 *C. tomato sauce*
½ *C. white wine*

Sauté onions, celery and carrots in olive oil. Add spices and garlic, sauté 2-3 minutes. Add wine and reduce by ⅔. Add chicken stock, tomato paste, tomato sauce, Worcestershire and Tabasco. Reduce and thicken. Add fresh tomatoes, season with salt and pepper. Add Parmesan, mix well. Simmer 10-20 minutes. Stir frequently.

TROUT: Press trout in Italian bread crumbs, flesh side, and sauté until golden brown. Place on baking sheet and bake 5-10 minutes at 350 degrees or until trout flakes with fork. Top with marinara sauce, sprinkle with grated Parmesan cheese and top with sliced black olives.

MUSTARD CRUSTED TROUT
ON A BED OF MILD GARLIC MASHED POTATOES WITH
MUSHROOMS, TOMATOES, LEMON-SAGE JUS

2 pc. rainbow trout filets, diamond cut
*   3½ oz. each*
6 oz. garlic mashed new potatoes (recipe)
Dijon mustard
herb breadcrumbs (recipe)
2 T. sliced Cremini mushrooms
2 T. red and gold concasse, mixed
1 T. scallions, thin bias cut
4 oz. lemon-chicken broth (recipe)
2 T. butter
1 tsp. sage, chopped

MILD GARLIC MASHED POTATOES:
1 qt. cooked red new potatoes
1 C. garlic cream (recipe)
salt and pepper

Place potatoes in mixer with paddle attachment and beat until smooth. Add cream and seasonings, blend well. Remove and keep hot for service.

GARLIC CREAM:
1 C. cream
¼ C. butter
2 T. chopped garlic
¼ tsp. nutmeg

Combine all ingredients and bring to boil. Remove and allow to cool.

HERB BREADCRUMBS:
1 loaf white bread, crust trimmed
½ C. basil leaves, chopped
1 C. parsley, chopped
⅓ C. chives, chopped

Place ingredients in Cuisinart and chop together until mixture turns green and herbs are finely chopped.

LEMON-CHICKEN BROTH:
1 qt. chicken broth
½ C. lemon juice

Bring to boil and remove. Allow to cool. Prepare trout and sauce for trout à la minute in separate pans. Season trout with salt and pepper, coat trout heavily, flesh side only, with Dijon mustard. Press both sides into bread-crumb mixture. Sauté trout in enough oil (about 3 T.) for even browning without sticking. Cook flesh side first to golden brown (about 3 min.) turn and cook skin side about 3 min. Drain briefly on paper towels. Serve immediately. While trout cooks, sauté the Cremini mushrooms 1 min., add scallions, tomato concasse, sage, lemon chicken broth and whole butter. Allow mixture to boil so broth reduces and butter emulsifies the mixture. Season with a little salt and pepper. When broth reaches light sauce consistency, it is done. Place about ½ - ⅔ cup of potatoes in center of service plate. Spoon around the sauce mixture and place trout on top of the potatoes. Serve.

NEW ORLEANS SHRIMP

This item is a popular appetizer at Jax.

4 tsp. granulated garlic
4 tsp. granulated onion
1 tsp. cayenne pepper
4 tsp. basil leaves
2 tsp. thyme, ground
2 tsp. white pepper
4 tsp. Kosher salt
2 tsp. black pepper
2 tsp. marjoram leaf
2 tsp. oregano leaf
4 tsp. paprika
2 tsp. gumbo file
8 shrimp, peeled and tail off
½ tsp. Worcestershire
2 oz. beer
2 oz. butter, unsalted (soft)
1 oz. clarified butter

Lightly cover shrimp in spice mixture. Put clarified butter in sauté pan over medium heat. When butter is hot, put shrimp in until they turn golden brown. Add Worcestershire, beer and let reduce by half. Stir in soft butter, a little bit at a time, until all is melted. Serve with hot bread.

ALSACE POTATO SALAD

This unique potato salad is featured each week on Jax Sunday Brunch.

Equal parts of Polish sausage, sauerkraut and washed, cooked and quartered B-size red potatoes. Slice Polish sausage thinly in diagonal pieces.

Garnish with green and red peppers, red onions, ¼" dice, 1 med. green, 1 med. red pepper and 1 med. red onion to 3 lbs. salad.

Mix all of the above with equal parts salad oil, cider or malt vinegar. For 3 lbs. salad (1 pt. dressing) 8 oz. oil, 8 oz. vinegar.

Flavor to taste with garlic salt, cracked black pepper, caraway seed and/or dill weed and sugar.

BAILEY'S IRISH CREAM BANANA TORTE

Jax and Kozlak's Royal Oak are renowned for their desserts. This delightful torte is featured at Jax.

CAKE:
1 banana cake mix (Pillsbury Plus)

Make banana cake according to package. Make 2 - 9" round cakes. Let cakes cool and cut into 2 layers.

MOUSSE:
1 env. unflavored gelatin
1 T. COLD water
½ C. Baileys Liqueur
1 C. granulated sugar
7 egg whites
1 C. heavy cream

In a small heavy saucepan, soften the gelatin in the water. Add the Baileys and sugar and stir over a very low flame just until the gelatin is thoroughly dissolved. Do not let it boil or cook too long. Remove from the heat and let cool to a syruplike consistency over a bowl of ice water. This mixture must be completely cooled before being added to the egg whites. Beat the egg whites until very stiff. Still mixing, slowly add the gelatin mixture. Whip the cream until stiff and gently fold in. Take care to thoroughly incorporate all ingredients without deflating the eggs and cream.

ALMONDS:
3 cups finely chopped almonds mixed
with ½ cup sugar – 2 T. butter melted,
toasted at 350 degrees appx. 10-15
min. Do up ahead of time and let cool.

Appx. 4-6 large bananas, sliced

To assemble cake, spread a thin layer of mousse onto the bottom layer of cake, arrange bananas on top, then spread mousse over bananas to completely cover. Continue this using the next 2 layers. On top layer, spread mousse evenly and on sides. Press crushed almonds on sides. Mark torte into 16 pieces, and place crushed almonds in center to make a circle. Decorate each piece with a rosette of mousse, place a chocolate truffle cup filled with Bailey Irish Cream in top of each rosette. Refrigerate overnight. May be kept 5 days.

INDEX

Page numbers *in italics* refer to photos.

281

282

285